Advance Praise for *Bone Hash*

"Griffith has created a riveting work that successfully blends a chilling mystery and a revealing character study into a potent whole."
—Kirkus Reviews

"Skye Griffith writes intriguing stories rooted in archeology with a generous sprinkling of intrigue and twists along the way."
—Steven James, bestselling author of *Fatal Domain*

"Skye Griffith has written a page turner murder mystery novel set in an archeologically rich historically indigenous area of the Southwest."
—Virginia Mampre, CFEE, President & CEO Mampre Media International, LLC

"With a setting as rough and deadly as the antagonists, Skye Griffith's debut novel is a thrilling and gripping read. For fans of Anne Hillerman and Margaret Coel, *Bone Hash* has complex characters, lots of twists and a protagonist that mystery readers will love."
—Kathleen Donnelly, award-winning author of the National Forest K-9 series

"An exhilarating adventure from the very first page, *Bone Hash* took me on a wild ride along the remote trails of the high plains desert."
—Bonnie Kimmell, Adult Services Librarian, Jefferson County Public Library

An Archaeologist Aideen Connor Mystery

Skye Griffith

Artemesia
Publishing

ISBN: 978-1-963832-13-6 (paperback)
ISBN: 978-1-963832-27-3 (ebook)
LCCN: 2025932886
Copyright © 2025 by Skye Griffith
Cover Illustration and Design © 2025 Ian Bristow

Printed in the United States

Names, characters, and incidents depicted in this book are products of the author's imagination or are used fictitiously. Any resemblance to actual events, locales, organizations, or persons, living or dead, is entirely coincidental and beyond the intent of the author or the publisher.

All rights reserved. No part of this book may be reproduced or transmitted in any form or by any means, electronic or mechanical, including photocopying, recording, or by any information storage or retrieval system without written permission of the publisher, except for the inclusion of brief quotations in a review.

NO AI TRAINING: Without in any way limiting the author's [and publisher's] exclusive rights under copyright, any use of this publication to "train" generative artificial intelligence (AI) technologies to generate text is expressly prohibited. The author reserves all rights to license uses of this work for generative AI training and development of machine learning language models.

Artemesia Publishing
9 Mockingbird Hill Rd
Tijeras, New Mexico 87059
www.apbooks.net
info@artemesiapublishing.com

For Gary

CHAPTER 1

Sunday Night, Tuba City, Arizona, Present Time

A DUST DEVIL SWIRLED through the motel courtyard. The Navajo called them *chindi* and claimed they carry bad spirits when they spin counterclockwise. I covered my nose and waited for the funnel-shaped tower of sand to pass, then I climbed the exterior steps to my room.

I'd asked for nonsmoking, but the stale smell of cigarettes lingered. When I slung the heavy backpack onto the bed, it knocked a framed picture off the nightstand. I rubbed my shoulders where my bra straps had dug in and switched on the air-conditioner under the window opposite the bed. The antique cooling system rattled into action.

I sat on the bed and picked up the picture. A tarnished metal frame held the black-and-white photo of a girl of perhaps sixteen. Her thick, dark hair was arranged in the traditional squash-blossom style once customary among unmarried Hopi women, with large circular twists secured above her ears. Her delicate features invited the eyes to linger, but it was her direct gaze at the unknown photographer that piqued my interest. She'd stared straight into the lens as if delivering a challenge, a gaze uncharacteristic of a traditional Hopi woman.

I'd moved to Arizona less than three months ago to take a job as lead archaeologist at Moenkopi Ridge, an Ancestral Pueblo settlement. The background in the picture was blurred, but one of the buildings looked familiar. This photo had been taken in Hano, a village on First Mesa in the Hopi Reservation some sixty miles from my dig. The girl in the photo wore an elaborate silver necklace and a crisp black dress with a fancy shawl draped over her shoulders. She looked the part of a traditional Hopi bride-to-be dressed for her engagement ceremony.

The summer sky had begun to darken through the front window. Returning the photo to the nightstand, I decided to drop it off at the motel office in the morning. It looked far too personal to be someone's idea of room decoration.

I closed the drapes and ran a bath, tapping in a few drops of essential oil. The sharp scent of lemon balm rose with the steam. The trailer I lived in at the edge of my dig was small and required water to be trucked in. A hot bath would be a treat, even holed up in a no-star motel room in Tuba City, Arizona.

After a long soak I toweled off and threw on a lime-colored nightgown with an elaborate "AC" embroidered on the front. I hadn't worn it since my late husband, Clay, gave it to me when we lived in Philadelphia. Remembering the look on his face the last time I saw him made me wish I hadn't brought it. Clay had died in a violent, freak accident about a year ago when we'd traveled to Peru to hike the Inca Trail. A mudslide took him with such astonishing precision I remained physically unharmed when its unstoppable force snatched Clay from where he stood and left me a widow at thirty-four.

I checked the doorknob lock, set the deadbolt and the security chain, turned out the light at the switch by the door, and sank gratefully into bed.

Hard to say how long I'd been asleep before pounding loud as a machine gun blast jolted me awake. Light from the parking lot pressed against the thin drapes. The clock radio on the nightstand cast a greenish light onto the photo of the

Hopi girl. I finally focused on the door when I remembered where I was.

"Who is it?" I yelled, grabbing my jeans off the floor in the dark and slipping them on under my gown.

No answer. More pounding.

I crept barefoot to the door, hands shaking, pulse drumming in my ears.

"Who is it? What do you want?"

A deep voice rumbled, "You're in my room."

Moving the drapes aside revealed a tall, beefy-looking man wearing a black cowboy hat and jacket standing under the low-wattage bulb. His hair stuck out from under his hat in long, unruly hanks that swung when he turned toward the window.

"You have the wrong room," I shouted through the door. "Check the number on your key!" Jerking out of sight, I tried to remember where I'd left my phone. The pounding resumed, blast after ear-drubbing blast. When he caught me sneaking another look, he stared back like he was lining me up in the crosshairs of a rifle.

"I've called the police! Get away from my room!"

Afraid he'd see me through the drapes if I turned on the light, I backed away from the window and felt around in the dark for my phone. No luck.

"I just want the picture," he growled. "Give it to me and I'll leave."

"Picture? What picture?" I shouted.

"Left it in the room. Next to the bed."

That picture? I snatched the photo of the Hopi girl off the nightstand, took it to the window and held it against the glass.

"This?" I asked.

He squinted. "Yeah."

No way was I opening that door. "I'll drop it off at the motel office in the morning," I said, my voice strident. "You can pick it up there."

But he wasn't having it. He resumed his attack, and the door pulsed back and forth like a bellows. I feared it would soon splinter.

Later I realized how brainless it was, but my adrenaline had spiked, and I couldn't find my phone. All I wanted was to get rid of him. I scurried back to the window, pulled the drapes aside, and rapped on the glass to get his attention.

"All right, all right. I'll give you the photo. Back up!"

Tucking the photo between my knees, I checked the security chain and unlocked the deadbolt. Clasping the doorknob in my left hand, I turned it slowly and pulled the door to the end of the security chain. I stuck the photo through the opening with my right. Instead of taking the picture, he grabbed my wrist! Twisting my hand to break his grip, I yanked the photo back inside. Then I whirled around, slamming my back against the door and trapped his hand. He roared out a string of expletives. I let up, thinking he'd remove his hand, but he stuck the toe of his boot between the door and the jamb and pushed against the door like a bulldozer.

I pushed back with everything I had... and shrieked like a screech owl.

"Shut up, bitch!"

A voice from another room yelled, "Shut the hell up!"

He pushed again, hard, and withdrew his boot. The door slammed shut at last. I whipped around to reset the deadbolt. My hand shook so hard, I could barely turn the knob. Sirens blared in the distance. Hopefully someone had called the cops. When I finally dared another look through the drapes, he was gone.

I flipped on the overhead light switch and staggered to the bed, still clutching the photo. The phone on the nightstand rang, making me jump like I'd been jabbed with a hot poker.

"What's with all the noise?" the voice on the phone demanded.

"A strange man tried to break into my room. Call the police."

"They're here. I'm sending them up."

Most of the lights in the complex were on by the time I noticed the red smudge drying on the doorframe. I pulled a jacket from my backpack and put it on over my gown, found my socks and hiking boots and sat on the bed. When I bent down to tie my boots, I spotted a piece of cloth sticking out from under the bedspread. I kicked at it, then leaned over to see what it was. A pair of stiff, oily-looking, mud-streaked jeans. I shivered. My would-be assailant had abandoned more than his photo.

CHAPTER 2

Two tribal policemen arrived together—Officer Humetewa from Hopi and Sergeant Bedonie from the Navajo Tribal Police. Since Tuba City sits on Navajo land, I expected a Navajo officer but was surprised to see the Hopi policeman outside his jurisdiction. Indian reservations are self-governed by the tribe and also fall under federal authority.

Bedonie pointed out the room's only chair to Humetewa, and then stood at the back of the room, occasionally pacing.

Humetewa moved with the muscular self-assurance of someone who routinely works out. He swung the chair to the foot of the bed, sat down, and motioned for me to sit on the bed. He pulled out a ballpoint pen and a small spiral notebook from his shirt pocket and studied me with a steady gaze.

"The motel clerk said you told him someone tried to break into your room. What can you tell me about this assailant?"

I described every physical detail I could remember—estimating the man's height at about six feet, recalling how he was dressed, and noting his long unruly hair and deep voice.

"Why do you think he came after you?" Humetewa asked.

"Apparently he thought it was *his* room. He said he

wanted his photo back."

"What photo? Did you give it to him?"

"I noticed a framed picture on the nightstand when I first arrived. He claimed he'd left it in the room and that he wanted it back. I started to give it to him, but then he tried to break in."

"So you still have it? Let me see."

I plucked the picture from where I'd dropped it face down on the bed and handed it to Humetewa. His hand tightened around the frame.

"Someone you know?" I asked.

Humetewa ignored my question. He turned and said to Bedonie, "I'm taking this back to headquarters."

I shrugged. It wasn't my photo, but Humetewa's reaction to it sparked an uneasy feeling. Bedonie stopped his pacing. A look passed between the officers.

"I understand this encounter must have been a shock," Humetewa said. "But are you sure you don't know the assailant, haven't seen him around? That long red hair of yours tends to make you stand out. People up on the Hopi Reservation know about that dig you're running. Maybe he holds some kind of a grudge."

I brushed my fingers through my uncombed hair and wondered how much this policeman knew about my work.

"No, I don't know him. And why would he bear me a grudge?"

"Something to do with your dig, possibly? People on the Hopi mesas know you've found prehistoric bones. Some of the old-timers don't like having their ancestors disturbed."

"We're very respectful of how we treat human remains," I said. "And we do our best to be mindful of local concerns."

Humetewa slowly nodded and then asked, "Can you recall any other details about this assailant?"

"He left these behind," I said, yanking back the bedspread to expose the dirty jeans.

"He must have been in a hurry."

"Here's an evidence bag," Bedonie said. He came over to the bedside and plopped the dirty jeans and a wadded-up T-shirt he found underneath them into a large paper bag. I rubbed my temples, trying to ease a sledgehammer of a headache.

Humetewa glanced back at Bedonie and then looked toward the door to the room.

"How did that blood get on the door frame, Dr. Connor?"

Looking to where he pointed, I said, "I slammed the door on his hand after he grabbed me."

"I'm pulling it," Humetewa said to Bedonie.

"Hardly seems necessary," Bedonie said.

Humetewa shrugged. He got up and walked out, leaving the door open. Moments later I heard a trunk lid slam. He returned shortly leaving the door slightly ajar and carrying a small plastic box that looked like a first-aid kit.

Humetewa set the kit on the floor and pulled out a wide roll of clear tape and a pair of scissors. He cut off a length of tape, pressed it against the smudge, then took a credit card from his pants pocket and used it to smooth the tape against the white doorframe. He checked the seal and then yanked off the tape. Most of the bloody smudge came off in one clean go, leaving only rusty flecks behind. He transferred the tape to a clean, glossy-looking plastic card from the kit and used his credit card again to smooth it down. Turning to Bedonie he said, "I'm sending this to the state lab. I'll let you know what they find."

Humetewa's elaborate procedure with the bloodstain puzzled me. While finishing my Ph.D. in Philadelphia, I'd been mugged going home late, and the police called to the scene weren't half as thorough. And why had the Navajo policeman allowed the Hopi officer to take the lead in a Navajo district?

Having been jolted awake and now sleep-deprived, I felt

like a lab animal hooked to an adrenaline pump. As soon as Humetewa finished with the bloodstain, I stood and said, "I've told you everything I can remember. How about I call you if I think of anything else? I'm pretty wrung out."

Humetewa's demeanor eased a little, and he nodded. Each policeman gave me a card, and I tucked both into the front pocket of my jeans.

"How do we know this guy won't come back?" I asked.

"We don't. Do you have someone you can call to come stay with you?" Bedonie asked.

"No, I'm getting out of here as soon as it's light, but I sure don't want to run into that guy again while I'm waiting for the sun to come up."

"Where are you planning to go?" Humetewa asked. "We might want to contact you."

"Back to my work site. My dig's not far from here." I took a card from my backpack and gave it to him.

"I don't want to alarm you," Humetewa said, "but it's possible my department might call you about a murder investigation."

"Why? What does this break-in have to do with a murder investigation?" The draft coming through the door he hadn't closed made me shiver. I got up to close it.

"Maybe nothing. But if someone from Hopi Tribal Police calls asking if you've recalled more details about what happened here tonight, do your best to cooperate with them."

Humetewa's comment puzzled me, but I was too nonplussed and wrung out to question him further. I told him I'd cooperate and then asked both officers to wait a minute while I called the front desk. There was no way I was going to stay in that room the rest of the night. The clerk said the motel was full—no other rooms available. I told the policemen my predicament, and they waited for me to run in the bathroom and swap my gown for a t-shirt and then toss the rest of my belongings into my backpack. Then they walked me to the motel office. The employee working the front desk told me I could stay there until daybreak and to keep the door locked, he was going back to bed. I thanked the two officers and locked the door behind them.

Sleepless, my hair bedraggled and my eyes scratchy, I sat on the overstuffed fake leather couch next to my backpack waiting for the dawn. My eyes felt like I'd ridden a motorcycle in a dust storm. The aggressiveness of the stranger baffled me. If the photo meant so much to him, why had he left it in the motel room—along with his dirty clothes? There had to be something more to all this, but hopefully, it was no longer my problem.

#

At first light I used the office restroom to put on a fresh T-shirt and jeans from my pack. Then I drove out of the motel parking lot and stopped at a nearby park to think over my next move. A few days earlier, Valerie Robinson, a friend living in Taos, had invited me up for a visit. I'd planned to drive there from Tuba City right after meeting with the local museum director, but the meeting ran late, and I'd changed my plans to stay in Tuba City overnight. Now driving alone to Taos had lost its appeal, and the bitter coffee brought from the motel office was giving me the jitters.

The only person in the park besides me was a man in his mid-thirties sitting on top of a concrete picnic table under its *sombra*, checking something on his phone. He wore black cowboy boots that looked new despite their dusting of red desert sand. Coarse black hair and a red-brown complexion gave him the look of a Native American, but instead of wearing his hair in one of the long local styles, he looked like the regular customer of a Fifth Avenue salon. Sand clung to the bottoms of his jeans as if he'd taken an early walk in the backcountry, not the paved path meandering through the park. I looked away, but when I glanced back, I caught him staring at me. On a whim, I called the traditional Navajo greeting. "*Ya'at'eeh.*"

He returned his attention to his phone without a nod or a word. The hint of a smile crossed his face. This guy was no desert local. I wondered where he was from as I sauntered to the company van I'd driven and slid behind the wheel.

The drive from Tuba City took me through open terrain across the Navajo Reservation. I turned on the radio for company, tuned in to KTNN out of Window Rock, and listened to a country queen sing out her sorrow against showy guitar licks. A black pickup followed me out of Tuba City and stayed several car lengths behind. When I headed east on I-40 toward Winslow, the pickup went south toward Flagstaff. My shoulders eased a little. I blew out a breath and cranked up the radio for the rest of the drive to the dig.

CHAPTER 3

A LITTLE-USED GRAVEL road running north out of Winslow leads to Moenkopi Ridge, site of a village built some nine hundred years ago situated less than an hour's drive from today's Hopi Reservation. Ancient inhabitants had a 360-degree view of the surrounding terrain and would have seen strangers approaching from miles away. Whenever I took this road into the dig or hiked past the ruins of their stone watchtowers, I considered the intelligence behind their choice of sites.

I drove past my residential trailer at the edge of the dig and followed the unpaved road to the construction trailer we used as an office. Nova Banks, our site photographer, had volunteered to look after Dakota, my dog. Still shaken from the break-in attempt, I was glad to return early and looked forward to an enthusiastic greeting from Dakota.

As I neared the parking lot, a deeply tanned man I didn't recognize walked down the office's metal stairs and made his way to the graveled parking lot. His self-assured carriage reminded me of someone used to being in charge.

Burk Trenton, the dig's bio-archaeologist, walked up to my van from the opposite direction. In his late thirties, Burk wore his usual field attire: a pair of convertible cargo pants with the legs zipped off above the knees, a loose camp shirt, and heavy socks inside steel-toed boots. He covered his blond hair with an old straw hat, its band darkened from sweat stains. As bio-archaeologist, Burk studied the human remains excavated at the dig, which helped us develop a fuller picture of the culture being studied.

"I saw you take the turnoff. Why're you back early?"

I climbed down from the van and told him about the nighttime intruder. He whistled.

"Did you recognize the guy?"

"No."

"You must have been scared shitless."

"That's one way to put it."

Burk shook his head. "Need help with anything?"

I slipped my cell phone into my pocket and said, "No, I'll collect my backpack later."

"There's something I want to show you before you go inside and get embroiled in paperwork," he said.

Before I could respond, the man I'd seen exiting the office when I drove in waved to Burk from the far end of the parking lot and walked toward us.

"Who is he?" I asked.

"Lyle Henderson."

I knew Lyle Henderson, the former site director, by reputation only. He'd published an impressive number of articles about a new research method he'd invented for dating ancient ceramics that established him as a leading expert in Ancestral Puebloan pottery. The man approaching looked to be in his mid-fifties. Although he easily had some twenty years on me, he hardly looked ready for retirement.

"You must be Dr. Connor," he said. "I stopped by to introduce myself on my way to a coin show in Salt Lake. Lyle Henderson," he added, extending his hand.

"I'm honored to meet you, and please, call me Aideen. You're a coin collector?"

"Yes, collecting coins has become part of my retirement strategy. You'd be surprised what some coins are worth, and they tend to hold their value." He smiled. "The office staff said they weren't expecting you back for a few days."

"Change of plans," I said, returning his smile.

"Good to see you, Burk," Lyle said. "How's progress at the kiva site?"

Burk thumped him on the back. "Going well, Lyle. How're things with your new business?"

"Picking up. I hope you'll come visit my gallery soon and see for yourself."

"You've left archaeology?" I asked.

"Yes. Made a big change, but I'm still consulting."

Lyle took a silver cardholder from his back pocket, removed a card, and handed it to me. "I left some reports on your desk. If you have any questions, please call me here."

His card had a deep red background with the drawing of a black-on-white ceramic vessel at its center—the kind of pot from the Pueblo period so popular with collectors. His card read, "*Desert Rose Gallery, Sedona, Arizona.*"

"You're specializing in Native American art," I said.

"The only kind I know much about," he said, laughing. "I should be going. I have a long drive. Good to meet you, Aideen."

Burk and I watched him walk to his car.

"Why did he leave his position here?" I asked.

Burk hesitated. "I guess it's no secret. He had a series of surgeries for melanoma. First time I've seen him in months."

"Too bad about his health. Makes sense he left a job working a lot of hours in the sun."

Burk and I resumed our walk. "Heard anything from those cops yet? I suppose it's still early."

"No, but the Hopi cop sure asked me a lot of questions. Odd since Tuba isn't in his jurisdiction."

"It's probably because of that murder up at Hopi last night."

"A murder?" I echoed. "That cop *did* say something about

a murder investigation. You have any details?"

"A woman living in the village of Hano was brutally stabbed to death in her home last night. A neighbor discovered her body when her dog wouldn't stop howling outside her door. A friend that works at the Hopi Studies Center just called to tell me. Everyone up at First Mesa's on edge and talking about it."

Officer Humetewa's behavior with me last night fell into place. Hano, a village on First Mesa is small and a tightly knit community. He probably knew the victim, no doubt the reason for his interest in the photo left in my room.

"The officer didn't give me any details about a murder, but he did say they knew we'd dug up more bones."

Burk looked west toward the excavations. "That's why I need to show you something first thing. Before you run into someone on the NAAC."

The NAAC, or Native American Advisory Committee, governed the handling of human remains and funerary artifacts at the dig. Four Hopis from the nearby communities served on the committee. The most vocal member was Juanita Joshwecoma, an attractive woman in her forties who lived on Second Mesa. She usually took the lead at committee meetings and voiced interest in our treatment of human remains and ceremonial artifacts we uncovered at the dig. She frequently questioned me about our views on ancient practices, as did Tony Ahote, another NAAC member who worked at his family's restaurant in Tuba City.

"What's the new excavation got to do with the NAAC?" I asked.

"There's strong evidence we've uncovered a bone hash," Burk said.

"A bone hash? You're sure?"

"As sure as I can be without running more tests."

"That's going to upset the folks on the NAAC."

CHAPTER 4

Burk and I took the footpath across the mesa toward the excavations. High-desert plants were in full summer display, their yellow and fuchsia buds poking through the sharp, thorny crowns of prickly pear cactuses. Throngs of bees swirled around the yellow blossoms of piñon pines, buzzing loudly enough to hinder conversation. Allergic to bee stings, my skin crawled when we passed a tree that hummed with activity.

A side-blotched lizard with its characteristic mottled brown-and-yellow markings skittered in front of my footsteps to the safety of low-lying branches. Pungent sagebrush owned most of the real estate on the mesa. During hot spells, its pleasant fragrance intensified, but hidden beneath its gray-green branches lived a dark world of black beetles, scurrying rodents, mottled snakes, and the occasional scorpion. Despite the protection of heavy boots, I was careful where I stepped, and I routinely tucked a clasp knife and an EpiPen in my pocket whenever I walked rough terrain.

Excavations at Moenkopi Ridge began six years before I arrived. Most of the dig's supporting buildings were temporary prefabs or construction trailers like the office. The collections building, the only permanent structure on-site, stood to the far west and housed our lab and a secure artifacts room where all artifacts discovered at the dig were stored and locked up.

Burk and I continued on the footpath behind the collections building and across the mesa to the trench containing the newly discovered human remains. The few wispy clouds we'd seen earlier had evaporated in the heat by the time we reached the new site.

Lonny Nampayu, a field archaeologist, stood beside a mound covered with a dark brown tarp and stopped working when he saw us. Lonny usually bunched his long, dark hair into a man bun when he worked outdoors. He liked to listen to heavy metal music turned up so loud I sometimes had to wave to get his attention. He pulled out his ear buds, and a thrumming beat disturbed the morning stillness.

"You've told her?" he asked.

Burk nodded and motioned to Lonny who jerked back the tarp covering the new trench. The sound of the sudden movement of stiff canvas amplified my anticipation.

I moved in closer. Multiple skeletons lay exposed in haphazard disarray, obviously abandoned rather than buried. Most startling was the color of the bones—a dark red. Not the brown red of dried blood, but the red of a deep crimson staining agent.

"I've asked George to test the stain," Burk said. "We think it's red ochre."

George Hargood, the project's research archaeologist, ran our on-site lab.

"Good call," I said. "If it is red ochre, it's the first use I've heard of at a Southwestern site."

"There's more physical evidence," Burk said. "Look at this." He removed a skull from the exposed pile. The top third was missing, the edge smooth and even. "And this ..." He pointed to a femur that had been severed in half.

I picked up an arm bone from the jumble and found similar marks. The cartilage was long gone, but deep cuts penetrated the top of the joint—the kind of cuts we commonly found on prehistoric animal bones that were hunted and butchered for food.

I felt my adrenaline spike. Not only were the tops of skulls missing, the backs of some were also black and charred.

"These cuts look like they were made after death," I said.

"Right," Burk said. "The bodies were dismembered post-mortem."

Burk's theory that we'd uncovered a bone hash looked spot on. "Bone hash" is a term archaeologists use to describe human bones found in a haphazard pile left after butchering. Such piles are markedly different from burials.

Ancient cannibalism was a behavior I wanted to better understand. I knew many prehistoric cultures practiced it, including my own Celtic ancestors. Clay and I had visited the Gough's Cave archaeological site in Southern England, home to ancient Britons. Human remains were discovered in the cave dating back 15,000 years, each of four skeletons showing irrefutable evidence of cannibalism. Recent research has uncovered similar sites throughout Europe.

Despite the discomfort of learning about cannibalism among my ancestors, I knew it was my job to understand, not to judge ancient people. We knew from tree-ring dating the early inhabitants at Moenkopi Ridge struggled through a long period of severe drought between 1130 and 1180 CE. Big game animals like deer were already gone, as were many smaller animals hunted for food. Eventually the springs slowed to a trickle or stopped flowing altogether. Only the most drought-resistant food plants continued to grow beside the remaining natural springs before the last people to live in Moenkopi Ridge abandoned their homes and moved on.

My fingers gripping the arm bone grew cold. The three of us huddled close without speaking. The extent and frequency Ancestral Pueblo people practiced cannibalism remained a highly controversial subject among modern descendants for both emotional and political reasons. The media had played up the sensational aspect when cannibalism was discovered at other sites, and some Native Americans claimed news coverage of these discoveries had been used to demean them. Any mention to the media of this find would have to be carefully orchestrated, if we disclosed it at all.

"I don't envy you your next conversation with the NAAC," Lonny said. "That bone pile is going to piss off a lot of my local relatives."

I returned the arm bone to the pile. There was no denying he was right. The members of the NAAC had cooperated with me so far, but I knew that could change. They would regard these bones as ancestral. I hadn't worked at Moenkopi Ridge long enough to have developed a strong relationship with the committee members, and every one of the original four had been recruited by my predecessor, not me. Recently, I'd asked a fifth member to join the committee, Cha'tima Honovi, a Hopi medicine man who lived in the ceremonial village of Walpi on First Mesa with his wife, Chosovi. I hoped that he would bring a balanced voice to the committee.

Lonny pushed a long strand of hair away from his face. "What's next, Aideen?" he asked.

"I'll let you know after I speak with Rodgers."

Our employer, Rodgers & Associates, was the private archaeological firm contracted to excavate this site by the Moenkopi Ridge Educational Foundation, the nonprofit organization in charge of the dig. Dr. Gerry Rodgers was my boss.

"For now," I told them, "Keep this trench covered. Go back to screening the kiva site until you reach the original floor. Hold off work on this trench until we have confirmation from George on the identity of the red stain and I give you the go-ahead to resume."

Burk and Lonny nodded, then both headed west toward the kiva site. I took photos of the bone hash with my phone to email to Rodgers.

I'd come to this position hoping a new environment would help me heal the grief of losing my husband, but the job had challenged me from the beginning. Adding to my duties of directing the excavations and managing the employees, I now faced an emotionally charged interaction with the site's descendants.

I pocketed my phone, secured the tarp over the bone hash, squared my shoulders, and hiked back to the office.

#

Nova let my dog out when she saw me walking toward the office. Dakota bounded to me, all long legs and paws. I shed my concerns for a moment and leaned down to pet her. Her tail thumped a welcome beat, and she turned in a circle, as if chasing her tail—her delightful way of telling me she was glad I was home.

I'd rescued Dakota from a locked SUV parked in full sun by a trailhead in Utah. She lay gasping in her own excrement on the back seat of the overheated car. I couldn't walk away.

I smashed a rear door window using a rock lugged from the trailhead cairn. When I pulled the dog out of the car, I poured water from my canteen over her and did what I could to get her to drink a little. Then I half-carried, half-dragged her into my car and rushed her to a vet in Blanding. There hadn't been time to leave a note for the dog's owner, but I figured the broken window and the dog shit on the back seat would tell the story.

After the vet worked to bring the dog around and predicted she'd live, I'd named her "Dakota" after the Dakota Gulch Trail where I found her. No one seeing my ninety-pound husky-mix dog now with her robust build and glossy gray-and-white coat would guess her history.

Nova stood in the office doorway sporting a new pair of pink running shoes. Her dark hair was pulled into a ponytail that exposed oversized hoop earrings. She wore a *Hike Grand Canyon* T-shirt and a pair of khaki cargo pants with the pockets loaded to the gills since she refused to carry a purse. I thanked her for taking care of Dakota and promised to catch up with her after I'd called Rodgers.

Dakota and I headed for my office in the back. I closed the door, put the phone on speaker, and dialed. Dakota curled up in her favorite spot beside my desk.

Gerry Rodgers, my boss, picked up on the first ring. I took a deep breath and told him we'd unearthed evidence of cannibalism. "Looks like at least a dozen skeletons, but Burk is still sorting that out and running tests. And that's not all. The bones were stained red. George is conducting tests to confirm, but it looks like red ochre."

Rodgers's voice sounded distant, like he was wearing his headset. I heard his chair scrape across the acrylic shield under his desk. He cleared his throat. "Use of red ochre in the Southwest is certainly unusual. Who knows about this find besides you, George and Burk?"

"Just Lonny."

"Already too many. Why am I on speaker?"

"Makes it easier for me to take notes."

"Pick up. I don't want this getting back to the NAAC or the foundation until we have a plan worked out."

I balanced the receiver against my shoulder and wrote myself a note to buy a headset. Rodgers took a minute. I imagined him fidgeting with his ballpoint pen the way he did in meetings when he mulled something over.

"There's a lot of interest now in cannibalism that occurred here in the Southwest," he said. "I believe we can use this discovery to ferret out grant money, especially since the bones have that red stain. Getting research underwritten would help our case with the NAAC and the foundation, but they'll still be worried about mishandling the media. We've got to keep this quiet until we know more."

Rodgers paused. His chair squeaked, as if he'd just sat down. "Weren't you going to Taos for a few days? I thought you wanted time off after meeting with that museum director in Tuba."

"Yes, but I can hold off."

"No, that's not where I'm going with this. Weren't you going to visit someone?"

"Yes, Valerie Robinson—one of the volunteers I met here at the dig."

"Good. Make the trip. You can leave tomorrow morning. There's a foundation close to Taos interested in prehistoric cannibalism—the Southwestern Cultures Foundation. Go pitch them for grant support. Take photos of the bone hash with you and ask them to keep it confidential while we wait on test results. I'll call ahead and make an appointment for you—I know the funding committee chair. I'll be in touch tomorrow with more details."

I held back from telling my boss about the attack I'd experienced in Tuba City. As the first female director at Moenkopi Ridge, I didn't want him thinking I lacked mettle. Instead of driving a company van, I'd take my own car and bring Dakota along.

I went out to the parking lot and transferred the backpack I'd left in the van into the trunk of my 351 Boss. Once my husband's pride, Clay enjoyed racing the dark blue 1967 Mustang so much I couldn't bring myself to sell it after he died. The Boss evoked memories of happier times. Its power on the road and Dakota's protectiveness would help me get over my concerns about driving alone after the break-in scare.

CHAPTER 5

TAOS IS A GOOD day's drive from the dig, close to 400 miles from Winslow, the nearest town. Dakota and I hiked down to the office parking lot early the next morning when the sun began to color the mesa. The dog jumped into the back seat of the Mustang, tail drumming out a beat against the headrest as soon as I opened the door.

Rodgers called me on the drive mid-morning to say he'd set an appointment for me at SCF for eleven o'clock the following day. I promised to call in a full report right after the meeting.

On the outskirts of town, I saw a sign pointing down a country road that led to Taos Pueblo. I'd heard the pueblo was home to some of the best silversmiths in the West. My friend, Valerie Robinson wasn't expecting me until after dinner, and besides, earrings have always been my downfall. The thought of a new pair of turquoise-and-silver danglers commandeered the wheel, and I swerved off the highway without signaling.

The driver I'd noticed following behind me since I'd crossed into New Mexico leaned on his horn, then he sped up and streaked past me in his black pickup. I shook my head wondering why he hadn't passed earlier. It wasn't like we were driving in Philly's rush-hour traffic.

The road to the pueblo looked deserted. At the gatehouse, three black-and-white sawhorses blocked the entrance. The middle sawhorse held a beat-up cardboard sign with a faded message: Pueblo Closed for Private Ceremony.

Disappointed, I checked the rearview mirror to back out. The black pickup that passed me earlier turned down the gravel road and crawled forward right behind my car. It sat there, engine idling, like a big black vulture waiting for its meal to die.

I looked for a way around the truck, but a thick row of scrub trees grew alongside the road to my right, and sagebrush covered the mesa to my left. The truck completely blocked my exit from the narrow road. Its windshield was heavily peppered with dead bugs, making it hard to see inside, but it looked like the driver wore his hair long under a black cowboy hat.

He opened the door and stepped down from his truck, standing knees bent, as if ready to spring, but it was his swollen and bandaged hand that cinched it.

I figured I could either sit there dumbstruck, or I could drive helter-skelter across the sandy terrain and get the hell out of there.

I backed up the Mustang the few feet I could, wrenched the wheel a hard left... and floored it.

Dakota slammed against the door. Gravel shot from beneath the rear tires. The engine revved when I shifted into second. The Mustang nose-dived into a shallow ditch between the road and the open field. I downshifted. Dakota righted herself in the shotgun seat. Tail pipes rumbled. I bulldozed through vegetation that scraped against the undercarriage and swerved to miss a boulder. Dakota leaned against me. The steering wheel felt slick from sweat, but my hands went cold when the rearview mirror framed the truck blasting through the high-desert underbrush, closing the distance between us.

"Down!" I yelled to Dakota.

I swerved right, then left, driving in a zigzag. Black Hat matched me zig for zag. I straightened the wheels and prayed I could outrun him. The tires shot sand and plant debris through my open windows. The car had little traction in the sandy soil.

Dakota popped up, whined, and turned her head just in time to avoid the bullet that shattered the rear window and exited the windshield, leaving a hole in the front pane and a spiderweb of cracks.

I sucked air and stood on the accelerator, struggling to see through the cracked windshield. We gained a little speed. I took my hand off the wheel to grab Dakota by her collar as the car broke through an old coyote fence, gray posts flying past us on either side. I swerved to miss a cedar tree and nose-dived straight into the dry river bottom. My jaw ached from gritting my teeth. The Mustang slowed to a creep, dragging in the deep sand of the arroyo. We rolled past sharp rocks and the gray, skeletal-looking remains of long-dead cactus.

My panic rose like floodwater when I checked the rearview. The truck had topped the hill right behind me. The Mustang barely moved in the deep sand. We gained another few yards before it bottomed out.

I threw open the door, let Dakota out, and stuffed the car keys into the front pocket of my jeans. We ran.

A few minutes later an ear-shattering crash disturbed the backcountry stillness. I took a huge breath, struggled to run faster, and fought the urge to hide.

"Come on, girl," I called to Dakota. I had no idea which direction the arroyo ran. With luck it would lead us back to the pueblo and a chance to find help.

I listened for sounds of pursuit, but all I heard were my own ragged breaths. My hands balled into fists as I fought for control. We ran around a curve. Dakota shot ahead. The sides of the arroyo loomed high, carved by a recent flash flood. I ran toward a cluster of cedars on my right, grabbed onto a low branch, and hauled myself up the steep side of the arroyo. Dakota stood waiting at the top.

I spied a low outcropping with a shallow cave a few yards beyond. We ran for it. I crouched down, and we scooted inside. I turned around to scan the landscape. No movement. I duck-walked out and around the back of the outcropping, Dakota following. Beyond lay nothing but sand, clumps of sagebrush… and open desert.

CHAPTER 6

DAKOTA AND I RACED across the mesa, the dog falling in step beside me like she did on morning runs at the dig. I lost my footing when we came to a steep ravine and slid down the slope a good ten feet on my butt. Dakota ran up the opposite side and disappeared over the top. I pushed myself to catch up with her, fixed my eyes on the white underside curl of her tail, and followed as closely behind as I could.

The clouds cast oddly shaped shadows onto the mesa, reminding me of Hopi tales of witchcraft. Dakota ran down a steep slope. When I caught up with her, I realized she'd led us back to the arroyo. We ran along the dry river bottom in silence, Dakota sometimes far ahead. The driftwood on its sandy floor reminded me of sun-bleached bones.

I heard wild barking before rounding a blind curve—and slammed straight into Black Hat.

I screamed.

But no one was around to hear me.

He shoved me hard. "Go ahead... scream your goddamned head off. It's not gonna do you any good."

Dakota growled and snapped at him before running off. He raised his rifle and fired. Dakota went silent. I strained to see her in the split second before he turned and aimed the smoking black hole at me.

I gripped my hands together in front of me to stop them

from shaking. My eyes blurred, darting from him to where I'd last seen Dakota.

"Looking for your dog?" he asked. "I got it good. Betcha it's dead by now. Turn around."

I figured if I turned, whatever was behind me would be the last thing I saw. I stalled. "What do you want?"

"Shut up. I said turn around."

His eyes bored into mine like two steel drill bits. He leveled the rifle at me, using his bandaged arm for balance.

I turned. He jabbed me in the back with the rifle prodding me to take steps. Pain shot through my spine with each blow. "Pick it up, bitch." His voice behind me sounded like metal on a rasp, and some inane part of me wondered how many packs a day he burned through.

Why didn't he just shoot me instead of marching me across the arroyo? I looked up, and then I knew. He'd pushed me toward a massive formation of boulders in the middle of the arroyo. I looked from side to side, hoping to see Dakota.

"Walk over to those rocks."

"What is it you want?" I gasped.

"I want my goddamned photo. What have you done with it?"

"I don't have it. One of the cops took it!"

He fired a shot overhead from behind. I jumped so hard I lost my balance, fell backward, and landed face up in the sand. For a moment I couldn't hear. Then he leaned over me and spat out, "Get up."

Struggling to regain my footing, I looked directly into his eyes. A cold hazel. Instead of another shot, I heard a faint clatter. The sound grew louder. Hoofbeats! He glanced sideways just long enough. I dashed behind the boulders and ducked out of sight. He fired, blasting the massive rock protecting me.

I inched up and dared a quick glance. Riders! Three horsemen charged toward us. I knew they couldn't hear me, but the rider in front had a rifle, and it was aimed at Black Hat. I had to try.

I stood and frantically waved my arms and called to them. "Help me!"

The first man to arrive held his rifle steady and shouted at Black Hat. "Lower that firearm. What's going on here?"

Black Hat pointed his rifle toward the ground.

"Just showing my girlfriend a few sharp-shooting tricks."

"He's not my boyfriend! He stalked me and tried to kill me! He shot my dog!"

The lead man looked older than the other two and exuded an air of authority. He studied me for a moment, then turned to face Black Hat.

"She looks really scared and messed up to me," he said. Leaning to his right he said something I couldn't hear to the younger man sitting astride next to him.

Desperate, I called again, this time in Tiwa, "Help me!"

The older man spun around in his saddle. "You speak Tiwa?"

"Barely." I pointed at Black Hat. "Not my boyfriend. Shot at me," I attempted mostly with gestures and the few words I could remember in Tiwa. I stared at the man who seemed to be in charge. "Please help me," I said in English. "I don't know this man." Tears I could no longer suppress spilled down my cheeks.

The leader signaled again to the man on his right. The younger man dismounted, and the lead man stayed on his horse and kept his rifle aimed at Black Hat.

"Hand over that rifle," the man now on foot demanded of Black Hat.

But Black Hat stood his ground, eyes narrowed. The third horseman pulled his rifle from a holster on his saddle and aimed it at him.

"You're on Taos Pueblo land," he said. "Hand over your rifle, then hands in front of you."

Black Hat turned his firearm broadside and shoved it at the man on the ground, who handed it up to the leader. He then went to his horse and took a length of rawhide rope from his saddle and walked back to Black Hat and tied his hands in front of him.

The lead man turned to me and said, "Is your dog still alive?"

"I don't know. She ran off," I said, a catch in my voice.

"You have five minutes to find her. There's a funeral at the pueblo. We have to get back."

Unsteady from the rush of adrenaline, desperate to find Dakota, and fearing the worst, I ran along the arroyo calling her name.

No sign of her.

No response.

Finally, one of the riders called to me, "Come on, miss. You can't stay out here alone. You have to go back with us."

"But my dog," I said. "I have to find her!"

"We'll handle that later. You have to come with us."

The man on the ground wrapped the loose ends of the rope binding Black Hat's hands around his saddle horn. When that *Taoseño* remounted, and the three of them began to move, I prayed Dakota was alive. The third horseman turned his horse and came back for me, leaning over to give me a hand up. We moved ahead in a slow walk with Black Hat jogging and huffing alongside.

CHAPTER 7

THE RIDE BACK TO the pueblo took less than fifteen minutes. The three *Taoseños* stopped at the gatehouse, and all of us dismounted. The man who'd given me the ride called tribal police on his cell phone. Wondering what would come next, I waited silently while the men tied their horses to a nearby hitching post. The gatehouse was a small wooden tower with windows on all four sides that reminded me of the stone watchtowers at my dig. The leader told me to go inside. A beat-up metal desk stood near the wall opposite the door with two wooden chairs in front and a rolling desk chair behind it. The three horsemen followed me inside, guiding Black Hat along by the rawhide rope tied around his wrists.

I turned and glared at him. "Who *are* you?"

He gave me a lopsided smirk. "You knew who I was last night, baby. Couldn't get enough of me."

"Who the hell do you think…?"

The leader motioned with his palms out for me to be quiet. "Our tribal police will get to that. Right now, we'd like to know what you were doing in our arroyo. That part of Taos Pueblo is closed to outsiders."

"I was running from him!" I shrieked, my hands tightening into fists.

"Why'd he come after you?"

"I'm not saying any more with *him* in here."

The man who'd given me the ride took Black Hat outside. The leader closed the door and turned to me. "Okay. What else?"

I told them how the same man they'd just found shooting at me had showed up at my motel room two nights before demanding that I give him a photo he claimed to have left in the room.

"Why didn't you give it to him?" the leader asked.

"I started to, but then he grabbed at me and tried to break in. I broke his hold and yanked the photo back inside. When the police finally got there one of the officers took it."

As Rodgers had instructed, I said nothing about the bone hash or why I was in Taos. I still had the business cards from the two cops in Tuba City tucked in my jeans pocket. I pulled them out and handed them over.

"Call these policemen. They'll confirm I'm telling the truth."

The leader looked at each card and jotted down names and phone numbers on a pad he picked up from the desk. He handed the cards back and said, "You'll have to wait here while we sort this out with our tribal police. Luis, the man who gave you the ride, will stay here with you. When our police are done questioning you, you can leave."

"But I've got to find my dog! Can't Luis take me back to the arroyo to find her?"

"No, you can look for it later."

The two men exited the gatehouse, leaving me alone with Luis. I struggled not to break down, knowing Dakota could be lying in the backcountry hurt and in pain, if not dead. Luis sat in the chair behind the desk.

I took a deep breath. "What's your last name, Luis?" I asked.

"Lujan."

"Don't you have a Tiwa name?"

"The priests gave us Spanish names when they first came here." He gestured toward a chair. I dragged it to the front of the desk and sat down.

"How did you learn those words in our language?" he asked. "Pretty odd for an outsider to know any Tiwa."

"My great-grandmother spoke Tiwa. Because of her, I listened to a few old recordings of Tiwa speakers at the university. I've forgotten most of what I learned."

"Your great-grandmother was Indian?"

"So I'm told. She died a long time before I was born."

"What is it you do?"

"Archaeology. I work in Arizona." I shifted my weight on the hard-backed wooden chair and met his eyes. "You know, Luis, I'm really worried about my dog. I need to find her and take care of her if she's hurt. Can't you help me?"

Luis shrugged. "You heard what Jesus said." He used the Spanish pronunciation.

"Hay-ZEUS?" I asked.

"The guy who led our patrol. He's a big deal on the tribal council. I've got to go along with him."

My sigh was long and exaggerated. "I don't get it. Some crazy guy tries to kill me, and the *help* I get is being held against my will while my dog could be lying somewhere in pain. She's the only family I have out here."

He gave me what could have been a sympathetic nod and handed me his phone. "You can make a call if you want. Best I can do."

Valerie Robinson's number was stored in my phone with all my other belongings abandoned in the Mustang. I didn't know her number by heart, but maybe I could remember it if I could calm down a little. I closed my eyes. Most of northern New Mexico had the same area code. I punched it in and gave memory a try. Several wrong numbers later, luck switched to my side. The call went to Valerie's voice mail. I left her a message that I'd been detained and didn't know for how long but would call her later. I asked Luis to hand me a pen from the gatehouse desk. I copied Valerie's number from the phone's display onto the back of Humetewa's card.

Out of ideas, I returned Luis' phone and stared out the window behind him, miserable but determined to hold myself together.

Two magpies sat chattering on a wire stretching from the gatehouse to a nearby power pole. Startled, they leaped from the wire and flew off. Then I heard what had startled them: scratching on the gatehouse door. I jumped up to open it and found Dakota wagging her tail so hard it looked like her rear end might wag right off. I crouched down and threw my arms around her, burrowing my face in her ruff. I ran my hands over her legs and belly and leaned back to look at the rest of her. No blood, no wounds. The shot had missed her.

"You really love that dog," Luis said.

I rubbed my eyes and heaved a sigh of relief.

Dakota followed me back to the chair I'd vacated and gave my hand a lick before she turned around three times to curl up beside me.

"You don't have anyone else? A husband? Some kids?"

"Parents and a sister—all living in Philly."

Luis scraped his chair backwards and propped his feet on the desktop. "No boyfriend?"

I looked past him out the window. "My husband was killed a year ago."

Luis let out a shrill whistle. "That really sucks. My girlfriend dumped me, but I guess it's not the same. How'd he die?"

"I don't talk about it."

Outside a car approached, crunching gravel. I opened the door to look out. A tribal police van pulled up and parked, with Black Hat in the passenger's seat. Jesus stepped out from the driver's side, and two other men climbed out of the van's side door and walked toward the gatehouse. Luis left to join them.

Two men came inside—a uniformed Taos Tribal Police officer, the second a man in street clothes who flashed a badge I didn't recognize. The policeman slipped past me and stood leaning against the desk. He folded his arms over his chest and looked me up and down without comment. Dakota came over and stood beside me with her ears back, watching. I rested my hand on her ruff to calm her, absently combing my fingers through her thick coat.

My face must have conveyed surprise to the man in street clothes. His shirt was different, but he wore the same dusty black cowboy boots, jeans, and the sunglasses he'd worn the day before when I saw him in the park in Tuba City.

"Aren't you Aideen Connor?"

"…Yes," I said slowly, "How'd you know my name? Who are you?"

"Special Agent Frank Nakai with the BLM."

"What's this got to do with the Bureau of Land Management?"

"BLM special agents investigate crimes on federal land. I came here earlier on official business. I'd like to talk with you when Lieutenant Ramirez here is finished taking your statement." He turned to the tribal officer and said, "Rudy, I'll wait outside. Let me know when you're done."

With that, he turned and left. The newly identified Lieutenant Ramirez moved around behind the desk to the chair Luis had vacated and motioned for me to sit opposite. He eyed Dakota. "Jesus said you claimed that guy we picked up shot your dog. It looks all right to me."

I remained standing and sighed. "Fortunately, he was a lousy shot."

"You realize it's his word against yours."

I frowned. "Didn't Jesus tell you that man was shooting at me when they rode into the arroyo?"

"They didn't see him shooting *at* you, but they did say they heard shots, and he was the one with the weapon. Why don't you tell me your version of what happened?"

My *version*? For a moment, I couldn't speak. *What had Black Hat said they found so compelling?* Ramirez picked up a pad and pen from the desktop.

I sat down in front of the desk, took a deep breath, and gathered my thoughts. Dakota nuzzled my hand. I gave Ramirez a detailed account of what had happened two nights ago at the motel and what had happened here today. He jotted down notes without interrupting.

When I finished, he asked, "How long have you been dating this guy?"

"That man tried to kill me! Didn't you hear anything I said? You're suggesting I'm *dating* him?"

Ramirez stared back, his jaw set. "He claims he's been seeing you. The two of you had a big fight, and he came to your room in Tuba City to make up. He followed you here when you wouldn't talk to him."

I stood up. "He's lying! If you don't believe me, go look at the windows in my car! Then tell me that creep and I are dating."

"Look... Dr. Connor, is it? I know things can go sour when people are seeing each other. We haven't seen this car you're talking about, and we can only act on what we know happened here on our land. I'll call these two officers in Tuba City, and we'll hold this guy while we look for evidence and check out your stories. That's all I can promise."

My face felt hot inside the stuffy gatehouse. I shook my head and glared at him.

Ramirez looked at me for a moment and then shrugged. "I'll tell the BLM guy we're done."

I took a few deep breaths to calm myself and hid my

hands behind my back when the BLM agent walked in so he didn't see them shaking. I looked at him coolly and gave him a nod.

"I had a couple of questions regarding a different matter," he said. "Did you know protecting ancient sites is one of BLM's mandates?"

"Yes." *Where was this going?*

"And you're aware there's a big problem with looting at ancient sites out here?"

"Yes, the remoteness of some sites makes the looting problem worse."

"Meanwhile thieves keep getting smarter and BLM's budget keeps going lower. Lately we've seen a surge in stolen artifacts turning up for sale. To be fair, gallery owners don't always know the true sources of their inventory."

"Why are you bringing this up with me?" I asked.

"Some of the items we've seized in the last few months could have come from your dig."

Folding my arms, I said, "I don't see how. Artifacts are locked up in a secure room after we've photographed them *in situ*. Only one staff member besides me has a key to the secure room."

"What about human remains?"

I twitched like a few dozen horse flies were marching across my back.

"Human remains are left where they're found or carefully moved until we work out repatriation or reburial with the descendants."

"And you personally follow protocol?"

"Of course I follow protocol. It's an important part of my job. You know, Agent Nakai, I'm way past my limit. I've been held against my will, scared out of my wits, shot at, worried sick about my dog, and now, are you actually *accusing* me of something?" I realized I was yelling. "Sorry," I said, taking a deep breath. "This has been a real day from hell."

He took a step back and raised his hands, palms out. "I'm not accusing you of anything. We know you've been in charge of that dig for only a few months. Mostly, I'm here to warn you because you could be in danger."

"Right. Now *there's* a surprise. What kind of danger are we talking about? Something worse than some crazy guy trying to kill me? You want to help me, why don't you clue me in on who that guy is who shot at me? None of this is making any sense to me."

Nakai sat on the desktop and motioned for me to take the chair in front of it, but I declined. He shrugged. "Sure, I'll tell you. You could probably find out on your own, anyway. Name's Ray Alonzo. Arrested twice for assault. Busted and jailed for cooking meth. Could be why he got so violent. Meth makes users super strong and a little crazy."

I gripped the back of the wooden chair in front of me, knuckles whitening. "He acted more than a *little* crazy."

"Understood. Just one of the reasons you need to be careful."

"Careful how? Isn't he going to jail?"

"They'll detain him, but they may not find enough to hold him for long. Do you have security at your dig?"

"No."

"Add it. Be on the alert for anything unusual."

"Unusual how?"

"Staff acting secretive. Things disappearing."

For the third time in twenty-four hours, a law officer handed me his card. I glanced at it briefly, then stuck it in the front pocket of my jeans with the other two.

"Call me if you notice anything suspicious. I wrote my cell number on the back."

"I'll keep it in mind. Are we finished now?"

He smiled. "Let me check with the tribal officer. I can give you a lift into Taos if they're done with their business."

His easy smile irritated me. "That would be great if I had

anything with me besides my car keys and my dog. I abandoned everything else in my car when that man came after me."

The muscles in my shoulders throbbed. The adrenaline rush that was keeping me going had all but played out. I slumped down onto the hard-backed wooden chair and put my head in my hands. Dakota sat beside me and leaned against my leg.

Nakai went outside to talk with the tribal cop. I wondered how I was ever going to make it to my meeting at the foundation the next morning, let alone get my wrecked car home and recover my belongings.

CHAPTER 8

Agent Nakai re-entered the gatehouse and said he had clearance from Lieutenant Ramirez to drive me to my abandoned Mustang. Ramirez would follow in a tribal SUV.

It was past dusk when we located my car. The three of us approached, leaving Dakota in the BLM van. Ramirez swept his flashlight over the car's exterior, pausing at the shattered rear window and the smashed trunk lid.

"Did that damage occur when you were in the vehicle?" Nakai asked.

"Only the shot through the rear window. The trunk was intact when the car bottomed out and the dog and I abandoned it."

Nakai tried to raise the trunk lid, but it wouldn't budge. Ramirez went back to his SUV and returned with a tire iron. He stuck it in the gap between the lid and the body of the car and gave it several strong jerks upward. The trunk creaked open, and Ramirez shone his flashlight into the opening.

"What the hell is that?" he asked.

I looked inside at the circle of light cast by his flashlight. And froze. My backpack and other personal items sat in a viscous red-brown puddle. My old Penn State sweatshirt had been slashed to pieces. Two painted sticks bound together with blue yarn were pinned to one of the pieces. A bloody turkey feather dangled from one of the sticks. The trunk emitted the metallic, putrid odor of decaying blood. Someone had made a *paho*, a Hopi prayer stick, attached it to a piece of my sweatshirt and set the whole mess in a pool of blood.

"Oh my God." I doubled over from the shock and the nauseating smell, willing myself not to retch.

Nakai put his hand on my shoulder. "You should go wait in the car."

My tightening stomach trumped any impulse to argue. I stumbled to the van and climbed into the passenger's seat. Dakota inched forward from the back and gave my cheek a lick. I put my arms around her and gave her a reassuring hug, as much for myself as for the dog. A little later, Nakai approached the van. I turned when he opened the rear door and the interior lights came on. He dug around in a large plastic box in the back.

"I'm going to bag the contents in the trunk. Tomorrow I'll send up a tech team for a full search."

"I need my billfold and my clothes out of that backpack," I said.

"Sorry, can't release your backpack or its contents. It's evidence."

"Evidence?"

"It's a crime scene."

I looked at him like he was nuts. "How am I supposed to pay for anything without my billfold? I haven't eaten since breakfast, my dog is hungry, and I'll need a place to stay."

"I'll see if BLM can guarantee your tab until you can access your accounts."

"But what if they won't?"

Nakai ignored my comment.

"There's a granola bar in the glove box," he said. "Help yourself."

The rear door slammed, and the van went dark. *Oh, great*, I thought. *I can have a granola bar, never mind my driver's license, phone, cash, or credit cards.*

I laughed a shrill laugh that sounded more like a shriek. Nakai walked around to the passenger's side and leaned in through the open window.

"You all right?"

"A granola bar? I've had a complete day from hell and you're offering me a freaking granola bar?"

"Better than nothing, if you're hungry."

I started to protest, but he was already heading toward the blood-soaked mess in my car. I wondered who could have put blood in the trunk. Alonzo would not have had time to stage something so detailed in the time between my abandoning the car and later running into him in the arroyo. I remembered that I hadn't opened the trunk before leaving. I'd packed up everything the night before. Someone at the dig could have done it though, in the night or the early morning before I drove off. I shivered at the realization.

I watched as Nakai slipped on latex gloves within the tight circle of light cast by Ramirez's flashlight. He placed each item from the trunk, including my backpack, into its own brown paper bag.

I opened the glove compartment and hunted around for the granola bar. Peanut butter. I gave Dakota half. Her piece was gone in one gulp. I nibbled at mine. "I hope it stays down," I muttered.

When Nakai returned, he opened the rear door again and placed all the bagged evidence in the large plastic box in the back of the van and left the lid off. A copper-like stench suffused the interior.

He slid into the driver's seat, and I gave him a dirty look. Nakai responded with an amused grin, started up the van and drove the rutted road back toward the pueblo. I ignored him until curiosity got the better of me. "Why did you use paper bags?" I asked.

"The blood hasn't completely dried. Paper bags allow it

to dry and are less likely to cause contamination."

He turned onto the highway to Taos and handed me his phone from a pocket on the door. "Probably best if you find a place on the plaza that has a restaurant. Keep it all on one tab."

I found a hotel online that took dogs and gave Nakai the name and address.

"I know where it is. Was there anything unusual in your trunk when you left?"

"I don't know. Nothing was out of sorts the night before when I packed, but I didn't look in the trunk before I left this morning."

I stared through the window into the deepening darkness and rubbed my hands down the front of my jeans. "I can't imagine why someone would use a *paho* like that. It's sacrilegious in the worst way possible. Like drowning a kitten in a holy water basin."

Nakai grunted and stared straight ahead. We clocked off several miles without speaking. The unfamiliar landscape loomed ghostly under the darkening sky. Nakai eventually turned toward me with eyes that looked black in the darkness of the van. "What was it you said to me yesterday morning in the park? Do you remember?"

"*Ya'at'eeh*. The Navajo greeting."

"Did you think I was Navajo?"

"Tuba City sits on Navajo land, and you have the coloring."

"I am Navajo, but I didn't grow up out here. My parents worked in D. C. Sometimes I heard them speaking Navajo at night, but they only used English with my brother and me. Do you speak it?"

"No. It's a complex language, hard to learn."

"Then why did you greet me that way?"

"I wanted to see what you'd do."

Nakai shrugged and focused on the road. The sky had

deepened to an inky purple. I remembered times when Clay and I rode together without talking, how the quiet passed pleasantly between us rather than awkwardly like it felt now.

"Lieutenant Ramirez told me you'd run into Alonzo before."

"Yes, I think he followed me here."

"From where?"

I told Nakai about the odd break-in attempt in Tuba City.

"He came back to the motel looking for a photo?"

"It's all he asked for, but he'd left some dirty clothes in the room as well."

Nakai turned down a narrow street at the main intersection in town and drove past a large public square he said was Taos Plaza. The common area, well-lit by streetlamps, showed off a good-sized bandshell, park benches, and the imposing bronze sculpture of a man standing with his arms outstretched. He pulled up to *El Valiente*, the hotel I'd booked online, and parked in a diagonal space in front.

"I'll go in with you to get things set up," Nakai said.

I stepped out of the van, opened the side door, and grabbed Dakota by the collar. We approached the front desk—the well-groomed law officer and the disheveled woman in dirty jeans and a rumpled T-shirt clinging to the collar of an off-leash dog. I started to say something to the clerk at the front desk, but Nakai interrupted.

"This is Dr. Aideen Connor. We're going to charge her room to my BLM account. She doesn't have any ID with her, so I'll give you the billing information."

Nakai turned to me. "Why don't you go on upstairs? I'll give you a call in the morning."

I took the key from the scrubbed-looking guy behind the desk, thanked Nakai, and headed upstairs with my dog.

#

Dakota needed a walk, and both of us were beyond

ready for food. I ordered two cheeseburgers from room service, one for Dakota and one for me, no fries, and we headed for the hotel's back stairs that opened onto an alley. Leashless, we jogged up and down the alley until Dakota did her business, then we returned to the room to wait for room service.

After the meal I stuck my collection of cop cards on the nightstand, headed for the shower, and scrubbed myself until the water ran cold. Then I washed all my clothes, even my jeans, in the bathroom sink and rolled each piece in a towel and stood on it. I hung the wet clothes over the shower rod and kicked the bathmat under it to catch the drips, but the kick didn't rid me of the fury I felt after my encounter with tribal police. Ramirez said he'd look for evidence in the arroyo to corroborate my "story," but hadn't it been obvious to the three riders that Alonzo was shooting at me? Didn't they tell that to Ramirez?

I wrapped myself in an extra sheet and climbed into bed. Dakota came to the bedside and whined.

"Rough day, huh, girl?" I said and broke my number one dog-training rule and invited her to jump up beside me. Minutes later she was snoring. I envied her ability to fall asleep with such ease.

My life and my sleep patterns had changed so much after my husband died. Well-meaning friends advised me to stay in Philly where I had roots and family, to create a new life for myself surrounded by friends and familiar places. But the old landmarks only reminded me of what I'd lost.

Sometimes I felt my loss in a physical way, like amputees who claim they can "feel" lost limbs. I'd toss restlessly in the bed Clay and I shared, and sometimes I'd dream I felt his light touch on my shoulder. Then I'd wake with a start, only to remember I was sleeping alone.

I knew when I started ditching work to smoke weed and watch tabloid talk shows that I had to leave Philadelphia.

Now here I was, stuck in the middle-of-desert nowhere—with no transportation, no money, no credit cards, and a professional meeting I had no way to get to the following morning.

In Peru, Clay and I had argued the night before he died. I wanted to make a side trip to an archaeological ruin off the main route. Clay wanted to stick with our aggressive pace. His motto: Hike hard. Make camp early. Watch the sunset. But I'd insisted on taking the detour, and that put us behind schedule. We never made it to our planned destination. Less than twelve hours after we set out, Clay would be dead. Insisting on making that alternate route was something I'd have to live with the rest of my life.

I leaned across Dakota to turn out the light on the nightstand. She'd stretched out her long wolf-like legs with one big paw dangling off the bed. I loved studying her when she was asleep—a time she lay still enough that I could appreciate her markings—the brindled gray of her back against the white of her belly and the underside of her tail. Her masked face sported a pattern under each eye that looked like a lightning bolt. She was my masked warrior, the one support I counted on at the end of a wretched day.

CHAPTER 9

DAKOTA PAWED ME OUT of the nightmare. In the dream, I floated above the Peruvian rain forest where Clay and I spent our last night together. The sun was sinking behind the next mountain range over, the one we were supposed to have reached by the end of the day. Insects buzzed all around us. The smell of decaying plants permeated the air as the rising moon revealed dozens of bats darting mid-air and devouring insects. Clay was helping the guide dig a fire pit, but the ground was so saturated the hole kept filling with water. I thought back on that long, damp night and pulled the covers up to my chin.

The nightstand clock read 3:04 a.m. I lay in bed, feeling the despair brought on by the nightmare until it gradually faded like fog burning off with the dawn. When sunlight struck my second-floor window, I climbed out of bed, groggy and exhausted from another night of little sleep and put on my still-damp clothes. Dakota and I took the stairs to the hotel entrance for a walk around the plaza.

A workman loaded overstuffed plastic bags from metal trash cans into the back of a municipal truck. He dropped an empty can, and Dakota barked and chased after it until it slammed against a bench. The workman gave me a dirty look. "Sorry," I mouthed and called Dakota to me.

A tall man wearing a black cowboy hat entered the

square from the west and sauntered toward us. I gripped Dakota's collar and watched him venture across the square long enough to determine he was not Ray Alonzo, but Dakota growled when the man passed.

We returned to the room, and I used the hotel phone to call my office. Burk answered. Despite the comfort of a familiar voice, I couldn't shake the shadowy memories of Alonzo's violence or the recurring nightmare. I sat on the bed and worked a section of top sheet into a wad while we talked.

"Damn, Aideen, what *is* it with you? Where are you now?"

"A hotel in Taos. I'm waiting for the BLM agent to release my belongings."

"How long will that take?"

"He wouldn't say, but they haven't shown any sense of urgency."

"You sure you haven't run into that guy who came after you before?"

"Only in Tuba City. The agent said he was likely stoked on drugs."

"No doubt. How're you holding up?"

"Pretty well. The boss sent me here to make a funding pitch. I've got to keep myself together and pull that off later this morning."

"What can I do?"

"Have Lucy wire me some cash against my next paycheck."

"Where to?"

"There's a Money Exchange in the grocery store on Paseo del Pueblo. Ask her to wire it there, at least a thousand. Have her call Arizona Motor Vehicles and find out how I get a replacement license and ask her to email a photocopy of my old license to AMV and to me here at the hotel."

Lucy worked in our Phoenix office. We were both transplanted Easterners and made instant friends when I moved to Arizona. Sometimes I stayed with her when I had business in Phoenix.

Burk took down the name and phone number of my hotel. The phone buzzed as soon as we hung up. It was Agent Nakai.

"I hope you have some good news for me," I said.

"The bureau hasn't released anything, if that's what you mean. I drove the items I bagged from your car last night to our forensics lab in Santa Fe. It'll take some time."

"Can't I at least have my ID and credit cards? How hard can it be to check those first?"

"They won't release anything until the techs are finished with all of it."

"What am I supposed to do in the meantime?"

"Try to be patient."

"But I'm here on a work assignment. What will your techs be doing exactly?"

"The Santa Fe team is examining the contents I delivered from your trunk. I'm sending techs up to Taos Pueblo later to search Alonzo's truck. Your car will be next."

"If you'll keep me in the loop, I might be able to help."

"You could help me now by telling me about that fetish we found attached to your sweatshirt."

"It's not a fetish. It's a Hopi prayer stick called a *paho*."

"What are they used for?"

"It's part of a prayer ritual. I've never heard of one being used in the way we found it, though. You should let me examine it."

"Why?"

"I might notice something your techs would miss."

"Like what?"

"Like whether it's authentic. That could reveal a lot about who made it."

"Letting a civilian handle evidence isn't likely to fly with the director, but we can discuss it later. I'll drive up to meet you when I'm done here."

"Where are you?"

"My office in Santa Fe—about an hour and a half away. There's a café in that hotel where you're staying. Meet me there at one."

#

It was a few minutes past eight when we hung up, and I wondered what Nakai had in mind when he asked me to meet him later in the day. I still had plenty of time to make my eleven o'clock appointment at the Southwestern Cultures Foundation—*if* I could figure out how to get there with no money, no transportation, let alone look presentable enough to give a sponsorship pitch. It was a tall order.

The foundation was a few miles north of Taos. I figured if I worked out a ride, I could leave Dakota in my room with the "Do Not Disturb" sign on the door and be back in plenty of time to meet the BLM agent. That left working out what I was going to say at the foundation—without access to my notes or the photos of the bone hash stored in my phone. I found Humetewa's card with the others I'd left on the nightstand and dialed Valerie's number that I'd scrawled on the back. I held my breath and counted the dial tones. She answered on the fifth ring.

"Aideen! What happened? I tried your cell, and it kept going to voice mail."

"My phone was confiscated." I filled her in.

"Good grief, Aideen. Somebody shot at you? Are you okay?"

"Working on it. I could really use your help, though. Could we get together this morning?"

"I have a little time to meet with you, but not much. Since I didn't hear from you, I made appointments in Santa Fe with a few gallery owners. You can still stay at my place if you want to, though."

"I don't think I'd want to stay there alone, but thanks. I need your help on something else."

"Sure. What?"

"Two things. Could I borrow a white shirt and a pair of black pants? I think we're about the same size. I have to make a presentation later this morning."

"No problem. What else?"

"Would you give me a ride to the Southwestern Cultures Foundation? It's a few miles north of town."

"I know where it is. Where're you staying?"

"El Valiente."

"I'll meet you there with the clothes in an hour. I should have enough time to give you a ride before I head down to my first appointment."

#

I left Dakota in the room with water in a hotel ice bucket and traipsed downstairs to the espresso bar off the lobby. I charged a dry cappuccino and two egg sandwiches to my room—one for me and one for Dakota—and then carried the plate and mug to a red wooden stool at the bar by the window.

Looking out on the morning's activity, I mulled over the strange events of the preceding night. The bloody mess in my car was obviously put there to scare me, but why the *paho*? Prayer sticks were not something I associated with fear or violence, and from what I'd learned about Alonzo, it didn't seem likely he'd made the *paho*. It made no sense that a man with a drug habit and a criminal record would make a Hopi religious object, although he might have been the person who planted it in my car.

Alonzo must have found out where I lived and followed me to New Mexico. The Mustang was an old car, and the trunk didn't lock automatically like on new cars. Maybe the BLM agent was right. Maybe the dig needed security.

Unable to answer my own questions, I carried my empty cup to the bus tub and headed upstairs to give Dakota her egg sandwich.

#

Valerie arrived in the hotel lobby half an hour late carrying a freshly ironed white shirt on a hanger and a pair of black slacks draped over her arm. Her streaked blonde hair looked disheveled; her face pinched.

"Sorry I'm late. Took longer than I expected."

"Do you have enough time for coffee?"

She smiled. "Sure, long as it's quick."

Valerie handed me the clothes. She knew her way around the café and led us to a small table in the corner. I draped the clothes on a chair, gave her a quick hug, and thanked her for showing up on short notice.

"Let me treat," she said. She put in our orders at the counter and returned shortly with two mugs.

"How are you doing? Can't believe someone shot at you."

"Not as calm as I'd like, but at least the tribal police arrested the shooter. I'm more worried now about the presentation I have to make this morning. I'm not prepared."

"You can wing it. I've seen you do it before at volunteer meetings. Did you know some of my paintings have archaeological themes?"

"No, I hoped I'd get to see your work on this visit."

"Yeah, too bad we couldn't get together last night. I wanted to take you by my gallery, but we'll do it another time."

"Where do you show your work?"

"Now, only at the Taos Arts Cooperative. "I'm trying to get my paintings into galleries in Santa Fe and Sedona for tourist season."

"Is the Arts Cooperative close by?"

"Right off the plaza a few blocks from here." She scribbled the address on a napkin and handed it to me. Then she pulled a phone from her woven straw bag and checked the time.

"Sorry, but if you're going to change into those clothes and want me to drive you, better go do it. I have to leave in a few minutes."

#

I asked at the front desk if the hotel offered guests emergency supplies. The receptionist obliged me with a small cellophane package containing a mini hairbrush, a travel-sized toothbrush, and toothpaste.

"Your office emailed this and asked me to give it to you," the receptionist said, handing me a printed email message from Burk and a copy of my Arizona driver's license.

Dakota greeted me at the door to my room. I gave her a quick hug, then I read Burk's message.

Lucy had wired me the thousand dollars I'd requested. He also mentioned they'd had a visit from Mrs. Joshwecoma. She'd shown up at the office right after Burk and I talked.

I gritted my teeth. An unscheduled visit from Juanita Joshwecoma was usually a forerunner to trouble. Of the five members on the NAAC, Mrs. J. was the most outspoken and vehemently opposed to making public any information about her ancestors that she considered negative. Prehistoric cannibalism likely qualified, and Burk's note said she knew about the bone hash. He'd asked for her source, but she wouldn't say.

George had confirmed that the red stain on the cannibalized bones was definitely red ochre. He believed the stain was applied many years after death, maybe as much as a hundred years. He would run more tests to get a better read on the timeframe.

That bit of information was significant and worthy of disclosure in my pitch to the foundation. We could be looking at evidence that pointed to a previously unknown ritual.

I glanced at my watch and realized I'd been gone nearly fifteen minutes. Quickly I changed into Valerie's shirt and pants, brushed my teeth, and ran the tiny plastic brush though my hair. I gave Dakota a quick pat and headed for the door.

#

Valerie was not in the lobby or the espresso bar. I ran out the hotel entrance to find her sitting in a silver SUV with the windows down and the engine running. She motioned for me to climb in.

"We've gotta hustle."

She hit the gas before the door closed, left the square, and drove to the main intersection. We turned north as the light changed from yellow to red.

"How're you getting back?" she asked.

"Damned if I know. Maybe I'll hitch."

"You can't be serious."

"Serious as a heart attack." I cringed at my own bad joke. Maybe I'd get lucky and bum a ride with a staffer. "How far is the foundation from my hotel?"

"Fifteen miles."

"Glad I'm wearing hiking boots."

CHAPTER 10

The Southwestern Cultures Foundation operates from an imposing building that reminded me of pictures I'd seen of Taliesin West, Frank Lloyd Wright's Arizona residence. From the look of its headquarters, the foundation controlled some serious money.

With a deep breath, I went in, grateful I had close to half an hour before my presentation. I asked the receptionist for a note pad and pen. She obliged and pointed me to a large waiting area that resembled a layout in an architectural magazine. Three crimson leather couches arranged in a *U* flanked a square glass table. Two potted palms in enormous black ceramic containers stood on either side of the middle couch, their fronds reaching for the natural light from a pyramidal-shaped skylight overhead.

My hiking boots squeaked crossing the polished marble floor. I took a seat on the middle couch and considered the best way to pull off the presentation without the photos I'd taken of the bone hash. Those photos would have given the funding committee a good idea of the size and scope of our find, but they wouldn't help me now stored in my phone, held by the BLM.

My thigh muscles cramped when I sat on the low couch, a reminder of my tangle with Alonzo. I scribbled talking points on the note pad and mentally reviewed the details that set this discovery apart.

We'd uncovered evidence that cannibalism existed at Moenkopi Ridge. Although cannibalism had been discovered at other Southwestern sites, the stain on these bones added years after abandonment was highly unusual, possibly making our discovery more significant. I'd read of finds like ours at northern European sites, but nothing like it here in the Southwest.

Deep in thought, I startled when someone said my name, and I looked up to see Lyle Henderson.

"Lyle, what a surprise. Do you consult for SCF?" I stood and extended my hand. His handshake was firm. For a moment, he appeared to fixate on my attire. Valerie was taller and a good size larger than me.

"No, I head up the foundation's Grant Committee as a volunteer. I didn't have enough time to convene the full panel, but I recruited three more of the seven."

"Thanks for helping us out on such short notice. I apologize for showing up dressed like this. It's a long story, but my luggage was lost."

"You're fine. Did you fly in?" he asked, sounding surprised.

"No, other complications."

"Running a dig in the middle of nowhere can wreak havoc on your wardrobe," he said with a laugh. "We're meeting in the board room."

I followed him, noting the brilliant shine of his Italian leather loafers and the well-ironed creases in his tan slacks that, even from the back, could have sliced butter. With luck, I'd be able to give my pitch sitting down.

Lyle led me into a sunny room as imposing as the lobby. Sixteen dark brown leather chairs arranged around a hefty table reminded me of the conference room at my dad's law firm.

Lyle introduced two women and a man—all seated

across from me and each presented as a voting member of the Grant Committee. Dr. Turner, an elegantly dressed gray-haired woman, asked me to summarize our project and the details of our capital request. Her erect, long-necked posture reminded me of a sandhill crane.

If my trip had gone as planned, I would have studied each director's bio on the foundation's website beforehand, but with the exception of Lyle, I had no information on the directors he'd recruited.

"Please proceed, Dr. Connor," Dr. Turner said.

I made eye contact with each director. When I looked toward Lyle, he gave me an encouraging nod. Briefly, I glanced at the notes I'd made. "A few days ago, Moenkopi Ridge archaeologists excavated a new trench that produced a pocket of prehistoric human bones. The remains did not show evidence of ritualized burial—instead, they were tossed in a haphazard pile. The bones did show striking similarities to human remains found at other Southwest sites where cannibalism was eventually confirmed. In other words, we believe we've uncovered a bone hash."

Dr. Turner leaned toward the woman next to her and murmured something inaudible to me. I waited for her to finish before continuing.

"Our find has one striking difference to other sites showing evidence of prehistoric cannibalism: All the bones unearthed at Moenkopi Ridge bear a deep stain that I just confirmed tested out as red ochre. I also learned that we have evidence the stain was applied in prehistoric times but *many years* after the people of the bone hash were killed." I paused for emphasis.

"To our knowledge, human remains stained long after death have *never before* shown up at sites in the American Southwest. Since SCF identifies prehistoric cannibalism as one of its areas of interests, I'm here to request funding to support research into why the bone hash ended up altered at a later date. We may have unearthed evidence of a previously unknown ritual."

The committee members asked a lot of questions—details about the size of the bone hash and the number of skeletons and if I had a theory about the significance of the red ochre. I left the meeting believing I'd presented well and that our request for funding would be seriously considered.

Lyle walked me to the lobby.

"I'll do what I can to shepherd your request through quickly," he said. "Did Gerry tell you we'll be working together if this project gets funded?"

I blinked. "No, he didn't say anything about it."

"Gerry wants me back as a consultant."

I clamped my teeth together. Working with someone of Lyle's prominence would be interesting. But it could be awkward and compromise my authority as site director.

"Looks like I've taken you by surprise," he said. "Gerry said he'd be discussing this with you. I assumed you knew."

For a moment I was speechless. It took all the control I could muster to say, "My phone was lost with the rest of my gear. I'm sure he's tried to reach me."

He smiled. "No doubt. Gerry's asked me to handle dating the bone hash. We want to identify the time between the occurrence of cannibalism and when the bones were stained."

Lyle grasped my hand warmly. "I'll get back to you and Gerry as soon as the committee decides. We could be working together as early as next week."

"Thank you, Lyle. I'll wait to hear from you," I said. Inwardly I dreaded the added stress Lyle's presence would heap on my already packed work schedule. I wished I'd had a chance to discuss the details with Gerry.

The clock behind the reception desk showed I had less than half an hour before my meeting with Frank Nakai. I asked the receptionist if anyone on staff planned to drive into town for lunch. She told me the full-timers brought their lunches or bought tacos from a food truck that made the rounds. I asked if I could use her phone. She pointed to one on the glass table in the waiting area. I dialed the cell number on the back of the BLM agent's card.

"Agent Nakai? It's Aideen Connor."

"On my way."

"Well, unfortunately, I'm not."

"But the café's right in your hotel?"

"Have you heard of a place north of town called the Southwestern Cultures Foundation?"

"Yes, why?"

"I'm there now. Could you pick me up? I have a wire waiting at the Money Exchange over on Paseo. If you'll give me a lift we can catch up on the way."

#

The BLM van pulled into the foundation's circular drive and stopped at the front entrance. Nakai was on his phone and reached across the inside of the cab to open the door for me.

"How do they justify that? He should be charged with attempted murder," he said. After a few minutes he disconnected and jammed the phone into a pocket on the door. "Bad news as far as you're concerned."

"How's that?"

"Alonzo was released. Tribal cops said they don't have enough evidence to hold him. They found a few spent shells in the arroyo where the riders found you, but since you weren't physically harmed, and neither was your dog, they didn't hold him. He admitted to going to your room in Tuba City but said it was to make up. They decided it was a lovers' spat, so Rudy drove Alonzo out to his truck, and he took off. Any truth to what he said about the two of you having a relationship?"

"Are you kidding? That man tried to kill me! How could they just let him go? And what about the weird scene in the trunk of my car?"

Nakai tapped his fingers against the steering wheel. "They claimed with no hard evidence, it was your word against his. And they decided there was no evidence Alonzo had anything to do with the blood in your car."

"Maybe you should just drop me off at the hotel, Agent Nakai. At this point, I've had my fill of lame law enforcement."

He smirked. "Sometimes I've had my fill of it too. Relax. Let's get your dog before we hit the wire office. There's a park on the way where we can walk her. And please, call me Frank. The way you just said 'Agent Nakai' set my teeth on edge."

I smiled despite my frustration and said, "Sounds good. I'm Aideen."

#

The Money Exchange was located inside the grocery store next to the customer service desk. Regardless of the nice walk in the park with Frank and Dakota, I still felt steamed over Alonzo's release. When we pulled into the grocery's parking lot, I let the dog out of the van, thanked Frank for the lift, and told him not to bother waiting for me.

"Don't you want to get your stuff back?" He grinned at the look I gave him. "Thought so," he said. "I'll wait here for you."

Dakota followed me to the entrance, and I told myself to cool off. Maybe if I acted a little more cordial BLM would return my belongings. I put Dakota in a down-stay and went inside.

A well-dressed couple speaking German stood ahead of me divvying up dollars the clerk counted out for them. When they finished, I stepped up to the counter and showed the clerk the color photocopy of my driver's license.

"Aideen Connor. I'm expecting a wire."

He gave a cursory look at the photocopy of my license,

checked his computer, and counted out ten, hundred-dollar bills. I stuffed them into the pocket of Valerie's borrowed pants, took the paperwork he handed me, and walked to the main entrance to check on Dakota. She wagged when she saw me. I stepped outside and gave her a quick pat, reinforced the stay command, located a grocery cart, and rolled it inside.

I dropped in a cloth billfold, a toothbrush and paste, deodorant, a hairbrush, a gold-colored T-shirt sporting a red imprint of the flag of New Mexico, and a pair of oversized sunglasses. In the pet section I threw in a six-foot leather leash, an extra-large dog bowl, and Dakota's favorite high-protein kibble.

I paid and went outside, toting two plastic grocery bags. There was no sign of Dakota. I whistled and called for her, but instead of her usual quick response, no dog. Then I saw why she'd run off. In the shadow of a store entrance opposite the grocery stood Ray Alonzo wearing the same dirty clothes he'd worn the day before in the arroyo, but he'd added something—a long hunting knife in a leather sheath attached to his belt. He looked at me and grinned.

CHAPTER 11

ONE LOOK AT ALONZO, and I bolted for the parking lot, but Frank wasn't parked where I'd left him. I scanned the aisles of parked cars, but no van drove up, and still no dog. I ran helter-skelter between parked cars and still not seeing Frank's van, I sprinted back toward the grocery store. Alonzo followed. He gained on me when I neared the front door but stopped short of coming inside.

"Where's security?" I asked the first employee I saw.

"Take aisle twelve through the double doors. Ask for Al."

I rushed down the aisle, grocery bags swinging, and bumped into cans stacked next to the cardboard cutout of a celebrity spokesman. The collision added a serious dent to his cardboard smile.

The security office had one gray metal desk facing out. A uniformed man sat in a swivel chair behind it thumbing through papers.

"Al?"

"Yes. What's the emergency?"

"A man who tried to kill me just followed me in here. Call this cop." I handed him Frank's card. "He knows me."

"Whoa, wait a minute! Who are you? Who tried to kill you?"

A sharp noise loud as a gunshot startled us both. I ducked behind Al's desk.

"Take it easy," he said. "It's only somebody unloading produce. Sit down and I'll call. What's your name?"

I told him. Al punched in the number.

"There's an Aideen Connor in my office asked me to call you… Yeah, she looks okay… My office is in the back next to receiving."

Minutes later, Frank appeared with Dakota. He'd looped his belt through her collar in lieu of a leash, his elaborate sand cast silver buckle next to her face.

"Sorry, but we don't allow dogs back here. Health ordinance," Al said.

Frank put Dakota into a sit and stuck out his hand.

"BLM Special Agent Frank Nakai. She's a service dog, Al." Frank removed his belt from under the dog's collar. Al's eyes narrowed, but when Dakota walked around the side of his desk and put her head under his hand, his eyes softened.

"Where's that vest they're supposed to wear that says Service Dog?"

"Must have left it in the van," Frank said. "Aideen, you okay?"

"Yes, where were you? Where'd you find Dakota?"

"I figured something went wrong when she shot past me. I whistled and got her inside the van. Then I went looking for you."

"You saw Alonzo?"

"Yeah, he split when he saw my uniform. I alerted local police. They should be searching for him by now."

Frank worked his belt back through his pants loops, and I attached Dakota's new leash to her collar. He reached for the grocery bags, and I thanked Al on our way out. When we came to his van, Frank opened the side door for Dakota.

"Someone may want to talk with you after our techs search your car, but right now, you should get out of Taos," Frank said. "Once they find him, the police can't detain Alonzo for very long without cause."

"How am I supposed to leave without my ID?" I said.

"I'm driving back to my office in Santa Fe after I meet with a local cop. Why don't you ride down with me? Maybe the techs will be ready to release your backpack by the time we get there. You can rent a car and drive home from Santa Fe."

"When could we leave?"

"In about an hour. I'll take you and Dakota back to the hotel. Go ahead and check out. I'll pick you up soon as I'm done with my meeting."

#

I figured it was time to check in with my boss when we returned to the hotel. I put fresh water in the ice bucket for Dakota and sat on the bed by the phone. My presentation at SCF had gone well, and I believed we had a good chance of being funded. But from what he'd told me, Henderson believed he'd be hired as a consultant if the grant was approved. Since he appeared well-liked by the employees, managing the dig with Henderson around could cause me problems if we disagreed.

Rodgers picked up on the first ring. "Where have you been? My calls keep going to voice mail."

I told him about being chased and shot at and that law enforcement had confiscated my belongings.

"Somebody shot at you? Christ, Aideen. Were you hurt?"

"No, I got lucky."

"Who came after you? What did he want?'

"He must have followed me from the dig. Then he cornered me at Taos Pueblo."

"Wait a minute, who was following you? What were you doing at Taos Pueblo? What's going on, Aideen?"

I hadn't wanted to tell Rodgers about my run-in with Alonzo in Tuba City, or my stop at the pueblo, but the whole story spilled out, including meeting up with Frank Nakai.

"Why did this BLM agent seize your belongings if you

were the victim?" he asked.

"I drove my Mustang rather than a company van," I said. "When he took me back to my car, we found a Hopi *paho* in the trunk sitting in a lot of blood. The agent declared the car a crime scene and seized everything inside the trunk."

The line went silent for what seemed an eternity.

"But you're all right?"

"Yes."

"What about the appointment I set up for you at SCF this morning?"

"I made the pitch as planned."

Rodgers blew out a breath. "How'd it go?"

"Lots of questions. Excitement about the unusual red ochre."

"That's encouraging," he said. "What else?"

"I spoke with Lyle Henderson after my presentation. I didn't know he chaired their Grant Committee. He said you asked him back as a consultant—if we get funded."

"Yes. He'd be a big help."

"I wish you and I had discussed it first."

"How am I supposed to discuss something with you if you can't answer your phone?"

I sighed. "Understood. How do you see Lyle's role?"

"He'll manage dating the bone hash."

"Will he report to me?"

"No, too awkward."

My hand tightened around the receiver. "Since he's switched to consulting, wouldn't he be used to reporting to the project director?"

"I'll discuss that with him and work something out. When will you be back?"

"As soon as BLM releases my stuff."

"How long's that going to take?"

"They wouldn't say. I'm pushing for today."

"I'm sorry for your scare, Aideen, and I'm thankful

you're all right, but you shouldn't have been at Taos Pueblo in the first place. You seem to have a knack for attracting trouble. This morning I got another call from Mrs. Joshwecoma. She knew about the bone hash. How'd she find out about it? I told you not to disclose it. She's worried we'll leak it to the media."

I twisted the phone cord around my finger and sighed. "I don't know how she found out. I didn't leak it—to her or the media."

"If the foundation gets another complaint about you from Juanita, we have a big problem. *You* have an even bigger problem. You've been here less than three months, so you're still on probation."

"Please reassure her that no one will be contacting the media," I said. "I'll meet with Juanita when I get back."

"She's not going to wait until you're back if she decides to make a stink."

"Do you want me to call her today?"

"No, I'll take care of it," he said.

"Gerry, there's something else we should consider—now that we've dug up the bone hash. The BLM agent told me there's been a run on thefts at sites out here, and he believes we need security at the dig. I'm starting to think he's right. Especially now that we have a discovery that's likely to be controversial to manage," I reminded him. "I'm sure if the foundation decides to fund our research, they'll want us to secure that new trench. How about I price out security costs and call you back with options later today?"

"How do you propose we pay for it? We've already wasted this year's discretionary funds on that equipment you wanted."

The new ground-penetrating radar equipment I'd ordered had already saved significant labor costs, but the timing didn't seem right to point that out.

"Let me crunch some numbers in our operating budget

first," he said. "In the meantime, don't make any more unauthorized side trips. And get back to the dig as soon as you can."

CHAPTER 12

Once Juanita Joshwecoma got wind of a situation that concerned her, she wasn't known for letting up. In the few months I'd been director, she was the one committee member I hadn't won over. Now she'd gone behind my back and complained about me to my boss.

Dakota whined to go out, barked, and loped to the door. I needed to cool off and come up with a strategy for dealing with Juanita. Maybe getting out for a walk would clear my head.

The dog and I took the stairs down, and I asked the receptionist to recommend a quiet café or bookstore close to the hotel. She suggested a popular place on the north end of town that offered both. I thanked her and asked for directions. She gave me a map of Taos the hotel printed for guests and pointed out the easiest route.

Dakota and I passed the Taos Arts Cooperative along the way, and I remembered it as Valerie's gallery and decided to check it out. When I got to the door, a sign said it was closed for the next several days due to the death of one of its members. I made a note of the address and planned to stop by on my next visit to Taos.

A short jaunt later we reached the territorial-style two-story building that housed a café and bookstore. A large wooden sign over the entrance read *"Community Café &*

Reads." I tied Dakota's new leash to a parking meter right in front and ventured inside.

A blackboard-sized community message board crammed with the usual announcements stood just inside the entrance. There were photos of lost pets, people seeking roommates, apartments for rent… but it was the death notice that grabbed my attention. A full letter-sized page read "Celebration of Life for Taos Artist." Location and details were printed under the photo of a Native American woman:

The Taos Arts Cooperative is holding a memorial service this Saturday for the artist known as Tiponi, a noted jeweler and Taos Arts Cooperative member, following her tragic death in Hano, AZ, on the Hopi Reservation…

The shape of the woman's head in the photo and the erect way she stood looked familiar, but it was her striking facial features that proved unmistakable.

"Oh my God, it's *her*," I said aloud.

I yanked the flyer from the message board and figured strategizing about Juanita could wait. I dashed outside to collect Dakota. We jogged back to the hotel. Flyer in hand, I approached the woman I'd seen earlier at the reception desk. Her name tag read "Sandra."

"Beautiful dog," she said. "Something I can do for you?"

"I'm Aideen Connor in 212. I'll be settling my account today and wanted to remove the charges from the BLM's credit card."

Sandra consulted her computer and said, "I'm to cancel the charges on Mr. Nakai's card?"

"You don't mean his *personal* credit card, do you? He told me his agency would take care of it."

"You should check with him on that," she said. "Your room was charged to a card in the name of Frank Nakai."

She smiled. I felt heat rise to my face. "You can remove the charge. I'll be paying in cash."

"No problem. Was there something else?"

I hesitated for a moment, then handed her the flyer. "I found this on a public message board. Do you know anything about this woman?"

Sandra took a good look at the flyer then handed it back to me. "I didn't know her personally, if that's what you mean, but one of those flyers was posted in the laundromat I used this morning. I saw another one last night at my church."

"What happened to her?"

"They're saying murder. Someone told me she moved to Taos to get away from an abusive husband. I heard on the news this morning they still haven't arrested anyone."

Nakai found me talking with Sandra when he strolled into the hotel lobby.

"Take a look at this," I said handing him the flyer. "This 'Tiponi' looks to be the same woman pictured in that photo I found in my motel room."

"What makes you so sure?" he asked

"I'm used to remembering physical details from my work. Plus an employee at the dig told me a woman was murdered in Hano the night I stayed over in Tuba City. Sandra here told me the woman shown on this flyer was *murdered*, and the flyer says she died in Hano. "It has to be the same person. Hano is a tiny village. No wonder that Hopi policeman was so interested in that photo left in my motel room. He probably knew her."

"I might be able to find out the identity of the Hano victim," Frank said. "I'll make some calls while you gather your things and check out. Let's meet outside."

#

On the way to Santa Fe we stopped at a phone store, and I bought a burner phone loaded with 100 minutes. When I returned to the car, I asked Frank if he'd turned up information on the Hano murder victim.

"I did find out something. I called a buddy of mine at the FBI field office in Phoenix. Hopi Tribal Police reported a murder up on First Mesa, and the FBI is investigating. My friend said he'd call me when he has more details."

"Thanks, I hope you'll share that information with me. This whole situation has been really unnerving, and it's gotten me in hot water with my boss."

"I'll do what I can. I'm sure you understand there's only so much I can tell you in an ongoing case."

I had no doubt the picture I'd found in my motel room was the same woman as the one murdered in Hano, and now I knew her name: Tiponi. But what I couldn't figure out was how Alonzo was involved, and why he'd wanted her photo so much he'd followed me to Taos and shot at me to get it.

"Sandra told me you charged my room to your personal account," I said. "I removed the charges, but thanks for covering for me."

#

Along the highway from Taos to Santa Fe, stunted cedar trees, sagebrush, and cholla cactus vied for dominance in the high-desert landscape. The twisted, prickly shapes brought to mind the dark images I was trying to forget—Alonzo pointing his rifle at me. A blood-soaked *paho* not made in the traditional way. The death notice of a woman who'd been killed on the Hopi Reservation.

Tiponi was an artist, a jeweler, with most of her life yet to be lived. I thought of the contrast in the two pictures I'd seen of her—the loveliness of her face overshadowed by that look of defiance in the first photo. Her photo on the flyer announcing her death suggested she'd achieved a level of success. Finding that first picture made me curious about her. Now I knew I would never meet this woman, and that all that was left for Tiponi was for her killer to be brought to justice.

CHAPTER 13

WE DROPPED OFF DAKOTA in Frank's office in Santa Fe, then he led me down the hall to an open door marked "Director." A fit-looking man sat behind a massive walnut desk. Frank introduced him as Sherman Burrows, director of BLM's Santa Fe office. Burrows had the tanned, weathered look of someone who'd lived decades in the sun-drenched Southwest.

"Dr. Connor," he said, looking up. "Glad to get to meet you. Agent Nakai tells me we've inconvenienced you by confiscating your belongings."

"Nice to meet you as well, director. Releasing my cash and ID would sure make up for it."

"I'll see what I can do."

Burrows stood and walked around to the front of his desk, leaned against it, and faced me. "I've been an archaeology buff for years," he said. "Did you know one of the Bureau's mandates is protecting ancient sites?"

"Yes, I did know that."

"What's your take on the increase in artifact thefts in this region?"

I went on alert. He was the second BLM official after Frank to question me about artifact thefts. "Unfortunately, it's a common problem at ancient sites. Probably worse out here because there are so many remote and unprotected locations."

"True. We have a lot more land to cover in the Southwest and greater density of sites. What about human artifacts—bones, grave objects? What are you doing at your dig to protect them?"

The back of my neck prickled. *Had he heard about the bone hash?*

"We follow federal laws governing funerary objects and human remains. Agent Nakai recommended adding a security team at my dig, and I've passed that suggestion on to my boss."

"Good to hear you're willing to listen to Frank's advice. We've had a run on artifact thefts this month. Agent Nakai will see to releasing your belongings. Anything else I can do for you?"

I stood a little straighter. "There *is* something else. I'd like to visit your forensics lab and look at that *paho* left in my car."

"Why?"

"To see if it's authentic—made according to Hopi tradition."

He scowled. "We don't allow outsiders in the lab, let alone permit a civilian to handle evidence."

"Director Burrows, with due respect, I'm a scientist," I said, looking him in the eye. "I work with ancient artifacts on a regular basis—some of them quite fragile. I know how to be careful, and I know how to avoid contamination."

His eyes widened slightly.

"What if one of your lab techs supervised me?" I countered.

"Sherm, I think she has a point," Frank said. "It doesn't add up that a known meth user would have the inclination or know-how to make a Hopi religious object."

"All right, all right," Burrows said. "Frank, you're responsible for protecting the chain of evidence. Go with her and make sure she follows protocol."

\#

The New Mexico forensics lab provides analytical services in ballistics, fingerprints, drug analysis, and biological sciences for multiple state law enforcement agencies. Frank led me through the main entrance to the red brick building and turned down a hall to a door marked "Microscopy." A man in a white lab coat stood bent over a microscope in a well-lit workstation under a fume hood.

Visiting the forensics lab reminded me of a class I'd taken in physical anthropology, which is where I'd met Clay. We used the same workstation in the Penn State lab but at different times. He'd complained to the supervisor that I took up too much of the storage space. The lab head told us to set up a meeting and work it out between ourselves.

Clay strolled into the lab around ten at night for our first encounter, wearing an all-black look and a T-shirt full of muscles. The meeting hadn't gone particularly well, but I'd agreed to move out some of my equipment, which apparently satisfied him.

A few months later I ran into Clay at a campus beer tasting for grad students. We were surprised to learn we had common interests—love of wilderness, desert hiking, and a fascination with prehistoric Southwestern cultures. We had dinner at a local pub after the tasting to continue our conversation. A few days later Clay asked me out. At the end of the semester, he invited me to join him on a backpacking trip in the Pine Barrens. Six months later, we were living together.

Frank introduced the man in the lab coat as Jed Lightner, director of microscopy. He turned off the fume hood and said, "Director Burrows called ahead. I've set up a place for you."

Jed handed me a fresh pair of latex gloves and walked me to a metal lab cart set up under a bright overhead light.

The *paho* had been laid out in a tray on the cart, stiff with dried blood and still attached to a piece of my sweatshirt. I slipped on the latex gloves. At first glance, the *paho* looked traditional with the straight male stick painted black and the notched female stick painted red. The two elements were bound together with blue yarn. I noted the decorative beads on the front. At first, I thought the *paho* was made according to Hopi tradition. Then, turning the prayer stick over and lifting up the soiled fabric, I saw what was off. The prayer stick had no cornmeal pouch. Cornmeal is a symbol of fertility and abundance among Pueblo people and plays an important role in many of their rituals. A pouch of red, black, or blue felt containing sacred cornmeal is usually attached to a *paho*, but it was missing from this one.

Frank leaned over my shoulder to get a closer look. I shifted in my chair. "This prayer stick was either made by someone unfamiliar with Hopi beliefs, or purposefully put together with a vital element missing."

Frank straightened. "You said yesterday someone at your dig could have made it. Wouldn't they know that?"

"Possibly, depending upon who it was, but we don't know for sure what the perpetrator meant to communicate." I turned to Jed. "Did you find fingerprints on any of the items in my car?"

Jed looked at Frank. "Should we be telling her this?"

Frank nodded.

"We found prints, but no match with our database."

"What about the blood?" I asked.

Jed looked again to Frank, and he again nodded.

Jed continued. "Well, the blood part is really interesting."

"Why's that?" Frank asked.

"It isn't human."

"What kind of blood is it?" I asked.

"Sheep's blood. Isn't your dig close to the Navajo Reservation?"

"Yes, why?" My shoulders tensed. *Sheep's* blood?

"Lots of Hopi and Navajo families raise sheep. Hopi land sits right in the middle of the Navajo Nation's Big Reservation. It wouldn't be hard for someone to find a sheep camp close to your dig."

I returned the *paho* to the metal tray. Jed took digital close-ups of both sides and measured each section.

"Any chance you'd share those photos?" I asked.

"He can't," Frank said. "You're lucky you got a look at it."

Jed returned the prayer stick to the evidence room and came back with my backpack sealed in a large plastic bag. He unzipped the pack and handed me my billfold. My driver's license, cash, and credit cards were all inside just like I'd left them. I smiled and thanked him.

"Backpack's stiff with dried blood," Jed said. "Do you still want it back?"

"Guess not. How about my cell phone?"

Frank nodded, and Jed handed it over. I tried to switch it on, but the battery was dead. At least I still had the burner.

I thanked Jed for his time and the chance to inspect the *paho*. Frank drove Dakota and me to a car rental and came inside with me. I filled out the paperwork and rented a Jeep.

On the way out, he paused at the door and said, "I heard from Taos Police. They found Alonzo and detained him, but they won't be able to hold him much longer. You need to stay vigilant. He could be released at any time."

"But Alonzo must know where I live to have followed me to Taos. What about a restraining order?"

"Next to impossible to enforce with the multiple jurisdictions. Besides, he'd likely ignore it."

CHAPTER 14

DRIVING I-40 WEST OUT of New Mexico in the rental, I missed the Mustang and the power I felt behind the wheel. My mind drifted like the tumbleweed, blowing every which way across the highway. As far as I knew, security at the dig hadn't been an issue before Rodgers hired me, but after my talk with the BLM agent, apparently it was now. I wondered why Rodgers seemed reluctant to hire a security team and why he'd made such a point of bringing up my probation. I'd just about completed the three-month probationary period required of all new employees. True, Juanita had complained about me before, but sometimes her accusations seemed petty, and Rodgers had acknowledged that in past meetings.

As to the mess in the trunk of my car, the *paho* puzzled me most. Unless born Hopi, most people have never heard of a *paho*. The prayer sticks weren't typically elaborate in construction. The ritual was more about one's intention in the making of it. Only someone familiar with Hopi religion would know that. And sheep's blood? What kind of person would put sheep's blood in the trunk of my car, shred my sweatshirt, and attach a fake prayer stick to a piece of it? It was so creepy, I couldn't imagine anyone at the dig doing it, but it seemed impossible Alonzo would have had the time or the know-how to pull it off after Dakota and I abandoned the car.

I turned down the gravel road into the dig and parked the rental in my usual spot. The sun hovered low and colored the landscape a deep red. I unhooked my cell phone from the charging cable, opened the door to the Jeep and slid the phone into the pocket of my jeans. The revolting stench of dead animal hit my nose like a punch. I'd have to check around the trailer in the morning when there was better light and bury the source.

Dakota whined, and I let her out. She loped around to the back of the trailer vocalizing enthusiastic yips. Her excited, staccato barks sounded like she'd given chase.

"Not another jackrabbit," I groaned. But unlike the usual vocalizations that went along with varmint chasing, Dakota's cries turned muffled and strange. I turned on the flashlight on my cell phone and went around to the back of the trailer to check on her and heard her howl but didn't see her.

Metal panels fastened along the bottom of the trailer protected its tires and formed a cavity underneath that was accessible by a small door. The setup resembled a crawl space in a home without a basement. The access door was pushed in and slightly ajar. Dakota's cries were coming from behind it.

I pushed the small door open, and Dakota crept out, smelling worse than an autopsy lab. Red-brown filth coated her face.

I grabbed hold of her collar and used my free hand to point the cell phone into the opening. The beam hit the vacant, dead eyes of an animal lying in a thick congealing puddle. I staggered backwards and dropped the phone. Dakota lunged forward and tried to scrabble back inside, but I grabbed her collar and yanked her away, dragging her back to the Jeep. I reached inside for her leash and tied her to the door handle.

Returning to the crawl space, I picked up my cell phone and peered inside. The eyes fixed toward the opening belonged to a small white sheep. Its legs were bound together. Buzzing, swarming insects covered the bloody slash across its neck.

I slammed the door and backed up. My face felt hot. Bile filled my throat. I leaned over and retched.

When it was over, I tested the door to make sure it latched and walked Dakota to the outdoor spigot on the opposite side of the trailer. I doused her good, and then tied her to the spigot and hurried inside for soap and old towels. After a good scrubbing, I rinsed her off and rubbed her down, leaving the soiled wet towels on the ground to dry in the desert air.

Once inside I bolted the front door, then fished out Frank Nakai's card from my pocket and called him. He picked up on the second ring and sounded surprised to hear from me.

"I didn't know who else to call."

"You sound upset," Frank said.

I blurted out what I'd found. "How would *you* feel if you came home and some cruel nutbag had killed an animal in your basement?"

"Pissed off, but I carry a gun."

I blew out a breath. "I wish I *had* a gun right now. Sorry if this is spoiling your dinner."

"It's not very good, anyway. Aideen, have you called 9-1-1?"

"No, would someone even come out here? Our site is very remote."

"It's still in a county. Dispatch should be able to identify the correct county sheriff."

"We don't have an address. The dig keeps a post office box in Winslow. That's it."

"Doesn't matter. Hang up and dial 9-1-1. After you talk with them call me back."

#

The 9-1-1 operator said she was able to place my location from the phone and that a deputy would be out, but she wasn't able to say when.

"All depends on their schedule. Your case is what we'd call a suspicious circumstance. If they aren't dealing with more urgent issues, a deputy could be there soon. If they're dealing with a serious crime, they might not be out until tomorrow."

"What about the dead sheep?" I asked.

"Someone from animal control will be notified to take care of its removal."

I paced back and forth in my tiny living room. The idea of waiting around for an unknown length of time for a deputy to show up made me jumpy. I called Frank back and told him what I'd learned.

"Can you send someone over from BLM in the morning?"

"I can drive out, but what about tonight? You shouldn't stay there alone."

"Dakota's with me."

"She's a great dog, but she'd hardly stand up to a weapon. I can leave now and be there in five hours."

Someone banged on the front door. I jumped like I'd been jabbed and drew in a sharp breath.

"Are you expecting anyone?" Frank asked.

"No. Stay on the line while I see who it is." I left the phone face up on my dining table. The dim outline of a man filled the frosted window in the trailer's front door.

"Who is it?" I called.

"Burk. Saw the car and figured you were back. Came to ask you what else you want Lonny and me to do about the bone hash."

"Burk, I just got back from an assignment in New Mexico. I need to shower. Drive up to Walpi with me in the morning. We can discuss options then. I've asked Rodgers for a security detail, and I'm still waiting on his approval."

"Okay, but what's going on out here, Aideen? There's an unbelievable stench around your trailer. I could smell it halfway up the trail from the office."

"Dakota must have killed something before we left. I'll find it and bury it tomorrow."

"Won't be too soon," he said. "See you in the morning."

I gave Burk time to walk away then picked up the phone. "You heard?" I asked.

"Some of it. Do you trust this guy?"

"I think so."

"Then why didn't you tell him what's going on?"

"I'm not sure, Frank. Guess I'm too unnerved."

"What are you going to do until that deputy arrives?"

"There's a gun in my office we use as a last resort to clear out rattlesnakes. I'm going after it."

"Do you know what kind of gun it is?"

"It's a shotgun."

"A shotgun can have a bad kick," Frank pointed out. "Have you ever fired one?"

"No."

"Do you know how to tell if it's loaded?"

"A quick lesson can't hurt."

Frank gave me the basics and said, "If you have to use it, make sure you put the stock solidly against your shoulder before you squeeze the trigger. Take your dog and your phone. Call me when the shotgun's in your hands."

I disconnected and slipped the phone into my pocket, leashed up Dakota, and grabbed a flashlight and my keys. I started down the path to the office, then turned around to lock my door—something I rarely did—then Dakota and I took off down the path.

All the office lights were off, even the overhead outside. I aimed the flashlight to find the keyhole, unlocked the door, and flipped the lights on. We kept the shotgun in a locked gun cabinet on the back wall in my office. I sat behind my desk and rummaged around in the middle desk drawer looking for the key, then dumped out the contents onto the desktop. Running my fingers through the supplies, I cut a finger on a loose X-ACTO knife. I swore and wrapped my finger in the end of my T-shirt to stop the bleeding. Dakota stood up, growled, and moved closer.

When I looked up, I sucked in a sharp breath. Burk stood in my office doorway.

"You scared me out of my wits!" I said. "What are you doing here?"

"It's okay, Dakota," he said. The dog sat back down but stayed close, ears back.

"I saw the lights on and wondered what was up," Burk said. "That blood on your shirt?"

"Yes, sliced a finger," I said, my wits returning.

Burk stared at my filthy, blood-stained clothes. "Why are you here so late? Thought you were taking a shower."

"Hunting for the key to the gun cabinet."

"Why?"

"Saw a rattler by my trailer when we drove in," I said, wondering why I still felt so reluctant to confide in Burk.

"Rattlesnake won't bother you after dark. More humane to kill it with a hoe if it's still there in the morning."

"No thanks. I'm not getting that close to it."

"Are you alright, Aideen?"

"Burk, you really startled me, and I'm tired, and I still have to shower and prepare for that trip to Walpi in the morning."

"Sorry. Want me to call that tribal cop for you and ask him to go by Cha'tima's house to set up the meeting?" The last time we'd uncovered human remains, Rodgers sent me to Walpi to ask him to head the committee. Now I wanted his support dealing with the other NAAC members since we'd uncovered a bone hash, and I hoped he could offset the negative attention Juanita Joshwecoma had stirred up.

"Sure, call him. That'll save some time. Did I give you his number?"

"I have it," Burk said.

Spotting the key in the jumble on my desk, I went to unlock the gun cabinet. Burk tossed the rest of the supplies back into the drawer, then he followed me and removed an extra box of shells from the cabinet.

"Unless you're a crack shot, you might need these," he said, handing me the box. He looked at me hard for a moment. "*Are* you a crack shot, Aideen?"

My eyes narrowed. "Wasn't part of my job description."

"You know it's no trouble for me to walk you back to your trailer," Burk said, lingering at the door.

I'd wearied of Burk's company following his surprise appearance. "No, thanks. Now that I have the gun, I should be okay. Let's meet up in the morning as planned."

I watched Burk head south from the office and walk west towards his tent, then I let out the breath I'd been holding. Burk bunked on the far west side near the excavations. Navigating the rock-strewn trails required care, even during the day, but he'd come inside without a flashlight.

I loaded the shotgun, put as many extra shells as I could cram in my pockets, and left the box with the remaining shells inside the office. When I opened the door to leave a hot breeze blew my hair across my face, bringing with it the rotten smell of death. I locked the office door, put the gun's safety on, choked up on Dakota's leash, and ran like hell.

Inside the trailer I locked the deadbolt behind us, cranked up the air-conditioner to lessen the stench, and lit a stick of frankincense. Before calling Frank I closed the blinds all around.

"What took you so long?"

I told Frank about my odd encounter with Burk.

"What did he want?"

"Said he came inside to see why the lights were on."

"Do you believe him?"

"I'm not sure. It's almost ten. Not your usual time for an evening stroll."

"Aideen, it's no big deal for me to leave right now," Frank said.

"You should get some sleep. I feel safer now that I have the shotgun. Maybe I'll get lucky, and the deputy will show up soon." I gave Frank directions to the dig from Winslow and said I'd look for him around noon.

After we hung up, I took a quick shower, threw on a clean T-shirt and jeans, and lit several more sticks of incense, relying on the strong odor accompanying the thin trails of smoke to keep me awake. Then I turned on all the lights in the trailer to make it easy for the deputy to find me.

Someone was playing hardball with me. With luck, they'd leave me alone the rest of the night. And if my luck ran out, at least I had the shotgun.

CHAPTER 15

Sitting in the trailer with all the lights on, the shotgun across my lap and Dakota at my feet, my body craved sleep, but I couldn't rid my mind of the bloody scene underneath my living space. The lonely chirp of a cricket under a window or the hum of a distant jet reminded me that I lived alone and at the very edge of human companionship. The slightest sound made me jump, and the long periods of silence were worse. Any unexplained noise brought me to full alert, knowing the person who'd killed an animal under my trailer might decide to come back and kill *me*. I dialed the county's emergency number again around midnight, and the intake operator assured me my case was still in the queue.

"We had a shooting tonight. Emergencies like that take priority," she explained.

My cramped legs begged for a stretch. Careful not to disturb my sleeping dog, I slid out of my shoes and walked barefoot to the window in the front door, shotgun in hand, and looked out through a droopy slat in the blinds. In the deep blackness of the nighttime desert sky, the moon shone bright as a New York City streetlamp. Nothing moved. Still no sign of the deputy. Returning to the couch, I sat down with my feet next to Dakota, anxious for the dawn.

#

Dakota's sudden movement startled me awake. Her ears perked straight up, a low growl rumbling from her throat. I laid my hand on her neck. "Quiet," I whispered. We sat completely still.

At first the only sounds were familiar ones. Night birds calling. The occasional barrage of wind. Then, there it was again, a soft thumping that sounded like it was coming from underneath the trailer. Dakota lurched from my grip and charged into the bedroom, barking explosively. A shadow moved across the window shade. I scrambled into the bedroom and yanked the shade up, but saw nothing but moonlight on the dark desert landscape.

The phone vibrated in my pocket—Frank Nakai's caller ID.

"Where are you?"

"At your turnoff."

"You're here already?"

"Yes, I left after we hung up. Did a deputy ever show up?"

"No, you're the only person who's shown up, and I'm sure glad you're here."

"Your dog's barking. What's going on?"

"A shadow crossed my bedroom window... I heard a strange noise—sounded like it was coming from under the trailer."

"See anyone outside?"

"No, only shadows."

"I'll look around when I get to your trailer."

"Thanks. Do you drink coffee?"

"Do I drink coffee? I'm a cop. It runs through my veins. I just spotted your trailer."

I went into my kitchen, fired up the kettle, and put ground coffee in the French press. A car crunched the gravel driveway outside. I looked through the front blinds and spotted the BLM logo on the van in the breaking dawn. Frank stepped out clad in dark brown pants, a khaki shirt, and a holstered gun. He looked around the surrounding terrain, but no one was about.

I opened the front door. "You're armed?"

"Wish it could scare away the smell out here. Nothing personal, but your front yard smells worse than a slaughterhouse."

"Sorry it's so bad," I said with a heavy sigh. "Want to take a look now at what I found?"

He ran a hand through his dark, mussed up hair. "Let's go for the caffeine first. Fifteen minutes and we'll have more light."

Frank slid into the dining nook next to the kitchen. I moved the wooden incense holder onto the table, lit another stick, and handed him a mug of coffee. He stirred in two spoonfuls of sugar from the howling coyote sugar bowl I kept on the table. I scooted into the U-shaped nook to join him and smiled in spite of myself. I hadn't expected to see him again.

Dakota whined to go out, but I bribed her with a dog biscuit to wait until I could walk her on the leash, and eyed her as she settled in to crunch her treat.

"Tell me what happened from the time you arrived home until now," Frank said.

I told him every detail I could remember.

"Anyone here at the dig you don't get along with?" Frank asked.

I thought for a moment. "George Hargood—our research archaeologist. He's made it clear from day one that he wishes the former director was still here."

Frank looked thoughtful, took another slug of coffee. Abruptly, he said, "Sun's up. Let's take a look."

Frank used a bandanna from his back pocket to push the crawl space door open. He crouched down and aimed his flashlight inside… then turned to me with a puzzled look. I looked inside. The sheep carcass was gone. Coagulated blood the thickness and color of dirty motor oil remained on the ground under the trailer, but no dead sheep. And something new had been added: a small stand-up picture frame lay face down in the blood.

My breath caught. I knew what it was before I turned it over— the last picture I'd taken of Clay. I reached into the cavity and snatched it up. The picture usually sat on the nightstand in my bedroom, and I hadn't removed it. I stood up too fast and promptly doubled over at the waist to keep from passing out.

Frank put his hand on my shoulder. "Easy there. Need some help?"

I straightened and took a few deep breaths. Frank watched me and held on to me until I told him I was alright.

I wiped the picture frame on my T-shirt and avoided looking at him. Blood had leaked inside and soiled the picture—the only print of it I had.

Someone really wants me out of here.

"You shouldn't be handling that," Frank said. "Set it on the sand, and I'll get an evidence bag." He gestured at me when I didn't do as asked. "You're pale. Go sit down."

"No, I want to save the picture."

"There could be fingerprints on that frame."

"I don't care. It's important to me."

Frank shrugged. "You're making it hard for me to help you." He crossed his arms, looked at the photo still in my hand, and met my eyes.

"Who is it?"

"I need a minute." I turned to leave.

"Where are you going?"

"I've got to walk my dog and change my shirt. I'll find you as soon as she's done."

Frank looked annoyed, but he didn't move to stop me. Once inside the trailer, I sat down for a moment with my head between my knees. I wondered who had done something so vicious. Someone had broken into my trailer and taken the only photo I had at the dig of my deceased husband. Stolen it right off the nightstand in my bedroom and dropped it face down in decaying blood.

When the light-headedness cleared, I stashed the photo in the shower stall and closed the bathroom door to keep Dakota away from it. I hadn't talked about Clay's death to anyone at the dig. The person who did this had learned something about me I rarely shared and had set out to hurt me in the worst way possible. Not just scare me.

I marched back into my living room, took the shotgun from the corner of the room where I'd left it, made sure the safety was on, and hid it in the closet in my bedroom. I leashed up Dakota and walked her behind the trailer where Frank couldn't see us, grateful for a moment to myself.

Dakota finished her business, and I took a calming breath and sighed before we went looking for Frank. He waved from a spot about a quarter mile down the trail. Someone had dragged the sheep carcass and left it close to the office door. Flies swarmed the blood-soaked, matted wool around its neck. Dakota lunged at the carcass. I choked up on her collar and put her in a sit.

"This must be what that shadow moving across your window was about," Frank said.

"Someone wants to make sure my staff knows about it too," I said.

"Looks that way. What are your plans for today?"

"I'm meeting a Hopi medicine man up at Walpi later this morning."

"How far is that from the dig?"

"It's on First Mesa. About forty-five minutes from here."

"I'm calling the sheriff's department to make sure we get someone out here today. You should stick around."

"I can't get in touch with the medicine man to cancel because they don't allow phones in Walpi."

"Think about what just happened, Aideen," he urged. "Isn't this situation more urgent? The deputy that comes out is bound to have a lot of questions that only you can answer."

I knew he was right and that the other employees would expect answers when they learned what had happened. But I also needed Cha'tima's help with the NAAC.

"Frank, there's too much riding on this meeting. I can't skip it. I'll drive back here as soon as I can. We're only talking the difference of a few hours."

Frank sighed. "Can you make it back by no later than two this afternoon?"

"Absolutely."

The frown and the hardness around Frank's eyes softened a little but didn't entirely vanish. "I'll call the sheriff's department and update them about the situation here. I can ask them to send someone out later this afternoon as a professional courtesy. I have business in Winslow. I'll meet you back here, no later than two, agreed?"

"Agreed," I said.

We walked the path to his van, and I thanked him for coming such a long way. I waved as he drove off, but I don't think he saw me through the plume of dust kicked up by the tires.

#

I went inside to take another look at Clay's photo, hoping to save it. Dakota followed me inside and curled up in her favorite spot in the living room. I set the photo on the dining table and went to the kitchen for a damp sponge. When I turned the photo over, I saw the message lightly penciled across the cardboard backing:

You're next.

I dropped the photo on the table. The glass cracked across Clay's face. Dakota stood and raised her hackles. The back of my neck tingled. I jerked around and looked out the window by the dining nook, feeling like I was being watched.

    I called Frank, but he didn't answer. I left him a message, then grabbed Dakota's leash and the Penn Museum tote bag I used for a purse. We hiked to the office with the words, "you're next" rattling around in my brain like a sinister mantra.

CHAPTER 16

THE FRONT DOOR OPENED, and someone walked back to my office.

"Good morning, Aideen," Lyle Henderson said.

From the look on his face, I must have looked surprised.

"Gerry didn't tell you? Your grant was approved. I start consulting today."

"I haven't had a chance to talk with Gerry yet," I said. "But that's good news."

Lyle smiled. "I'm sure he'll be glad to know you're back." He held out his hand for Dakota to sniff.

"And who might this be?"

Dakota wagged her tail, and Lyle gave her a good scratch.

"Name's Dakota. Glad to see you don't have a problem with dogs."

"No, not at all. It'll be fun to have a dog around," he said, and gave her a pat. "How soon can you walk me out to inspect the bone hash?"

"Give me a minute—I should call Gerry first."

Nova arrived, gave me a nod and said, "Hi Dr. H! What brings you here?"

While Nova and Lyle caught up, I closed the door to my office, wondering what to handle first. The blood left under my trailer needed a fast cleanup, and now I had the former site director to deal with.

I called Rodgers at the Phoenix office.

"Where are you? I thought I'd hear from you yesterday," he said.

"At the dig. Got back late last night."

I told Rodgers what I'd learned in Santa Fe and the bizarre circumstances surrounding my homecoming.

"Sheep's blood in your car? A dead sheep under your trailer? That's bizarre, Aideen. What did the county sheriff have to say?"

"No one from the sheriff's office has shown up yet. Last night I called the BLM agent I met in New Mexico. He drove out, and he's also called the sheriff's office to make sure we get someone out here."

"Let me know what you find out—and have Lyle contact me. I'm making him the liaison with the foundation and the NAAC."

"Gerry, I can handle them."

"You have too much going on already. Solve the safety issues first."

"What about my request for security?"

"I'm still looking into it. I'll have to get back to you."

#

I left Dakota in the office, and Lyle and I struck off across the mesa for a look at the bone hash. Extra tarps had been piled over the mounded excavation as I'd directed. I'd messaged Burk to meet us at the site, but he wasn't around when we arrived.

While we waited for Burk, Lyle and I discussed what we knew about the cannibalized bones and the isolated boy's skeleton we'd excavated near the bone hash. Burk had reported the child's bones were thin, consistent with malnourishment. His skeleton measured only ninety-six centimeters, small for a child whose bones suggested he had died between the ages of four and five.

I looked out onto the mesa and imagined what he had last seen. Were people he knew part of a killing spree? Or had strangers come to his village—people desperate to survive in a time of severe drought? If the bone hash dated between 1130 and 1180 CE as we suspected, we already knew from tree-ring dating that period had experienced the worst drought ever to occur at Moenkopi Ridge.

The sun brightened the mesa under a crisp and clear blue sky that morning. Prickly pear cactuses gleamed in full bloom, their yellow and fuchsia flowers in brilliant contrast against the surrounding gray-green sagebrush. I wondered if those colors had existed in the child's drought-impacted world. I wondered what his name had been nine hundred years ago.

"I'm interested in hearing your theories about the red stain on the bones," I said to Lyle. "My understanding is the use of red ochre in burials is not typically found out here."

"True," Lyle said. "And those bones weren't typically buried, either, as you know. If what George told me pans out, red ochre was applied years after the cannibalism occurred. Could be similar to the hypothesis put forth by Danish archaeologists at paleo-European sites. Red ochre was used at sites there to warn people not to dig further, to leave the bones at rest because the corpses had been violated. These circumstances look similar—a different culture uncovered bones years after the people died. The later culture applied the red stain to warn people from exhuming the bones again in the future."

"Do you think the people who stained these bones had healing intentions?" I asked.

"That's an interesting question. Healing how?"

"Healing as in a spiritual sense."

"Not something we're likely to know since they had no written language. The only clues we'll have to interpret are physical ones—the condition of the bones and the artifacts found with them, if there are any non-human artifacts. Even with physical evidence, unless we find something similar to modern-day Pueblo practices, we may never know why those bones were stained."

"That's part of the mystery of archaeology, isn't it?" I said. "Even with physical evidence, everyday use of artifacts is still open to interpretation."

I checked the time on my phone and said, "Burk was supposed to go to Walpi with me this morning, but he's late. It's more important that you meet with him. Let's have a quick look at the bone hash, then I'll take off."

I walked around to the back side of the covered mound and was surprised to see tracks in the surrounding sand that looked like they'd been made by the small backhoe we used on-site. We removed the stones weighing down the tarps, and I flipped back a corner of the canvas. Nothing but dirt. I rolled the tarps further back.

I gasped. We both stared, dumbstruck. Most of the bone hash was gone. Mounded up red-stained dirt, a few small bones, and an assortment of excavation tools were all that remained under the tarps.

"What the devil ..." Lyle raked his fingers through the dirt in the top of the trench.

"I never had to contend with this level of theft when I ran this site," he said. "This is a first."

My heart raced. "Look at this," I said, indicating the back-hoe tracks. "They stop right at the mound. Must be how they got all those bones out so fast."

Lyle shook his head. "No telling how much damage they did."

I stood with my hands at my sides, speechless. We'd opened this trench less than a week ago. As far as I knew, only Lonny and Burk had known about it, and they'd agreed not to discuss it.

Lyle took in my distress. "You were right, Aideen. This

dig needs security. Immediately. We can't risk any other areas of the dig being vandalized. Here's what I think we should do. You're going up to Walpi to meet with Cha'tima Honovi, right?"

I nodded.

"I'll wait here for Burk and show him what happened. The two of us will keep it to ourselves. As soon as you're back, I suggest we have a conference call with Gerry—you, Burk, and me. I'll do what I can to help you. We've got to convince Gerry to get armed protection at this dig."

Lyle and I quickly replaced the tarps and re-set the heavy stones. Still no sign of Burk. The other field archaeologists were working farther west. With any luck, we'd keep the theft quiet until after we conferenced with Gerry.

"I'm sorry you've had to deal with this, Aideen, but it's not the first major theft at an archaeological site."

I sighed. "It's the first major theft *I've* had to deal with."

He briefly laid a hand on my shoulder and said, "Call me as soon as you're back."

I nodded. Brushing the dirt from my hands, I turned east to run the trail to the office wondering what was keeping Burk.

#

Dakota was alone inside the office. A note on my desk from Burk said he couldn't reach Officer Humetewa, but he'd learned from the Hopi website that a religious healing dance was being held in Walpi. There was a good chance I'd find Cha'tima and Chosovi either attending the dances or in their home in Walpi Village. Burk couldn't join me because Rodgers had told him to meet him in Winslow. I called Burk's cell, but he didn't answer. I left an urgent message asking him to call me.

The drive to the Hopi mesas wound through desolate country. I felt in no mood to drive it alone, but it was too hot to take Dakota. The dog and I took the trail back to my air-conditioned trailer. The smell of rot that assaulted my nose when we drew close reminded me of all the reasons I dreaded this meeting with Cha'tima.

CHAPTER 17

First Mesa sits high above the Polacca Wash, its fortress-like presence rising like a ghost ship that's visible for miles. From the air, the land formation resembles a blunt-toed boot. Walpi and the two outlying villages, Hano and Sichomovi, tower some three hundred feet above the valley below. A single road, too narrow in places for more than one vehicle, gives access to the summit. When I go to First Mesa, I keep my eyes straight ahead driving up, mindful of the steep drop-off. Hano is the entry village at the summit. Residents welcome tourists and maintain an office to take visitors on guided tours into Walpi. Only Hopis are permitted to enter the old ceremonial village without a guide.

The tourist office looked open when I arrived, but a handmade sign in the window said all tours were canceled until the following week. I pulled into a parking space in front. Across the road, a strip of yellow police tape marking off the front of a residence had snapped one of its moorings and whipped around in the wind like an angry serpent. Karen, the tour guide, sat at her desk thumbing through papers. Her daughter played at a child's table nearby, engrossed in a coloring book.

Karen looked up and acknowledged me but frowned slightly.

"We're closed this week," she said.

"Do you remember me from the last time I visited? I came to see Cha'tima and Chosovi."

"They aren't taking visitors yet."

"Why? Have the dances started?"

She gave me an odd look and shook her head.

"Then would you please send someone to tell them Aideen Connor is here? They're expecting me." Saying I was expected was a bit of a stretch, but on my last visit, Cha'tima had agreed to another meeting.

"I don't think they'll see you," she said. "But I'll send my daughter over to ask."

Karen's daughter, Roberta, was about six and wore a pink *Hello Kitty* sweatshirt, blue jeans, and purple sneakers with her dark hair pulled into a long ponytail. Karen spoke to her in Hopi, and Roberta took off down the gravel road leading to Walpi. Some fifteen minutes later, the little girl returned, grinning wide and motioning to me to follow.

We took the winding path through the villages of Hano and Sichomovi, Roberta skipping ahead, occasionally turning and smiling me on. Both villages were built in the traditional pueblo style around compact communal plazas. Many homes were one room. Second and third-story homes were stacked like blocks on top of the ground-floor residences.

The fragrance of simmering stews seasoned with herbs and chilies drifted through open doorways. A woman seated on the landing of her home patted out a plate-sized blue corn flour tortilla. Dogs ran and barked alongside laughing children playing atop the narrow mesa exhibiting no apparent concern for the unprotected drop-off.

Long ago, residents voted to keep Walpi a ceremonial village that would remain untouched by the changing world. They ruled against having running water, connecting to the electrical grid, and allowing other modern conveniences. As a result, Walpi functioned mostly as a place for religious dances and seasonal ceremonies. Only a few people still lived in the village year-round.

Roberta crossed the land bridge that connected Sichomovi to Walpi. She pointed to a steep trail that curved down to a cairn at the base of the mesa and marked the source of a natural spring that once provided water for all three villages.

Looking out over the endless valley, I felt I'd been transported to an eagle's aerie. The engineering required to erect this ancient village in such a steep and remote location stood testimony to the ingenuity of its original inhabitants. Many stones in these buildings had been carried up the mesa on human backs, one by one, centuries ago. The original trails used to reach the mesa top were still in use today, although most were off-limits to non-Hopi.

We climbed the stone stairs to the second level. Wooden ladders, polished by hundreds of hands throughout the centuries, protruded from a kiva close to our destination. Cha'tima told me during my last visit there were seven kivas in Walpi. Each round, subterranean room served men of a designated clan during secret religious preparations. The men of the clans owned the kivas, but the homes were the property of Hopi women in the tribe's ancient matrilineal tradition. When we reached Chosovi's home, Roberta hopped from one foot to the other while we waited for someone to answer my knock.

Chosovi pulled open the heavy wooden door. She had arranged her thick gray hair in the traditional married woman's style with a hank to each side of her face. Each ponytail was bound with a hand-crafted hair tie made of a leather disc elaborately embellished with tiny blue and white glass beads hand sewn to the leather in a geometric design. She grasped my arm warmly and motioned me inside. I smiled my thanks and complimented her on her beautiful hair ties.

Chosovi handed a piece of wrapped candy to Roberta and gave her a big hug. She watched Roberta skip back toward Hano until the little girl waved and turned out of sight.

A wooden table, painted dark green and surrounded by four plain wooden chairs, formed the focal point of the room. Katsina carvings stood on display in a bookcase against the back wall. A wood-framed bed was visible from the doorway into the back room. Natural light shone through white curtains covering a large window to the right of the entrance. Strings of chilies and dried herbs hung from wall hooks behind the stove.

Cha'tima rose from a cot near the wood-burning stove they used for cooking and heating their home in winter. Standing next to him I realized how tall he was, well over six feet, full-bodied, and muscular for a man past seventy. Scuffed brown cowboy boots poked from underneath the bottoms of dark blue jeans he'd topped with a silver-buckled brown leather belt and a blue chambray shirt. We shook hands.

"Thank you for meeting with me," I said.

"What is so important that it brings you here *today*?" he asked.

His brusque manner took me aback. During our first meeting he'd been friendly and helpful.

"We tried to contact you through a Hopi officer, but we weren't able to reach him. Should I come back another time?"

Cha'tima motioned for me to take a seat at the table. "I suppose it's as good a day as any, since you're here."

Chosovi glanced at me from across the room with a look that made me feel there was something she wanted to tell me. Instead, she went to the stove and asked if I'd like a cup of tea. I nodded. She took a handful of dried herbs from a glass jar and crushed them into a copper kettle on the stovetop. A few minutes later, a sharp minty fragrance filled the room. Chosovi let the tea steep a while then brought two cups to the table. Cha'tima's posture in the straight-backed chair relaxed a little when she set the mugs down, then Chosovi went quietly into the back room and closed the door.

Given Cha'tima's demeanor, it seemed best to get down to business and keep the meeting brief. I took a sip of Chosovi's tea and handed Cha'tima the list of funerary artifacts we'd excavated since our first meeting. I told him we had, again, uncovered human remains. Although the dig was located on private land, Cha'tima knew our procedures with grave objects and human remains still fell under government regulations.

I gave him time to review the documents then said, "There's something else I need to tell you."

Cha'tima studied my face from across the table. "Something that causes you concern?" He folded his weather-beaten hands expectantly on the tabletop.

I brushed back a strand of hair and took a breath. "The bones we uncovered this week had cut marks, Cha'tima. Some were severed into small pieces. The leg bones showed evidence of marrow removal."

Cha'tima frowned. His posture stiffened.

I continued. "The bones were abandoned in a pile, not buried—the remains of at least a dozen people."

"We had enemies long ago that attacked and mutilated our ancestors."

We stared into each other's eyes. I clasped and unclasped my hands under the table.

"Cha'tima, the marks and cuts on these bones look like the remains from other sites where archaeologists identified cannibalism. I wanted you to hear this from me first, before anyone else on the committee gets wind of it."

He straightened, his eyes narrowing.

I shifted in my chair and said, "The problem is, something even worse just happened."

Cha'tima slammed his fist on the table. "What could be worse than claiming my ancestors were cannibals? It's the Death Mound all over again."

I looked away and sighed. I'd feared he might have this reaction. The Death Mound was the name the tribe gave to human remains abandoned after a massacre in the village of Awatovi, a part of the Hopi Reservation now closed to outsiders.

In 1700, only ten years after the Pueblo Revolt, the people of Awatovi turned away from the Hopi religion under pressure from the Catholic friars sent from Spain to convert them. Early accounts claimed the friars led converts to their faith through miraculous healings; other accounts claimed villagers were coerced to convert through fear and threats.

When Hopis in the five neighboring villages learned Awatovi's residents had deserted the Hopi religion, they grew enraged. Chiefs from the other five villages quickly amassed a united army with the sole mission of punishing the religious deserters. The army struck Awatovi at dawn. Warriors advanced on each of the kivas and withdrew the ladders, the only means of escape from the subterranean rooms. Then they threw in burning logs and dried chilies, killing the Awatovi men below.

The warriors had agreed earlier to take the women and children back to their respective villages, but fighting broke out among the warriors. In an astounding act of violence, the marauders slaughtered the Awatovi women and children on the spot. Bodies were dismembered where they fell. Afterward, archaeologists claim the fallen were cooked and eaten as further warning against abandoning the Hopi religion. The bones of the victims were tossed into a massive pile—the Death Mound. Archaeologists studying Awatovi centuries later would regard this act of cannibalism as the extreme punishment the warriors deemed necessary to warn other villages against deserting Hopi traditions.

Soil accumulated over the bones of the massacred for three hundred years, and they lay undisturbed in the abandoned village until archaeologists excavated the site in the 1970s.

Cha'tima leaned toward me, his voice a sharp whisper. "Do you have any idea how much anguish the Death Mound has caused my people?"

I met his eyes. "I do, Cha'tima. That's why I want your help with this."

He looked at me warily.

"There's more," I said. "All of the bones we uncovered were stained with red ochre. We think it was applied many years after the people died. That an entirely different group of villagers stained the bones."

"What is it you think *I* can do about this?" he asked, his voice louder.

"I'm not sure. Unfortunately, all the bones in the death mound at my dig... are now gone. I need your help disclosing all this to the other NAAC members."

Cha'tima spoke in a voice low-pitched and measured. "Last time you came here you said the ancestors' bones would not be removed until after that committee you asked me to join arranged for reburial."

"That's true, Cha'tima, but I didn't order the bones removed. They were stolen."

Cha'tima raised his voice. "Stolen? What do you intend to do about this? There are people full of evil who *sell* ancestral bones."

"I know. I've seen ads on the internet. That could be their motive. Especially if the thieves believed the bones had been cannibalized."

He looked at me, his face in a scowl, then he pushed his chair away from the table, turned, and stared at the wall behind him, as if looking into the past. My eyes followed his gaze to the display of Katsinam—the hand-carved wooden figures arranged in his bookcase. The carvings appeared to stare back at me, accusing me.

I'd met with Cha'tima only one time before, and although I felt we'd begun to build rapport, it probably wasn't enough for him to trust me.

He saw me looking at the carvings and said, "Katsinam teach us appropriate behavior and the consequences of unacceptable behavior."

I went to the bookcase for a closer look, hoping to dispel the awkwardness between us. The small, detailed carvings, each representing a unique Hopi spiritual messenger, did not prepare me for what else I would find in that bookcase. Propped between two Katsinam, as if held in a state of protection, was the framed photo of a young woman. My breath caught. I pulled it out, knocking a Katsina to the floor—Crow Man—known for making war on Hopi clowns at the Plaza Dances. Crow Man's job was to warn off non-Hopi behavior. I snatched up the carving with my free hand, shuddering at the look of its forbidding black-winged mask, and hastily returned it to the shelf.

Then I looked at the photo I still grasped in my other hand.

Cha'tima took hold of my wrist and squeezed it hard "You must put that back."

I held on to the picture. "How do you know this woman?"

He peered into my face for a moment. Lines deepened around his eyes and across his forehead. A feeling of dread engulfed me. I took hold of the bookcase to steady myself, remembering the police tape flapping in front of the Hano residence when I drove in. Cha'tima stared into my eyes with a look of such pain that my breath caught. He released my arm and his next words cut deep.

"She was Tiponi, our only granddaughter. Humetewa gave me this photo after she was murdered." Cha'tima's voice trailed off. "It's one of the few pictures we have of her."

"Your *granddaughter*?" I whispered.

My heart felt squeezed as if in a vise. If anyone knew the agony of losing a loved one from a violent, untimely death, it was me. My eyes filled with hot, stinging tears. I placed my hand gently on his arm, but Cha'tima turned away.

"Oh my God, Cha'tima," was all I could say. "Oh my God, how awful."

CHAPTER 18

Cha'tima walked back with me to Hano, moving slowly, as if every step aged him. I'd apologized for visiting so soon after his granddaughter's death. He'd placed his hands gently on my shoulders and said, "We should have refused to see you, but Chosovi holds a certain affection for you. You'll have to manage that committee on your own, Aideen. I can't be involved right now so soon after losing Tiponi."

Thunderheads gathered in swirls as Cha'tima led me to the parking lot under a darkening sky. He briefly took the hand I offered, then opened the car door for me. Across from the tourist office, strong winds scattered the vendors selling Katsinam. The parking lot was full, despite the sign placed in the window stating all tours of Walpi were canceled. Then I understood. The healing dances Burk mentioned in his note were meant for Cha'tima and his family. In remembrance of Tiponi.

I watched Cha'tima's retreating figure hunched against the wind before I drove down. My hands felt clammy on the steering wheel and my eyes smarted. Rain and hail splattered the windshield halfway down the narrow road as I drove off First Mesa.

My thoughts reeled in a maelstrom of unanswered questions, flickering like black-and-white film caught in an old-time projector. What could I do to comfort Cha'tima and Chosovi over the loss of their only granddaughter? How would I deal with the remaining members of the NAAC without Cha'tima's calming support?

By the time I reached the turn-off to the dig some forty miles down the road, I'd outrun the rain but not the dark clouds that had followed me from Walpi to cluster over Moenkopi Ridge. I pulled onto the shoulder at a high spot where cell reception was usually good and called Lyle.

"Have you talked with Gerry yet about the stolen bone hash?" he asked.

"No. Wanted your input first."

"I don't have any new ideas, Aideen. Better to go ahead and tell him. Let me know after the two of you've talked, and I'll call him and put in a good word for you."

He was right. The longer I waited, the worse the situation and my anxiety would become.

"Lyle, I found out something important while I was in Walpi. That woman murdered on the Hopi Reservation last week was Cha'tima's granddaughter."

There was a pause. "What woman? What are you talking about?"

"Remember when we first met? I'd just come back from Tuba City after I ended up staying there overnight. I found the picture of a young Hopi woman left in my motel room, and later, a man appeared in the middle of the night claiming the photo was his and demanding it back. Long story short, he tried to break in, and the police were called. Later I learned the woman in the photo was murdered, probably that night. Today I just learned the murder victim was Cha'tima's granddaughter. I have this sinking feeling that our dig is in some way involved in that murder."

Lyle was silent for what seemed like a long time.

Finally, he said, "That must have been a very uncomfortable meeting. But I can't imagine how the dig would be

involved. What a terrible loss for the family."
"Cha'tima quit the NAAC because of it."
"Not good."
"Can't really blame him," I said.
"Nor do I. I've been thinking all morning about the red stain on those stolen bones. If the victims were attacked during extreme drought, I'm sure the attackers would have been extremely cautious about showing up in a strange village. The drought years would have brought on intense fighting for the limited resources."
"Yes, extreme drought would have spawned extreme offensive actions."
"Or worse. More like the way some archaeologists believe the cult at Chaco Canyon operated—using human sacrifice and cannibalism to control people," Lyle said. "There's a significant number of archaeologists who believe the drought brought on a time of unusual violence. I tend to agree with them."
"Some family groups began migrating during that time as well," I said. "The villagers remaining had to have lived in constant fear and stress. I only hope we get the chance to study those bones. Will you be on-site later this week?"
"Yes, I drove down to my gallery after you left this morning. I'll be back at the dig some time tomorrow after the storm. Good luck with Gerry."
We disconnected. I sat in the car looking out over Moenkopi Ridge, contemplating the mysteries the site held. Archaeology can be a painstaking process. Physical evidence is uncovered slowly to avoid damage to artifacts that are old and often fragile. Yet, consequential damage to a site's descendants could be swift and brutal. I wondered how Tiponi's murder was connected to our newest discovery, if at all. And how was Ray Alonzo connected to any of this? What about Tiponi's picture was so compelling for him that he'd chased me across two states to get it back?

My phone buzzed.

"It's Frank. I just listened to your message. Where are you?"

"At the turn off to the dig."

"You all right?"

"Yes, but I have lots to tell you. Any news about Alonzo?"

"Yes, the Taos cops released him this morning, but a warrant went out for his arrest about an hour ago. The Feds found the weapon that killed that woman in Hano. And by the way, you were right. The picture you saw on that flyer in Taos was likely the same woman in the photo that Alonzo keeps demanding. The name of the victim was Tiponi. Tiponi *Alonzo*. Turns out Alonzo was her ex-husband. You didn't hear it from me, but his prints were all over the murder weapon."

CHAPTER 19

I ARRIVED HOME TO find my front door ajar and the air-conditioner running full blast. The trailer looked the same as when I'd left, nothing out-of-place or missing—except my dog. I retrieved the shotgun from my bedroom closet and walked outside from one end of the trailer to the other, calling Dakota. There was no sign of her. I jogged down the trail, thinking someone might have taken her inside the office. Jill and Nova sat at their desks working on their computers.

"Have you seen Dakota?"

Jill, the site administrator looked up and shook her head. "Why do you have that shotgun?" she asked.

"Had a break in. Dog's missing."

"Thought Dakota was with you," Nova said. "Pretty weird having a break in out here. Can I help you find her?"

"Would you check the dining tent? I'll see if she's back at the trailer."

Running up the trail I spotted a turkey vulture circling in and out of the clouds. Vultures are known to have a keen sense of smell, and the stench coming from under my trailer had likely attracted it. I realized then that I hadn't checked the crawl space.

My breath caught when I saw the heavy stone jammed against the small door. It took a lot of effort and several precious minutes to lug it away. Dakota lay inside in the overheated space, her mouth open from panting, her breathing slow. She half-opened her eyes.

I crawled inside the foul-smelling enclosure, my knees sinking into the bloody quagmire, my arms shaking. I grasped Dakota under her rear legs and backed out, dragging her with me as gently as I could.

I ran to the hose attached to the spigot at the back of my trailer, turned it on full blast, pulled it around, and sprayed Dakota from end to end. She shuddered when the water hit her. I soaked her and ran back to turn it off. The external water tank held only 500 gallons, and the delivery service had missed our last scheduled stop.

Inside, I gathered every hand towel I owned and drenched them in the kitchen sink, then I carried the wet towels outside in a large pan and placed each one over the dog's major blood vessels—on her belly and groin, in each armpit, under her neck, against the pads of her feet. I'd learned from the vet who saved her in Utah that a wet towel completely covering the dog could hold heat in. I dribbled water from a soaked towel into her mouth. She swallowed a little. I gave her a moment to rest, then continued coaxing her to take more water.

With my head in my hands, I rested a minute beside Dakota and asked her to hang on. The person who'd trapped my dog had to have known I depended on her for protection, but it was doubtful anyone knew how much I counted on her for emotional support. When she stretched out her paw to touch my arm, I grabbed hold of it and cried.

I heard a car pull in and park and, figuring it was Frank, I called to him to come around back. He found me sitting on the ground beside Dakota covered in filth.

He stopped mid-stride. "What happened?"

"Heat stroke. Someone trapped her inside," I said nodding toward the crawl space.

"What about using ice?"

"Ice can constrict the blood vessels. Air conditioning would help cool her off, though. I know she's soaking wet, but would you move her inside?"

Frank wrapped a couple of the damp towels around Dakota and lifted my ninety-pound dog in his arms as gently as he could. I followed him inside.

Frank set Dakota on the kitchen floor, crouched beside her, and stroked her head. I took her bowl to the kitchen sink and turned on the water. The faucet sputtered. Both water tanks had run dry.

"What do we do now?" I said.

"Isn't there water in the office?" Frank asked.

"Yes, but it's trucked in like it is here." I retrieved my phone from where I'd left it on the dining table and called the office.

"Did you find Dakota?" Nova asked.

"Yes, but she's overheated, and my trailer just ran out of water. Would you check the office tank?"

"Don't have to. I can tell you we're out," Nova said. "Barely enough left this morning to make coffee. Jill called the delivery service, and they won't be back out here for a few days."

"Tell her to call them again and say it's urgent." Replacing the phone, I said to Frank, "The only water available on-site is in the collections building. It has its own system, but it's at least a mile from here, and there's only a trail down, no road."

"What about your dining tent?" Frank said.

"We usually keep two five-gallon jugs there in dispensers, no running water. Frank, I'm sorry to ask, but would you drive to that market in Winslow? We've got to get water, and I should stay here with Dakota."

"I don't mind helping, Aideen, but leaving you alone here after what happened with your dog is a bad idea. What if the perp who trapped Dakota comes back for you?"

"Look, Frank, none of us will be okay in this heat without water. I can protect myself with the shotgun if I have to."

"Where is it?"

"The closet in my bedroom."

Frank shook his head and sighed. "Okay, I get it about the water. I have a change of clothes in my van. Maybe there's enough water left in the bathroom pipes for me to wash up."

#

"Anything else?" Frank asked on his way out.

"There's no food in the trailer."

"I'll pick up whatever I can score fast," he promised.

"Good idea. The weather's not likely to hold much longer."

Frank shot a look at the sky through the kitchen window. "You could be right. I'll make it quick. Leaving you alone here is still against my better judgment."

"I'll be fine. It's the middle of the afternoon."

I went back in the kitchen after Frank left and halfheartedly picked up the tea kettle I'd left on the stove. Water sloshed inside. I smiled at my stroke of luck and poured what there was into the dog's bowl. She lapped a little. The cool air inside the trailer seemed to be reviving her.

I sat on the floor beside Dakota, grateful she seemed better and wondering who had trapped her. It wouldn't have been hard to entice her inside with the smelly sheep's blood still in the crawl space. Alonzo was the only person who came to mind. I figured he'd had enough time to drive to the dig after confronting me in Taos.

"Aideen," a voice called from the doorway.

I jumped. I hadn't heard the door open and turned with a start.

"What happened? What's that crap all over you?" Nova asked.

"Nova," I said, relieved to see who it was. "Someone

trapped Dakota in the crawl space. We've been struggling to bring her around."

"That's awful! What's that stain on your clothes?" she asked with a frown. "Looks like blood. Is Dakota gonna make it?"

"She'd better," I sighed. "Sit down if you want, and I'll tell you the whole story."

Nova settled into the dining nook and crossed her long legs under the table. I stayed on the floor beside Dakota, giving her an occasional pat and urging her to drink more water every few minutes.

"Why would someone want to kill Dakota?" Nova seemed offended on Dakota's behalf. "She's such a good dog. Didn't give me an ounce of trouble when I was watching her."

Dakota lifted her head when Nova spoke and looked up at her. Nova went a little pale. She sat, arms crossed. "Are the rest of us in any danger out here?"

"I don't know, Nova. I'll ask the deputy what he thinks when we get him out here."

"That tarp covering that foul-smelling mound by the office—is that the dead sheep?"

I nodded.

"Better bury it soon." She shook her head. "All we need is another predator lurking about."

"The sheriff's department is supposed to send out someone from animal control to get rid of it."

"Is there anything I can do to help, Aideen?"

"Thanks, I don't think so."

"Then I'd like to get home before the storm hits. It's almost four..."

"Good idea. I'll catch up with you in the morning."

#

Dakota's breathing had eased, and she looked comfortable lying next to her water bowl. A sudden flash of lightning followed by a loud crack of thunder startled me. Rain began a light tattoo on the metal roof. Frank had already been gone an hour and a half. Winslow is a thirty-minute drive from the dig, one way. I hoped he'd make it back before the worst of the storm hit. With a sigh, I reminded myself that weather always sounded worse sitting inside the trailer with its thin walls and metal roof than it did outside.

I found a can of chicken soup in the pantry and poured it into the dog's bowl, then I sat beside her on the floor to encourage her. It was a relief to see she was plenty eager to lap it up on her own.

When I stood to have a look at the storm through my kitchen window, an angry face glared back at me.

Alonzo.

CHAPTER 20

ALONZO THREW THE FRONT door open. I raced to the bedroom and dove into the closet for the shotgun, Alonzo on my heels. I whirled around and aimed the gun at his chest. He skidded to a halt, blocking the bedroom door.
"You're not going to shoot me," he said.
"Do you really want to find out? Hands up."
Alonzo squinted and raised his hands.
Dakota growled weakly and rose on shaky legs.
Alonzo turned to look at her. "What's wrong with your mutt?"
"You should know. You're the one who tried to kill her."
"You're psycho," he scoffed. "I didn't do nothin' to your dog."
He started to lower his hands. I lowered the shotgun to gut level.
"Easy," he said, palms out. "I just want my photo. I'm not here to hurt you or your fucking dog."
"Right. Just give me a reason to shoot you," I said. "Back up."
My breaths came in fast, shallow bursts. I had to get to my phone to call Frank, but Alonzo had followed me when I dashed to the bedroom to get the shotgun, and he was blocking my way to the dining table where I'd left it. He took another step toward me.

I aimed high and squeezed the trigger. The china cabinet over the kitchen sink blew up behind him. Debris flew everywhere—pieces of wood and plastic and what was once my dinnerware. Dakota yelped, shook, and staggered into the living room. Dust and smoke clouded the air. Alonzo blinked, rubbed his eyes, and batted at the back of his head, shaking off pieces of cabinet.

I racked another shell. "I said back up." My ears buzzed. I had to shout for him to hear me.

Alonzo backed up.

I pointed with the shotgun. "Stay facing me and back into the living room. Keep your hands up."

Alonzo slowly backed past the dining nook, now wary of sudden moves.

I leveled the gun and slid my phone across the dining table to where I could work it one-handed. I hit redial and set it on speaker, keeping the shotgun and my eyes on Alonzo.

Frank answered, "What's up?"

"I need you back fast. Alonzo's here. I have the gun on him."

"I'm at your turnoff. Hang on."

Rain on the roof sounded like a stampede. Water splashed in through the front door Alonzo had left open. Dakota growled but didn't get up from her new spot by the couch.

"Why did you try to kill my dog, you sick bastard?"

"What would that get me? I told you, I don't give a flying fuck about you or your dog. Just give me my photo."

Alonzo lowered his hands.

"Keep your hands up where I can see them!" I sidestepped to the front door and tried to close it, but didn't get it to latch. "Did you give a flying fuck about your ex-wife when you killed her?"

His face contorted. "You crazy bitch. Tiponi's not dead!"

"Oh? Then why is there a warrant out for your arrest—

for murdering her?"

Alonzo's head jerked backwards like he'd been punched. He thrust his hand behind his back, yanked a pistol from the waist of his jeans, and pointed it at me. I raised the shotgun to fire but stumbled backwards, slipped on the wet linoleum by the front door, fell, and dropped the shotgun. Alonzo came at me. Hovered over me and jammed his pistol in my face. I raised my arms in front of me. Dakota barked weakly and stood.

"Where's my fucking photo?" he yelled.

"I don't have it," I rasped. "I told you before! The cop in Tuba took it!"

Tires crunched on gravel.

"You'd better not be lying," Alonzo said.

He pushed past me and leaped out the front door over the trailer steps. A car door slammed. "Hold it!" Frank yelled and fired. Rain had churned the trail to soup. I stood in the doorway and watched Alonzo charge down the path toward the office and disappear into the downpour.

#

"I knew I shouldn't have left," Frank said, latching the door behind him. "I've put out an APB."

"Alonzo acted surprised when I said he was wanted for Tiponi's murder."

"Like most suspects," Frank said. He nodded at the shotgun lying on the floor where I'd dropped it.

"Is that why there're pieces of crap all over the place?"

"Yeah, pretty much." I told him what happened.

"You blew up your dish cabinet?"

"Yep. After that Alonzo was more cooperative. Until I fell on my ass instead of shooting him."

Frank shook his head. "I'm staying here tonight, no argument. The road from Winslow ran like a creek. You're lucky I made it back."

Frank sat on the couch in the living room. Dakota

scooted close to him and put her head on his knee. He scratched her gently behind the ears. Dakota lay down and rolled over with a contented sigh, and Frank gave her a belly rub.

"Want a comforter to throw over your soaked clothes?" I asked.

"Not now. I picked up a frozen pizza and some beer. I'll go back out and get the stuff in a minute."

"I can unload," I said, reaching for the slicker I kept on a hook by the door. "Toss me your keys."

"Not a good idea, Aideen. Who knows where Alonzo is? I'll go. Let me borrow that slicker."

Frank checked his gun, holstered it, threw my slicker over his shoulders and then headed to his van. He returned shortly with a large frozen pizza and a six-pack of Blue Moon. He made a second trip and returned lugging a five-gallon jug of water on his shoulder.

He set the water jug on the counter in the kitchen with the spigot pointed into the sink. "I'll bring in the rest of the water in the morning. I need to dry out."

"Me too," I said. "I need to wash up and get out of these filthy clothes."

"Good idea. You're looking pretty scary," Frank said, giving me a quirky smile.

I cleaned up with a pan of water carried into the bathroom then returned to the kitchen. Fragments of cabinet and dishes lay scattered everywhere. I sponged up debris off the stovetop, lit the propane oven, and set the pizza in to bake. Then I set about sweeping up the rest of the mess.

Frank pulled off his waterlogged boots and socks. I draped a comforter over his wet shoulders, and he stretched out on the couch, watching me for a few minutes. I lowered my eyes when he said, "I get the feeling there's something big going on out here that you're not telling me."

"Like what?" I asked, looking up.

"Who was it who banged on your door last night when we were on the phone?"

"Burk. I told you that."

"I heard him say something about bones," Frank countered.

"He was talking about a new trench we just opened. I told him we could talk on the way to Walpi. But this morning he left me a note saying the boss wanted to meet him in Winslow and for me to drive up without him."

Frank took a moment to mull this over. "Pretty insubordinate of him. Why don't you sit down and give me the whole story?"

I finished sweeping up the remains of the china cabinet, then I ditched the broom and sat opposite Frank in the living room. I stared down at my dirt-trashed hands and picked at a hangnail. No matter how helpful he'd been, Frank was still a BLM agent, and Rodgers had warned me not to tell anyone outside the dig we'd unearthed evidence of prehistoric cannibalism. Given the amount of trouble I was in already, I felt reluctant to reveal anything that could add to Rodgers's disapproval.

Frank noted my frown. "I'll keep what you tell me to myself. You have my word."

I glanced out the window at the rain and considered what might have happened to me if Frank hadn't made it back when he did.

"Have you ever heard the term bone hash?" I asked.

Frank shrugged. "Sounds like bad canned meat."

I laughed. "That's a good one." I explained what it meant, which was more involved for someone without the necessary background.

"Pretty gruesome," he said.

"Some would say that. But a lot in life depends upon circumstances. It's hard for people in modern times to understand what prehistoric people had to endure. And there's something else that makes this discovery unique. The bones we unearthed were covered with red ochre."

"Why does that matter?"

"We think it was applied by a different group of people *years* after the bones were discarded. Red ochre stains are common at European burial sites, but not out here. The staining could represent a new discovery about Ancestral Pueblo beliefs."

"Then I'd think your new find would present interesting scientific opportunities. Why is it a problem?"

"The discovery isn't the problem."

Frank looked puzzled. I continued, "I stopped by the trench with the former dig director before I drove to Walpi this morning."

"And?" Frank said.

"Gone … Most of the bone pile went missing. Apparently stolen. And like I said, Burk never showed up to meet us like I'd asked him to."

"How many bones are we talking about? Wouldn't removing them take a long time?"

"Maybe a dozen skeletons. And, yes, it would take a very long time to remove the bones *properly*, but it looked like the thieves used our backhoe."

Frank looked flabbergasted as he contemplated the idea. "You use a backhoe at an archaeological dig?"

"Only for moving earth in non-critical areas. Obviously, we can't use it for trench work. I don't even want to think about the damage those thieves did."

Frank shrugged. "I suppose the idea of owning cannibalized human bones would beguile some people."

"Unfortunately, that's true. I've actually seen 'Indian' bones for sale on the internet. It's not going to go well for me when I tell Rodgers what happened."

"So why did you insist on leaving the dig this morning?

"To ask for help from the medicine man. Cha'tima was to

be the head of our Native American Advisory Committee. He helped make decisions about the grave objects and human remains we discovered. I wanted his support dealing with the rest of the committee members. If it gets out the dig lost human remains, some locals will claim we failed to show proper respect to prehistoric people."

"I can understand that," Frank said. "Less than fifty years ago, museums still displayed Native American skeletons in glass cases."

"True. Some people in the local Native American communities believe their ancestors' early practices have been used to demean them."

"What do you believe?"

I twisted a tendril of hair around my finger then tucked it behind my ear. "I think Native Americans have had their share of denigration by the media."

Lightning streaked across the window behind Frank. For a few long moments, neither of us spoke. Then he said, "Are you thinking the threats against you in Taos and the threats to you out here are connected with this bone theft in some way?"

"I do think that, and I believe all of it is connected to that woman's murder up on the Hopi Rez."

"That's a big a stretch, Aideen. How'd you come up with that idea?"

"I found out something that shocked me when I visited Walpi this morning. Tiponi—the Hano murder victim—turns out she was Cha'tima's granddaughter."

"And he's that medicine man you told me about?"

I nodded.

"That is an odd coincidence. But what's it got to do with you?"

"It's not so much what it has to do with me as what it's got to do with Alonzo. You just told me Tiponi was married to him, and Alonzo followed me to Taos and came here just to get back that photo of her. He didn't act like he meant to kill me when he came here. He just insisted he wanted the photo like he said. He acted surprised when I told him I'd heard he was accused of murdering Tiponi."

"But if all he wants is the photo, why would he be pulling the kind of scare stunts happening here? Doesn't make any sense."

"That photo is tied to something he values. As to the scare tactics directed at me, I haven't figured that out yet."

"It's not adding up for me, Aideen," Frank said. "I get it that for whatever reason he wants his photo back, but why try to scare you away from your job? Big waste of his time."

"I don't know, Frank. Maybe I'm way off base."

"Alonzo carrying out elaborate plans to scare you out doesn't make any sense. Could someone here at the dig be trying to force you to leave?"

"Can't think of who it would be."

"Let it sit for a day or two. And make sure you're careful. Is that pizza ready yet? I haven't eaten all day."

I checked the oven and took out the bubbling pizza. Then I opened the fridge and twisted off the top of two beers and handed one to Frank. Rain streaked down the kitchen window in wide rivulets. "I'm glad this thing sits on high ground," I said.

Miraculously, there were two intact dusty plates sitting in the dish drainer. I brushed them off with a clean dish towel and dished up the pizza.

"We still haven't connected with someone from the sheriff's office," Frank said.

"No deputy in his right mind would come out in this weather. Why don't you call them again after we finish the pizza?" I suggested. "Maybe by then the rain will have slowed down a bit."

CHAPTER 21

INSTEAD OF LETTING UP, the storm uprooted clumps of sagebrush and cut gullies in the sand around the trailer. Frank called the Navajo County Sheriff's office again, and the dispatcher promised a deputy would be out as soon as someone could navigate the road to the dig. Sitting in the dining nook, Frank opened another beer and continued to question me about the strange threats against me since I'd returned from Taos.

"Tell me about that picture we found stuck in the crawl space this morning. I got your message that someone wrote a warning on it, but you were upset about it before you even noticed. Why?"

It was a question I'd been dreading. "It usually sits on the nightstand beside my bed. *I* didn't remove it. That means someone broke in here and stole it out of my bedroom."

"Hmph. What have you done with it?" Frank said. "Let me see it."

I retrieved the photo from the shower stall, giving Dakota a few pats when I passed her curled up on the kitchen floor. She raised her head and licked my hand. I set the photo on the dining table and stood beside Frank. "You're next," in barely visible writing was scrawled on the cardboard backing. Frank turned the picture frame over and laid it face up on the table. Clay's smile beamed through cracked glass. I shivered.

"Who is this, Aideen?"

My eyes drifted to the poster in my living room of a young couple strolling hand in hand in a Philadelphia city park.

"Aideen?"

"It's Clay."

"Clay? Who's Clay?"

My voice broke. "My husband."

Frank did a double take. "You're married?"

"He was killed."

"Killed? When?"

I crossed my arms. "About a year ago."

Frank scooted over on the dining nook's padded bench. "Sit down, Aideen."

I slumped in beside him.

"Was he murdered?"

"No."

"How can you be so sure?"

"Because I was there, Frank. He was killed in a mudslide. I watched him die and couldn't do a thing to save him. It was the worst moment of my life."

Frank went silent. I took several deep breaths, aware he was watching me.

"Do the other people who work here know about Clay's death?" he asked.

"I've never talked to anyone here about it."

Frank turned to look out the window. "I wonder what's keeping that deputy? I thought he'd at least call me back after the last conversation I had with the dispatcher."

"It's the weather. Or bad cell reception."

"I'm giving them another call. Excuse me for a minute." He slid out of the dining nook, stepped into the kitchen, and dialed with his face turned away from me. I was glad for a little time alone with my thoughts. Finding the picture of Clay deposited in a puddle of blood had unnerved me far more than I wanted to let on. Frank's sudden need to call the sheriff right then told me learning about Clay had unnerved him, too. And I wasn't ready to talk about Clay's death. Not to Frank, not to anyone.

"Did you hear what I just said?" Frank asked. He pocketed his phone and slid back into the dining nook beside me.

"No, sorry."

"The sheriff's department couldn't give me an update on when the deputy'll get here because of the weather."

"Probably not until tomorrow—and that's if we're lucky and the road doesn't wash out."

#

Hours later, night had set in without any let-up from the storm, and Frank and I were talked out. Wind howled around the trailer, rattling the windows and sometimes so strong the trailer shuddered. Rain drumming on the metal roof made further conversation difficult.

I took an extra blanket from my closet and one of the pillows off my bed and handed both to Frank. Dakota took a drink from her bowl in the kitchen then followed me into the bedroom and settled in her spot next to my bed. Soon her breathing was slow and even. With a sigh of relief, I closed my bedroom door, grateful that Dakota seemed to have recovered and I didn't have to spend the night alone after Alonzo's attack.

#

Clay and I are in Peru. An overnight downpour has left deep puddles on the trail. We clamber over stones laid down by the Inca some seven hundred years ago. The trail is so uneven and slick our progress is tedious and slow.

Tired after taking a side trip off the main trail, and failing to reach our planned destination before dusk, we come to a mountain gap the guide tells us is Dead Widow's Pass. He laughs when I quiz him about the strange name and points straight ahead to peaks in the distance that form the silhouette of a reclining woman.

"Why not 'Sleeping Woman's Pass?'" I ask.

He shrugs. "She never leaves."

The guide takes the pack llama to a flat area off the trail to prepare dinner while Clay and I admire the view. The deep valley suddenly turns dark. Clouds drift below us and infuse the air with a rich, earthy smell. I step closer to the side of the mountain toward the steep edge of the trail and dig in with my hiking poles. A noise from higher up, like a branch cracking, flushes a murder of crows. They fly down in dark swoops, cackling as they drop into the gorge. Clay ventures further up the trail and stands close to the abyss. My hands tighten on the handles of my hiking poles.

He turns and calls, "Come join me. The view is amazing!"

I smile up at him. "I can see just fine from here."

Clay knows I'm uneasy in steep, high places and doesn't insist. Instead, he turns to face the gorge, lifts his arms, and throws them wide. He shouts an exuberant "hello" that echoes off the far side of the gorge. His T-shirt stretches tightly across his back, his muscles well-defined from all the exploring we've done. I've never seen him looking so fit or found him more attractive. I drop my hiking poles and reach into my daypack to pull out my camera. I call to Clay, and when he turns, smiling broadly, I snap his picture.

A swath of spindly burned-out trees pockmarks the edge of the trail between us. They hold low at a strange angle and suddenly topple like skeletal marionettes with their strings gone slack. Clay whirls around, his face pinched, and calls to me over the roar... And then he's gone.

#

Dakota stood inches from my face barking without pause, but it was my own scream that woke me. Rain pounding the trailer roof matched the pounding in my chest—and the pounding on my bedroom door. I blinked, scrambled out of bed, and went to the door but didn't open it.

"It was a nightmare, Frank. I'm okay. Go back to sleep."

"Open the door, Aideen. I want to see that you're all right."

I opened the door wide enough that he could see my face. "Sorry I woke you."

"I thought someone had broken in. What the hell were you dreaming about?"

"The rain brought it on. Go back to sleep." I started to close the door, but didn't get it to the threshold in time.

Frank shoved his hand between the door and the jamb and said, "What's going on, Aideen?"

"I told you. I had a nightmare."

"Does this happen often? After scaring the hell out of me, at least tell me that."

"Yes."

"Yes? That's all I get?"

"Look, I told you what happened," I said. "This isn't the first time I've had a bad dream. Go back to sleep. We both can use some rest."

"Will you be able to sleep? It sounded like someone attacked you."

"Who knows. Let's talk in the morning."

Frank removed his hand, his face a mixture of concern and confusion. I backed away and closed the door with a hand that wouldn't stop shaking. Whomever had stolen Clay's picture off my nightstand had successfully conjured up memories I'd been struggling to forget. I knew the time had come to let them go—and to figure out how Tiponi's death was tied to my fate at Moenkopi Ridge.

CHAPTER 22

FRANK WAS NOT IN the trailer the next morning, but there were four more five-gallon jugs of water lined up in the kitchen. I took Dakota out for a walk on sand so saturated it felt unstable and squished under my boots. While Dakota sniffed at clumps of sagebrush, I closed my eyes for a moment wondering how the day would play out. I couldn't put off calling Rodgers any longer. I took in a deep breath of the rain-drenched scent of the desert and summoned calm.

Dakota and I followed footprints around to the back of the trailer and found Frank inspecting the interior of the crawl space. He twisted and glanced over his shoulder when he heard us. "Good morning. Dakota looks like she's doing okay?"

"I think so," I said, smiling.

"You're lucky. Your dog's alive, and the stench is dead."

"Sure glad it didn't go the other way around. Can we bury the sheep carcass now? That stench is overbearing."

"Let's leave it to show the deputy when he gets here. I just gave their office another call."

"Then come on inside and have some coffee."

Frank followed Dakota and me around to the front of the trailer and back into the kitchen.

"Did you get any sleep?" he asked.

I stood in the kitchen with my back to him. Sleep had

eluded me like it usually did after the nightmare. I lit the stove with a long-nosed metal lighter—the very kind Clay had used to light the last campfire we'd shared together. I set the kettle on the stove, scooped coffee into the French press—which luckily had escaped the shotgun blast—and turned to face him.

"I slept well enough."

"When are you planning to call your boss?"

"Soon. Can't keep dragging it out."

The kettle sang a shrill whistle. I poured hot water over the coffee and set the carafe on a tray with spoons and two mugs. We slid into the dining nook side-by-side. Frank stirred two teaspoons of sugar into his coffee and took a sip.

"I believe I convinced the Sheriff's Department to send someone out today," he said.

I smiled and said, "I appreciate your help, Frank."

His phone rang. He checked the display and answered, "Hello, Sherm. Saw you called earlier. Yes, I'm still in Arizona... When did that happen?" He paused. "Can't it wait a few days? The people at this archaeological site have had some nasty threats... Yes, I called the county. We're expecting a deputy out shortly."

Frank scowled. "It's a five-hour drive... Yes, I'll leave soon if it's that critical..." He disconnected. "Aideen, I'm sorry, but I've been called back. New developments in a big case we're working."

I frowned in spite of myself. "You can't stay until the deputy arrives?"

"Unfortunately, no. There's a multi-agency sting brewing in New Mexico. Burrows said Arizona law enforcement could be tapped as well... But after the conversation I had with them this morning, I believe a deputy will show up soon."

He took another slug of coffee and held out his cup for a refill. "You should be in good hands once the sheriff has a look at your situation."

Frank upended his cup and gave me a long look. "I'm sorry, Aideen, but I'd better get on the road. Take care of yourself and Dakota. I'll call later to make sure someone from the county made it out."

I thanked Frank and walked him to the door. Dakota followed and sat leaning against me. Frank drove off and I waved, then rested my hand on Dakota's ruff. When his van made the turn onto the road to Winslow and slipped out of sight, I looked down at my dog and felt more alone than I had in a very long time.

#

I sat in the dining nook and called the Phoenix office to tell Rodgers about the stolen bone hash. Lucy said he'd left the office and was on his way to Winslow.

"Are you at the dig?" she asked.

"Yes. Came home to another mess."

"What happened this time?"

"You need to get out of there," she said after I told her.

"I can't, Lucy. I want to keep this job. I could use some help from you, though. Can you check some HR files for me?"

"Sure. Got a list?"

"Just two. George Hargood, the research archaeologist, and Burk Trenton, our bio-archaeologist."

"Anything in particular?"

"Anything that strikes you as unusual," I said, tired of grasping at straws.

"I'll call you if I find something."

I tried Rodgers' cell, but he didn't answer, so I left a message for him to call me. I collected my tote and my car keys. Dakota stood up and wagged. She seemed herself, so I leashed her up.

"We have business in Winslow too," I said to her with a faint smile. "There's no food in this trailer, for humans or dogs."

#

Winslow is a small town with most of its businesses on the main drag. The Two Horse Café is a popular breakfast spot and Gerry Rodgers' favorite local hangout.

I parked the Jeep across from the café and tied Dakota to a shady tree easily visible from the café's picture window. The café ran long and narrow with faux brown leather booths down both sides, reminding me of a galley kitchen. Drawings of famous Western brands hung above the catsup and menu stands. Towards the front, a few square tables stood opposite the counter, each sporting brown-and-yellow ceramic salt and pepper shakers made to look like miniature cowboy boots. An old-time brass cash register stood sentinel on the counter and sounded a loud *ka-ching* whenever the cashier rang up a ticket.

Two men, wearing brand new cowboy hats, sat on stools at the counter, each hunkered over a steaming mug. I sat next to the man in the dove-gray Stetson.

He tipped his hat. "Howdy, Little Lady."

I laughed. He had intense blue eyes set off by long dark lashes and a New York accent thicker than clotted cream.

"Doesn't sound like you're from around these parts," I said.

"Nope. Trying to get on as an extra in that movie they're shooting. Where're you from?"

"Philly, originally."

He stuck out his hand. "Joel Goldberg. What brought you to Winslow?"

"Aideen Connor. I work close by," I said, shaking his hand.

"Are you trying out for the movie?"

"No, what's it about?"

"A drug ring using canyon country to hide its operations. They need extras who can ride."

"You ride?" I asked.

He nodded.

"Good luck hiring on." I said.

Joel smiled and returned to his mug. It was hard to imagine him on a horse with such soft, well-manicured hands.

I stood to check on Dakota and drew in a sharp breath when I saw the two about to walk in.

Joel turned. "Trouble?"

"Maybe."

The door opened, and Gerry Rodgers walked in with Jill Linden, the office administrator. He saw me and blinked. Jill gave me a wide-eyed stare. "Hello, Aideen. I thought that looked like your dog outside," she said, recovering. "What're you doing in town so early?"

"Rustling up breakfast."

Jill and Rodgers headed for a booth, and I asked if I could join them. Jill and I sat on the side opposite Rodgers. "Are you planning on meeting me at the dig later?" I asked him.

"Yes, early afternoon."

"Shall we just say two o'clock? I'll make sure I'm in my office."

"That'll work."

I knew Gerry Rodgers kept an apartment in Winslow for times he worked at the dig. I wondered if the rumor I'd heard about an affair between him and Jill was true. I didn't make a habit of keeping track of dig romances—it was common enough for people to hook up in isolated dig sites—but Rodgers was married and had a family in Phoenix.

#

I left the Two Horse, relieved to be away from Rodgers and Jill and was driving down Main Street when Lucy called.

"Where are you? Sounds like you're driving."

I stopped at a traffic light. A fit-looking man with a thick, dark beard stood on the corner. George Hargood. I wondered what he was doing in Winslow so early; stores were barely open. The light changed. George crossed and continued on, apparently not recognizing me in the rental car.

"Hold on, Lucy. Let me pull over."

I drove through the intersection, took a parking space on the street, and watched as George ducked into a business at the far end of the block.

"Lucy, I just saw George Hargood. Did your sleuthing turn up anything significant on him?"

"George? I did find something. He was busted for drug use a few years after he'd been working here. Rodgers called him in and put him on probation, but no repeat incident reported since."

"I'm amazed Rodgers didn't fire him," I said.

"I was surprised too, but it was marijuana, and it became legal in Arizona after the incident, but Rogers isn't known around the Phoenix office for his empathy toward his employees. Makes me wonder if George knows something about Rodgers the rest of us don't know," Lucy said. "I found out something about Burk, too. Did you know he was trained in Special Ops? He spent two years in Afghanistan. Didn't finish his Ph.D. until after he was discharged."

"No, I didn't know. Wonder why he's never mentioned it?"

"Can't say, but there's a letter in his file says he received special commendation for rooting out drug lords. And there's a big gap in his résumé—almost five years unaccounted for."

"Interesting Rodgers hired him with an unexplained gap that big. You know how inflexible Rodgers is sometimes."

I pulled out of the parking space and drove past multiple businesses—a travel agency not yet open, a gun and ammo store, two tourist shops, and the High Desert Behavioral Health Center, but I didn't see George. I turned off Main Street and headed for the Shop 'n' Go.

"You meeting with Rodgers today?" Lucy asked.

"Yeah. Wish me luck. It's not likely to go well."

"What do you plan to do?"

"Start updating my résumé."

CHAPTER 23

A MAN IN A green-and-khaki uniform sat waiting for me in front of my trailer in a Navajo County Sheriff's SUV. He stepped out of his car and walked over to the Jeep.

"Deputy Marston," he said. "Are you Dr. Connor?"

"Yes, I'm Aideen Connor," I said, exiting the Jeep.

"I'm here about the suspicious activity you reported around your residence."

Marston was of medium height with a mid-section that had started to go soft. His sandy-brown hair showed a crease where his trooper-style hat had rested. I guessed him to be in his mid-forties.

"Nice to meet you, deputy. Let's get out of the heat and talk inside."

I let Dakota out of the car to run around for a few minutes and held the door open for the deputy. When I whistled for Dakota, she came inside and settled next to her water bowl. Marston took a seat on the couch. He carried in a small computer that looked like an iPad and used it to take my statement. Nodding at the hole in the cabinetry where the china cabinet used to hang, he said, "Agent Nakai told me a lot of things have happened here since your original call. That part of it?"

"Yes, my situation has gone *way* beyond finding a dead sheep at this point."

"When Agent Nakai called this morning, he said the animal killed under your trailer was dragged elsewhere. Is it still in the vicinity?"

"Yes. Do you want to take a look in the crawl space where I found it and then see where the remains were dumped?"

"Yes, but let's finish with your statement first," Marston said. "I'll call animal control for its removal. Any cleanup beyond that you'll have to arrange on your own."

"Okay. That carcass has already upset some of the staff. Not the kind of excitement we're used to out here in the middle of archaeological nowhere."

Marston grinned. "You said there were other things?"

"Yes, much more serious. Yesterday I discovered a collection of prehistoric bones missing."

His grin faded. "You mean like a grave robbery?" Marston asked.

"Worse than that. These bones were some nine hundred years old, and the people in our local Native communities consider them ancestral."

"Why would someone steal prehistoric bones like that?" Marston asked.

"It's hard to say not knowing who stole them, but there are people out there with some, pretty strange collections—including prehistoric bones. Plus, we believe these bones showed evidence of cannibalism and bore a highly unusual red stain. Those traits would make them of greater interest and higher value to some collectors."

That gave Marston pause. "Did I get you right? Did you say cannibalism was practiced here in prehistoric times?"

"It looked that way from our bio-archaeologist's initial inspection, but he wasn't able to run all the tests he wanted before the theft. In other areas in the Southwest archaeologists have documented incidences of prehistoric cannibalism. That's one reason we need your help recovering those bones, so we can study them further. And we want to keep this situation out of the media, in respect to the local descendants, until more is known."

Marston scratched his head. "That has to be the weirdest request my department has had since I've been there. I'll need to talk this over with the sheriff and get back to you."

"Okay. Has anyone else contacted your office from our dig recently?"

"Another archaeologist by the name of Burk Trenton called a couple of times, but apparently nothing came of it. Does that guy still work here?"

"Yes, he's our bio-archaeologist."

Marston looked puzzled as he contemplated the job title. "What does a bio-archaeologist do, exactly?"

"They examine skeletons at excavations to determine things like health, lifestyle, diet, other physical characteristics. Their work provides insights into the daily lives of the people in the culture we're studying."

"The dispatcher told me this Burk guy sounded a little weird. Do you think he could be behind any of these actions around your trailer?"

"Hard to say."

"We may decide to talk to Burk, and possibly other people employed here."

When Marston was finished with the interview, I showed him the still-bloody crawl space and walked him over to the sheep carcass. Despite the recent downpour, the desert heat had done its work on the remains.

Marston covered his nose. "Something else you should know is Agent Nakai asked if we'd keep tabs on you. "I can certainly come by, occasionally. And, of course, call us if anything else occurs. I'll get back to you on those stolen bones."

#

After my meeting with Marston, I left the dog in the air-conditioning and walked down to the office. I hadn't been at my desk twenty minutes before Juanita Joshwecoma blustered in with Tony Ahote, another member of the Native American Advisory Committee.

"Aideen?" she called from the front room.

"I'm back here, Juanita."

They stood in front of my desk, Juanita wearing her signature black tunic over jeans with red cowboy boots. She'd added an elaborate white shell necklace that gave her a regal look.

"You remember Tony?" Juanita said. "Old man Ahote's son. He's taking a more active role on council now that he's marrying that Loloma girl. They'll be living near me over on Second Mesa."

I stood. "Of course I remember Tony—from our meeting last month. Congratulations on your engagement," I said, shaking his hand. "Why don't the two of you take a seat?" I indicated the chair opposite my desk for Juanita. "Tony, there's another chair you can drag in from the waiting area."

I hadn't seen Tony since the last full meeting of the NAAC. He'd grown a trim, short beard that made him look older. His jeans were pressed, and he'd paired them with a long-sleeved brown cowboy shirt. The rumor was he'd landed a managerial job at a Navajo-owned construction company in Tuba City and had left the family restaurant. He gave me a nod.

"What brings the two of you in this morning?" I asked.

"We heard," Juanita said.

"Heard what?" I asked, though I figured I knew.

"We heard ancestral bones went missing," she said. "Your boss wouldn't give me any assurances that you'd involve the NAAC on how you'll handle any fallout with the media."

That didn't sound like Rodgers. He was always saying we had to keep the NAAC on our side.

"We aren't planning on making any announcements. It's

way too soon for that, and I have every intention of involving the committee. Where are you getting this information?"

Juanita ignored my question. "Aren't you going to report the theft? That'll bring a whole swarm of gossip-seekers over here. Some talking TV head will hear you've unearthed bones suspected of showing cannibalism and run another demeaning story—like they did when they suspected cannibalism at that Mesa Verde site. And if that's not bad enough, now the bones have gone missing because of your negligence."

I wondered if Rodgers had suggested to Juanita that the theft was my fault, never mind his failure to approve a security detail.

"Your concern is noted, Juanita, and we will do what we can to recover the remains."

"We have enough problems now, dealing with that murder in Hano," she said.

"Did you know the woman who was murdered?" I asked.

"Since she was a little girl," Juanita said. "She wasn't even living in Hano anymore. Moved to Taos to get away from her worthless ex and to sell her jewelry."

"I'm sorry you lost someone close to you."

Juanita held my gaze, eyes narrowed. "Now, maybe you understand the reason we don't need a lot of press hanging around—ancient practices of our ancestors are nobody's business. And that family needs to grieve."

Although I didn't agree with her "nobody's business" assessment of ancient practices, after meeting with the Honovis, I concurred with the need to give the family some privacy.

"No statements will be made from my office, Juanita. I'll contact the NAAC well before anything goes out. You have my word."

"I'll trust you to keep your word, then," she said. "Henderson always did."

#

Alone again in my office, I tried to make sense of the escalating threats at the dig. I'd relied on my wits and a loyal dog for protection, but someone had nearly killed Dakota and the flimsy lock on my front door was worthless. Lucy was right. I wasn't safe at the dig. So far, the bizarre actions around my trailer had been directed solely at me, but I knew that could change at the drop of a hat. The other employees had a right to be informed. I sent staff an email, copying Lyle, and called for a meeting in the dining tent for noon.

I mulled over what I'd learned from Lucy about Burk. Completing an advanced degree in bio-archaeology after spending years in the army tracking down drug lords seemed like quite a leap. Then there was that long gap in his résumé. I wondered if Burk had problems with PTSD, like so many vets returning from a war zone.

As if thinking about him conjured him, I looked up from my computer to see Burk staring at me from the doorway. He hadn't made a sound. I flinched and dropped my pen. He watched it rattle across my desktop, his face impassive.

CHAPTER 24

"**You know how much** I hate it when you startle me like that," I said.

Burk leaned against the doorjamb. "I heard you've been checking up on me."

"Who said?"

"Rodgers."

That was interesting. How had Rodgers found out? Lucy wouldn't have told him.

"Have a seat, Burk. It's uncomfortable trying to talk with you towering over me."

For a moment he didn't move, then he sat in the chair across from my desk.

Burk and I had gotten along for the most part in the short time I'd been on the job, but the day before he'd ditched going to Walpi with me. He could have told Rodgers we had plans. What else was he doing—or not doing—without telling me?

I studied his face for any sign of aggression. "Since you're here, I have a question for you. Are you the one who's been trying to drive me out?"

"What are you talking about?"

"There've been a run of weird activities around my trailer since I came back from Taos."

"Like what?"

"Yesterday someone tried to kill my dog. The night I returned I found a dead sheep under my trailer killed there and left to rot. Then later someone stuck a picture of my dead husband in its blood. Early the next morning someone dragged off the sheep carcass and left it outside the office where everyone would run into it. You know. Stuff like that."

Burk leaned back and crossed his legs. "I saw that dead sheep and wondered what the hell was going on. Why would you think I'd pull crazy stuff like that?"

"Maybe you want my job?"

He smirked. "I'm disappointed you'd think that."

"What should I think? You stood me up yesterday morning, then you dodged my calls the rest of the day."

Burk shrugged. "Yeah, I guess that would make you feel suspicious."

"No kidding. Why were you a no-show? And why are you here now?"

He lowered his voice despite the fact we were alone in the office. "I believe this dig's being used to hide drugs."

I felt a rush of adrenaline. "What? How did you come up with *that* idea?"

"I'm an insomniac. Fallout from the war zone. When I can't sleep, I crawl out of my sleeping bag and walk around at night. A few nights ago, I saw a couple of bozos going in and out of the collections building."

"Did you say anything to them?"

"No. I started to approach them, but they were carrying assault weapons, and I wasn't armed."

"Assault weapons?"

"Yeah, I watched them through binoculars. Smooth operation—in and out in fifteen minutes."

At first, I didn't speak. In addition to the potential threat to employees, we stored all the artifacts unearthed at Moenkopi Ridge in a locked room inside the collections building. Some of the artifacts we'd discovered at the dig had high street value.

"What's interesting is how they got inside the building," Burk continued.

"How?"

"Either they jimmied the lock, or they have a key."

"Holy crap," I muttered. "Have you told anyone else about this?"

"Not lately. About a year ago, when he was still lead here, I told Henderson about the first time I saw them. Same thing. Quick in and out. Heavily armed. Henderson called the sheriff's office. Deputy came out and searched the collections building, but he didn't find anything. After that no more activity—until a few days ago."

"What do they do?"

"Carry in bags the size of lunch sacks. I combed the collections building the day after I saw them and checked the artifacts room. Nothing missing, and nothing left behind, near as I could tell."

"What do you think's in the bags?"

"Drugs. You've probably read about the multitude of meth labs cropping up out here. "There are several canyons close to the dig that people rarely visit, and this area is really remote. Too remote and inhospitable for hikers. But there's still vehicle access from old mining roads. Possible to get an RV into a canyon if it has high clearance. They can be used for cooking meth. Likewise, our dig is in the middle of rough backcountry and a perfect place for hiding a stash."

"But you haven't found one, right?"

"True. So far, nothing."

"Did you tell Rodgers when you saw intruders here before?"

"Yes, but after a deputy came out and didn't find anything Rodgers agreed with Henderson. Said I should drop it."

"Interesting. You'd think Rodgers would want to rule out

foul play rather than just drop it," I said, considering. "Why did he insist on meeting you in Winslow yesterday? Didn't you tell him we'd made plans?"

Burk frowned. "I did tell him, but apparently it didn't matter. He said meeting him was more important, and not to tell you about it. But when we hooked up, all he did was ask a lot of questions about your management ability."

I'd begun to feel very uneasy about the direction this conversation was going. "What did you tell him?"

"I said it was obvious to me you had a lot less experience than Henderson, but in some ways, you were more organized."

"What did he say about that?"

"Nothing. He just dropped it."

Rodgers was checking up on me by grilling another staff member?

"What else did you and Rodgers talk about?"

"Sports. Progress at the kiva site. Nothing out of the ordinary."

"So, it wasn't an important meeting after all?"

"Guess not. I sort of wondered why he'd called me away."

"Have you done anything about this recent appearance of the guys with guns?"

"I called the sheriff's office this morning, but they put me on interminable hold, so I hung up."

"A BLM special agent who came out to help me also called them this morning to make sure a stop at the dig was on their schedule. A deputy from Navajo County finally came out today and took my statement. Given all the recent unexplained activity, I'm starting to think staff sleeping in tents isn't safe here anymore."

"Probably never has been," Burk said. "Like I said, this dig is right in the middle of drug country. But the prowlers I've seen don't seem interested in the employees. They're definitely focused on the collections building. If they show up again, I'm getting pictures."

"What do you mean, you're getting pictures? Wouldn't that alert them?"

"I have infrared equipment. They won't know."

I tapped my fingers on the desktop. Apparently, this dig had under-the-radar activity going on that potentially put us all at risk. First the theft of the bone hash, and now, if Burk was telling the truth, gun-toting intruders. I wondered if I could trust Burk on this.

"How do you protect yourself when you're out snooping around at night?" I asked.

"I own a gun. Next time I see them, I'll have it on me."

"You know having a gun at the dig is against your employment contract. Do you have a permit to carry it?"

"Of course I have a permit." Burk gave me a mocking smile. "If there's one thing you learn in the military, it's discipline. You're not going to tell Rodgers, are you?"

"No, I've got more pressing issues—like moving staff to a safer location until after this mess is resolved."

"Like where?"

"We'll take rooms in Winslow until we have a security team patrolling at night. We'll work out an emergency plan in the meeting today."

#

After Burk left, I took my time walking to the staff meeting mulling over our conversation and considering whether to call Deputy Marston. Burk's belief that the dig was being used as a hiding place for drugs seemed far-fetched, and I had only his word. Without any evidence, what would I tell the deputy if I called him?

Burk had worked on high-risk assignments when the army had him hunting down drug traffickers. That kind of stress doesn't necessarily go away after a person is discharged. It could be coloring his assessment of what was going on, but his comment about prowlers at the dig struck a chord. There'd been nights I'd heard odd noises outside my trailer and dismissed them, blaming the wind, or too much time living alone. But the next morning, I'd find footprints outside that were too big to be mine, or a piece of fabric snagged on a bush close to my front door.

Finding a cruelly killed sheep under my living space left no doubt someone was trying to run me off. But what was their motive? As I walked into the dining tent, I was starting to wonder who at the dig I could trust.

The tent we used for meals and meetings was a sizable forty by forty foot structure with sidewalls that could be lowered as needed. We erected it at the beginning of the excavation season and left it up until we moved off-site. The tent had electrical access and essential furnishings that included folding tables and chairs, a four-burner electric cook top, four five-gallon water dispensers, and a large refrigerator. Much of the time staff picked up prepared food in Winslow for lunches and took evening meals at restaurants in town when time permitted.

Staff members had already arrived and stood talking in clusters when I walked in.

"Could we all gather in one place? I have important information to share with you," I said.

Everyone but George Hargood carried folding chairs to the front of the tent.

I raised both hands for quiet. "For today, I'm going to suspend project reports because we have safety concerns."

I continued once I had everyone's attention. "After returning from my fund-raising trip to Taos I met up with some very strange circumstances." Then I recounted the threatening incidents of the past few days, starting with the events in Taos.

George stood in the back and said, "You need to get a grip on managing this site, Aideen. No bullshit like that went on when Henderson ran things."

"That comment was out-of-line, George. Move up and join us." I stared at him until he slowly migrated, scowling.

"Sounds like someone has it in for you, Aideen," Janet said. "I'm wondering if the rest of us are in danger?" Janet Livingston, our field operations supervisor, had worked at Moenkopi Ridge every summer since the project began and spent her winters teaching graduate courses at UCLA. She had a habit of tossing back her mid-length brown hair when she was nervous, and she was doing double-time tossing it back now.

"I can't rule it out, Janet. I don't know what we're dealing with yet. As you might imagine, the dead sheep incident really upset me. But I just heard something even more concerning. Burk told me he saw armed strangers going in and out of the collections building a few nights ago."

The room buzzed.

"Armed?" Janet said. "Have you seen them, Aideen?"

"No, I haven't."

Janet glanced at Burk, looked away and said nothing.

"To my knowledge, no one from our company has authorized unsupervised visits to the collections building after hours, but I'll confirm that with Rodgers. I've contacted local law enforcement, and I met with a deputy today. While we're sorting this out, I plan on hiring a security company to patrol the dig at night. Until they arrive, I'm asking everyone to sleep in town."

"What do you mean—sleep in town?" George asked.

"We'll reserve motel rooms in Winslow and commute for a few days. If anyone is concerned about working here during the day, I'll approve a leave of absence until we have the security company in place."

"How are we supposed to pay for rooms?" Lonny asked.

"I'll ask the company to pick up the tab. It shouldn't be for more than a few nights."

George stood with his arms locked across his chest.

"Who's going to organize it?"

"Hank," I said, "would you call around in Winslow and book rooms for us?"

Hank Benton worked under Janet's supervision as the second field archaeologist alongside Lonny. Lean and athletic from his early-morning runs, Hank had interned at the dig the preceding summer and was well-liked by the others.

"Sure, no problem," he said.

"Jill and Nova, you have apartments in town. Are you okay working here during the day?"

Jill nodded.

Nova said, "I'm sorry this week has been so stressful for you, Aideen. After what you just told us, I'm carrying my handgun when I'm here during the day. That'll make me feel safer."

As much as I liked Nova, the idea of an employee carrying a weapon to work didn't sit well, and it went against employment contracts. "Nova, you know that's not something I can authorize. You'll have to use your own best judgment. Burk haven't heard from you. Comments?"

Burk said, "You already know I'm in."

"Hank, let me know when you have rooms booked. If anyone wants to speak with me privately, my door will be open. Meeting adjourned."

CHAPTER 25

DESPITE BURK'S INSISTENCE HE'D found no evidence intruders were removing or disturbing anything from the collections building, I decided to have a look on my own. If anything seemed off, I'd call Deputy Marston.

The staff meeting had again exposed George's on-going hostility toward me, but at least I'd gotten him to cooperate during the meeting, albeit reluctantly. George was an excellent researcher but not much of a team player. Getting more cooperation out of him was going to take some work, and if he didn't continue to improve, I intended to fire him. I wondered if he was the person who'd orchestrated the sheep saga against me. I wouldn't put it past him.

Except for Janet, the others didn't seem all that concerned about the strange events I'd disclosed in the meeting. I'd speak to Janet privately after we had rooms worked out. Hopefully, she'd feel safer once security was in place.

I hiked back to my trailer to pick up Dakota, and we made our way down the trails to the west side of the dig.

The entrance to the collections building opened into a large room furnished with folding tables and chairs. Dakota and I took the hallway to the lab where George and Nova were cataloging grave objects. Dakota raised her hackles when she saw George. I gave her a firm "no" and put her in a down-stay while I looked at his drawings.

George's drawings emphasized the unusual attributes of the more significant artifacts we uncovered, and he took measurements of each item and recorded them beside each example. Nova photographed the pieces, sometimes including close-ups. At the end of the excavation season, all photos, reports, and drawings would be entered into the site's database for further study.

Though our dig was on private land, we followed federal dictates of the Native American Graves Protection and Repatriation Act, or NAGPRA, that required return of human remains and funerary objects to the control of a site's descendants. The NAAC would ultimately decide on the fate of these artifacts. Human remains were typically reburied. Sometimes the committee allowed unusual human artifacts to remain in our care for further research, although we had no guarantee of extended access—one of the reasons a trusting relationship with committee members was so essential to our work.

"Have you contacted the NAAC yet about these new grave artifacts?" I asked George.

"No, I need more time."

George's drawings were carefully rendered in black ink, a skill that required a good eye, a steady hand, and years of practice.

"Your drawings are very impressive," I said. George didn't look up, but I saw the hint of a smile on his down-turned face.

"I have information to present to the NAAC as well. Let me know when you're ready and I'll schedule a meeting." I didn't look forward to telling the rest of the committee members their ancestors' bones had been stolen after my confrontation with Mrs. Joshwecoma, but at least I would give them the courtesy of telling them in person.

George kept his eyes on his work and nodded.

"Have you noticed anything unusual in the lab recently?" I asked. "Anything out-of-place? Missing?"

George put down his drawing pen and looked up. "Nothing. I already told you; no one believes Burk's stories. I don't know why you do."

Nova glanced at George, rolled her eyes, and said she needed a break.

"If there's even a small chance Burk is right, we need to err on the side of everyone's safety," I said.

George shrugged. "Yeah, you could definitely view that sheep saga as a threatening act."

He picked up his pen and began another drawing. I released Dakota from her down stay. After she'd growled at George again when we entered the lab, I wondered if he'd been the person who trapped her in the crawl space. He was certainly strong enough to force her inside since it was unlikely he'd be able to coax her.

Dakota and I walked down the hall to the front room. The artifacts room was unfortunately no place for a dog; all excavated objects, some over a thousand years old, were stored there until transported to our Phoenix warehouse. I tied Dakota's leash to the handle of a large built-in cabinet near the entrance and told her to stay. I didn't think George would try to pull something with the dog in the middle of the day, and I didn't expect to be long.

Nova exited the restroom. "George on his good behavior today?"

"Hard to say. You two feuding again?"

"He's a little better since Henderson left. Only nagged me once this week about photographing the rest of the new finds."

"I'll tell him to ease up on you. Got a minute? Come check out the artifacts room with me."

Nova slung her camera bag over her shoulder and followed me down the hall. I unlocked the room and flipped on the lights. The room stank of stale air and a nearly imperceptible chemical odor I couldn't place. We'd outfitted the room on three walls with extra-deep adjustable shelves set at varied heights. A small wooden desk pushed against the open wall bore a thick network of spiderwebs between its dinged legs. I kicked a web, and a hairy black spider dropped onto my boot and then scurried away.

Haphazard footprints made a chaotic pattern in the dust on the cement floor. Nova set her camera bag down. A beetle with a missing leg crawled out from under the camera bag and caromed through the dust.

"Don't any of the archaeologists clean off their boots before they come in here?" she muttered. "What exactly are we looking for?"

"I wanted to see if there's anything here that looks out-of-place or if we notice something's missing."

"I photographed over a hundred items. I don't think I could remember all of them."

"I know—just a general impression—anything that looks off. Weren't you the last person Burk let in?" Burk and I were the only on-site employees who had keys.

"As far as I know."

We walked slowly past the shelves. I paused in front of noteworthy artifacts—unusual because of their size, a few that were exceptionally well preserved.

I picked up an atlatl—a spear thrower used in the Basketmaker period—one of the timeframes we were excavating. The atlatl increased the distance a hunter could throw his spear, much like a ball-throwing stick used by dog owners. The Pueblo period would usher in the invention of the bow and arrow as its replacement, but occasionally the two weapons were found in the same strata.

The atlatl felt smooth to the touch, its five-foot wooden shaft beautifully balanced. The finger loops, made of organic material, were still remarkably well preserved. I returned the ancient weapon to the shelf, feeling admiration for its craftsmanship.

A loud thud, and the metal door to the room slammed shut without warning.

"Freaking George," I said, startled.

"He can be such a jerk," Nova said.

I rushed to open the door, my heart racing.

The knob wouldn't turn.

My mouth went dry. I took a deep breath, remembering what I'd learned: "Deep and slow breathing produces calm." I consciously slowed my breaths and fumbled around in my pocket for my keys.

"One thousand and one," I muttered, my voice a low rasp. "One thousand and two …"

"What did you say?" Nova asked.

"One thousand and …"

The windowless room plunged into darkness. I felt along the wall for the light switch, stumbled, and dropped my keys.

"Nova, did you bump the lights?"

"No, stay where you are. I'll get a light from my camera bag."

Fear tightened around my chest like a constricting snake. I'd read constrictors were opportunists. When the victim exhaled, the snake constricted harder. The captive had less and less room to breathe. Suffocation was inevitable. How long it took was up to the victim—and how hard she fought.

I slid down the wall to the floor struggling to regain self-control.

"Doing okay?" Nova asked.

I didn't answer. The room smelled foul from where I sat—chemical-laced air that made me lightheaded. A thin line of light outlined the bottom of the door. Nova's voice sounded far away.

Something shattered. Nova gasped.

"Nova?"

"I cut my hand on something."

"Is it bad?"

She hissed softly under her breath. "I'm trying to stop the bleeding."

I slumped against the wall. "One thousand and one. One thousand and two..."

"Hang on, Aideen."

The sound of feet shuffling. A zipper. Nova rifling through her camera bag. A beam of light split the darkness. The ancient ceramic pots cast oversized shadows, reminding me of Hopi tales of witchcraft. Nova hunched over, hunting for the keys I'd dropped, the light in one hand, the other hand wrapped in her blood-stained shirt tail. She set the light on the floor, picked up the key ring and tried a key. Wrong one.

"Look for a red 'A' painted on the key. For artifacts room," I said.

"Got it."

She slid the key into the lock and pulled the door open. I crawled out and sat on the floor. The hall light was still on, but the lab across the hall was quiet and dark.

"Looks like George left," Nova said, joining me on the floor. "What a jackass."

"Much as it's tempting to agree, we don't know for sure George is the one who slammed the door or doused the lights on us," I said.

Nova gave me an exasperated look and shrugged. Dakota barked from the front room.

"I should go get her."

"Wait a few minutes. How do you feel?" Nova asked.

"Better." I ran my hand over my face. "Sorry I lost it."

"My aunt is claustrophobic."

"I thought I had it under control."

Dakota charged down the hall without collar or leash. I threw my arms around my dog and pressed my face against her neck. A few minutes later I sat up, took a few deep breaths, and got her to sit beside me.

"How long have you lived with this?" Nova asked.

"Maybe a year. Started after I watched my husband die in a mudslide. I couldn't do a thing to help him."

"God, how awful! I thought you were divorced."

"No. Widowed. At thirty-four. How's your hand?"

"Bleeding's slowed."

"Don't tell anyone about this, Nova, okay?"

"It's really nobody's business," she said. "But isn't it a problem in your work? I've seen you go into some pretty tight spaces."

"It's never happened before at work."

Nova gave me a sidelong glance. I stood. We walked down the hall together, Dakota following close behind. Nova set up two folding chairs. "Feeling better?"

"Yeah, thanks." I took a seat in one of the chairs she'd set up. "Would you take a look in the electrical box? Someone must've flipped a circuit breaker."

Nova opened the gray metal panel inside the broom closet at the far end of the room.

"One of these levers shows red." She flipped it back on.

"Let's make sure all the lights come back on in the artifacts room," I said.

"Sure you want to go back in there?"

"Like you said, occupational hazard. Can't let this control me."

I put Dakota's collar and leash back on, tied her to the cabinet a second time, and told her to stay. I put my arm around Nova's waist, and she put her arm around mine.

"Thank you, Nova. You've been a friend on more than one occasion."

She gave my waist a squeeze. "No problem. And your secret is safe with me."

With key in hand and jaw clenched, I made myself go back inside the artifacts room.

"Sure stinks in here," Nova said when she followed me in. "Smells like it does at the dry cleaners."

"You're right. And it's gotten worse."

"What's wrong?" Nova asked, seeing my scowl.

"Just the smell," I said, willing my voice to sound steady. Returning to the windowless artifacts room had elicited a strong urge to bolt. I needed to get out of there.

Nova gave me a concerned look and nodded.

CHAPTER 26

I DECIDED NOT TO call Deputy Marston after inspecting the artifacts room. Nova and I had seen nothing missing or out-of-place, much as Burk reported. Dakota and I jogged up the trail from the collections building to make it in time for my two o'clock meeting with Rodgers.

The dog and I stood in the office doorway watching for him to turn off the main road. When his car neared, I recognized Fiona, Rodgers's wife in the passenger's seat. He parked, and they walked up the dirt trail to the office, Gerry in front, Fiona struggling behind him in high heels. I liked Fiona, but she seemed out of her comfort zone at the dig, rarely forsaking the professional dress she wore for meetings with her interior design clients.

Jill, the office administrator Lucy has accused of having an affair with Rodgers sat hunched behind her computer, her blonde hair obscuring her face. Fiona ignored Jill and took a seat in the waiting area closer to Nova. She gave Nova a smile, a hello, and promptly pulled a design magazine from her oversized Gucci bag.

Rodgers followed Dakota and me into my office and sat in front of my desk. I closed my office door and sat in my desk chair with Dakota curled up on the floor beside me. Rodgers watched me for a moment before saying, "Aideen, I went out to inspect the bone hash yesterday."

My heart raced.

"I think you know what I discovered. No bones. And no dig director. When did you know the bone hash went missing? And where the hell were you?"

Pulse pounded in my ears. "I found out it'd gone missing right before I left to meet with Cha'tima in Walpi," I said.

"When was that?"

"Yesterday morning."

"You knew since then and you didn't call me? What in the name of Christ is going on here?"

I sat up straight and tried to slow my breathing. "In fact, I did call this morning, but you weren't in the office, and you didn't answer your cell. But if you knew yesterday, why didn't you call me?"

"You're the subordinate here, Aideen. I'm asking the questions."

I felt like I'd been smacked. "Then why didn't you say something when I saw you in Winslow this morning? Aren't we on the same team?"

His face turned dark red. "There was another employee present this morning, and this doesn't concern her, and then right after you left, I got another call from someone on the NAAC. They believe their ancestors' bones have been stolen. I told them the bones are prehistoric Native American, not identified with a specific tribe, but they don't see it that way. The NAAC is threatening to sue Rodgers & Associates if the bones are not recovered and returned immediately. Do you have any idea what that kind of action would do to this company? It could shut us down. This is the third time I've had a complaint from the NAAC about a problem on your watch."

"Gerry, I did try multiple times to reach you."

"But you didn't try to contact me as soon as you found out, did you?"

"No. Like I said, I had to leave for Walpi, and when I returned, I came back to another threat against me personally."

"What kind of threat?"

I told him how I'd returned to find Dakota trapped in the crawl space and near death.

Dakota stood up, looked at Rodgers, and moved closer to me.

Rodgers threw up his hands. "You've got to get rid of that damned dog. I never should've allowed you to keep it."

"Gerry, in all fairness, I have Dakota for protection. It's not like there are friendly neighbors living down the street from me. And regarding the bone hash, I did ask you to approve hiring a security company before those bones were stolen."

He glared at me. "Are you suggesting this was *my* fault?"

"No, of course not. Nor was it mine, and a security team would have made a difference. What more *could* I do? The only security tools I had were tarps and stones to cover the trench, and I had Lonny pile on extras of both."

"Aideen, I don't like your tone. This is serious, and I have to protect my firm."

"Gerry, I've been trying to protect the firm as well. That's why I've asked repeatedly to hire security. This site is remote, and I've also had plenty of nasty threats against me personally. Seems to me a security company could have been money well-spent."

"Your three-month probationary period is up in two weeks, Aideen. It's unfortunate I need to keep you on until I can replace you, but don't count on being director here after your probation ends. Consider this your two-weeks' notice. I have to do whatever it takes to protect Rodgers & Associates. Trouble from the Native American community would ruin us."

"But..."

Rodgers stood. "I don't want to hear anymore. Your failure to report this theft is unacceptable, and the NAAC's new complaint against you only adds to my resolve. You'll have a letter from me tomorrow summarizing what I said in this meeting. If you can't keep it together these next two weeks, you'll be terminated immediately. If you *do* keep it together through the end of your probation, I'll allow you to resign."

"Wait a minute!" I said standing, my voice way too loud. "I have important safety issues I need to discuss with you."

"Not another word. I'm calling Henderson to get his help containing this problem. This meeting is over."

Rodgers flung open my door. I scurried around my desk to follow him. Fiona stared up from her magazine. He grabbed her arm, and they left together.

I returned to my office, closed the door, and sat behind my desk, my knuckles pressed into my eyes. Dakota sat beside me and leaned against me. "I've been told to get rid of you," I said. Dakota moved her head under my hand. "Fat chance of that."

Dakota nosed my arm, and I dropped my hand to her ruff. "You're right. I don't have time to feel sorry for myself." I blew my nose, grabbed my cell phone, and left Dakota in my office.

"I'm taking a walk," I said to Jill and Nova. "Back in a few."

They looked up from their computers. Jill turned her face away, and I wondered how much they'd heard. Any of it would have been too much.

Nova said, "You know, Aideen, you'd be welcome to stay with me for a few nights."

"Thanks. I might take you up on it," I said, heading for the door.

I stepped out into the heat. Frank picked up on the second ring.

"Has a deputy shown up?"

"Yes, it was a good meeting. But my situation with the boss just got worse. He told me I wouldn't be here after my probation ends. Our meeting was so contentious I didn't have a chance to get his approval for hiring security."

"What are you going to do?"

"Unless I receive immediate written notice of termination, I have the authority to re-allocate budget in an emergency. I'm hiring a security team as soon as I can get one out here."

"Good call."

I told Frank about my earlier conversation with Burk.

"Do you believe him about these intruders?"

I shielded my eyes from the blinding sun. "I don't know, Frank. Sometimes he acts like he's trying to help. Other times he just acts weird. Trouble is, if he's right, the people here are in danger. I've got to do what I can to keep us safe."

"Agreed. Do you have a safe place to stay tonight?"

"I'm working on bunking most of us off-site until security shows up."

I hung up and returned to my office to make calls. The earliest I could get a security team on site was in two days. I hired them on the spot and charged it to my company credit card.

My cell buzzed.

"Aideen? It's Hank."

"What's the word on rooms?'

"Nothing available. All the motels are booked solid."

"In Winslow? What's going on?'

"It's that movie they're shooting. The film company reserved room blocks months ago. They've hired a lot of extras."

"Crap. Notify everyone to reconvene in the dining tent by six o'clock. I have a security company lined up starting in two days. We'll work out what we can do until then."

I called Frank back and told him about the room situation.

"What's Plan B?"

"I'm moving staff into the office trailer. Burk said he's

only seen the intruders go into the collections building. They probably come in off-road in a four-wheel-drive on the west side away from the office. There's at least a half mile between the two buildings and no road for vehicles in the gully connecting them."

Frank said. "Better than nothing, but what happens if the intruders decide to branch out?"

"Then we're sitting ducks."

CHAPTER 27

That evening everyone re-assembled in the dining tent and knew there were no rooms available in Winslow.

"So, what do we do now, Aideen?" George said. "Drive to Phoenix?"

"The security company will be here in two days. I believe we can be safe if we move everyone into the office at night. As an alternative I'll authorize a two-day leave for anyone who doesn't want to hole up here for two nights," I said.

"Paid leave?" Hank asked.

"Can't promise, but I'll lobby for it. There's something else you need to know before you decide. Burk volunteered to stand watch near the collections building until security gets here."

"Isn't that a little unusual?" Lonny said. "Asking an employee to stand guard at their work site?"

Burk stood and said, "She didn't ask me. I volunteered, and all of you are now witnesses to that."

We were treading water, and I knew it. Lonny was right. Surveillance wasn't in anyone's job description. Burk had hatched the idea of standing guard, and I'd gone along with him, but the plan left me uneasy. Maybe giving everyone a two-day furlough was a better option, but given the outcome of my meeting with Rodgers, I couldn't promise them they'd still be paid.

"You have experience in surveillance?" Hank asked.

Burk nodded

"Where?"

"Afghanistan."

Everyone looked at Burk. He raised his hands, palms out for quiet, and sat down.

"Let's have a show of hands if you prefer to try for rooms elsewhere tonight," I said. "There are motels along Interstate 40 going west that look reasonably priced."

Janet raised her hand. "I have a friend in Winslow. I can stay at his place."

"I don't think anything's going to happen," Lonny said. "We've been down this road before, and even if what Burk says is true, I'm not up for shelling out money I might not get back."

"Me, either," Hank said. "I'm struggling to save for tuition."

"I don't believe we're *in* any danger," George said. "Burk claimed something like this was going on when Henderson was here, and it never came to anything."

Burk gave George a dirty look but held his tongue, and I was relieved. We had enough to deal with already without fighting among ourselves.

"At least bed down in the office tonight, George. You'll be just as comfortable there as you would be in your tent," I said.

"If it'll make you feel better," George said.

I ignored his sarcasm and said, "Looks like George, Hank, and Lonny are staying here tonight. Be in the office with your bedrolls by nine. Janet, confirm with your friend that you'll be able to stay in Winslow, and leave me a number where you can be reached."

#

Dusk dressed the landscape in oranges and corals outside my kitchen window. I fed Dakota and threw a few items into my carry-all, hoisted my bedroll over my shoulder, and locked up. Animal control had removed the dead sheep, and I let Dakota run free as we headed down the trail.

Wary cottontails stood on their hind legs, wrinkling their noses as we made our way to the office. Hank let us inside, then he and Lonny went back to arranging their sleeping bags. George barged in and tossed his bedroll on the floor. Dakota growled at him, and I called her to me.

"Where's Burk?" George asked, his voice a snarl.

"Outside," I said.

George scowled at the dog, walked to the west window and looked out. "Where outside?"

"I don't know exactly, George. Let me drop off my gear and my dog and we'll go find him." I carried my bedroll to my office in the back and closed Dakota inside.

George took a small flashlight from his pocket and shone it on the ground. We crunched through the undergrowth down the ravine toward the collections building. Something small slithered away from George's tiny circle of light. He lurched backwards and bumped into me.

Hank had discovered bark scorpions under a water trough a few days earlier. Bark scorpions are the only Arizona scorpion whose stings can be fatal. Everyone at the dig went on full alert. Spotting them at night required a UV flashlight—something I hadn't packed. The small venomous predators showed up as eerie green blobs under blacklight.

We found Burk staked out behind a copse of cedars with a clear view of the front door to the collections building. Clad all in black, he wore a contraption over his eyes that looked like an elaborate set of goggles. He took them off when he saw us.

"What are those?" I asked.

"Night-vision infrared stealth goggles."

"What a mouthful," I said.

Burk set the goggles on top of a backpack he'd leaned

against a tree. The full moon illuminated George's face. He seemed agitated. Burk looked him over for a moment. "Something I can do for you, George?"

George rubbed the back of his neck. "If I were you, I'd move your pack away from that tree."

"I'm not concerned about bark scorpions," Burk said.

"Then maybe you're not as smart as you think you are. No way I'd risk it. I want to know why you're standing watch tonight."

Burk stood shoulders back, chin high. "Like I said in the meeting, I'm experienced in surveillance, so I volunteered to fill in until the security company gets here."

"Are you armed?" George asked.

"Yes."

"You could end up shooting one of us."

Burk spoke in a low voice. "I'm confident I can distinguish us from them, George. For one thing, staff doesn't dress all in black and carry assault weapons."

George grunted and turned to me.

"If we're in that much danger, you should contact law enforcement and Rodgers should know about it. You haven't told him, have you?"

"We don't have enough facts yet, George," I said. "Burk brought this up with Rodgers before, and he chose not to pursue it."

"Doesn't matter. Rodgers should know what you're pulling. I'm calling him."

George spun around and started to walk back. Burk grabbed him by the shoulder.

"Look, George, give it till daybreak. It's only the difference of a few hours before Aideen calls him."

George pulled away. "That's not good enough."

"It's good enough for the next few hours," I said. "You need to stand down."

"What's gotten into you?" Burk said. "We used to be

friends, and you used to be a team player."

"That was when Henderson ran things." George turned and stomped back through the vegetation, his penlight shooting narrow beams in front of him.

"What do you think he'll do?" I said.

"He'll call Rodgers, but if Rodgers is staying with Jill tonight, he won't answer."

"We're out of luck. Fiona's in town," I said.

Burk shrugged. "Doesn't mean he'll be staying with Fiona. Especially if the cat is out of the bag. How'd your meeting with him go?"

"Lousy. Rodgers told me I'm out in two weeks. He didn't stick around long enough for me to tell him about the intruders. Did he tell you he already knew the bone hash'd been stolen when you met him in Winslow?"

"Yes, that was the first I heard about it. Henderson had already left the dig before I got back after meeting with Rodgers. Lyle and I didn't discuss the theft until I called him later in the afternoon."

That was interesting. Burk knew the bones were stolen close to the time I found out—when he met with Rodgers in Winslow. But he hadn't brought it up. I hoped I'd made the right decision going along with his stake-out idea.

"I called you all day yesterday to tell you about the theft. Why didn't you answer?"

"I needed time to think, Aideen. I couldn't exactly run interference between you and Rodgers. He's still the boss. And it's not like you confided in me, either."

"I would have. If you'd called me back."

Burk shrugged and turned away. The moonlight illuminating his profile heightened his look of determination.

"Are you planning to stand watch here all night?"

"Yes."

"Then I'm covering the back."

"That's a crazy idea, Aideen. You don't have that kind of

experience."

"You don't know that. Besides, there are two entrances. You can't cover both of them."

#

I trudged back to the office. Lonny unlocked the door to let me in and then clicked it shut behind me. George stood at the west window watching the collections building. Hank sat on his sleeping bag, watching George. Dakota barked from behind the door to my office, and I let her into the main room.

A cricket chirped from the corner of the room. Hank tripped over a bedroll, cursed, righted himself.

"I'm going out to cover the back entrance," I said. "I'm leaving Dakota in my office."

"Covering it with what?" Hank said. "Do you have a gun?"

The slight bulge of the clasp knife in my pocket gave me no reassurance.

"No, but I'm good at staying out of sight. I want to see for myself if Burk's claim has any merit. Hank, let me borrow that windbreaker you're wearing."

Hank unzipped his black windbreaker and handed it to me.

"This is nuts," Lonny said.

"If strangers show up, one person could miss them," I said.

"So could two," George said.

"What're we supposed to do? You're acting like the reincarnation of John Wayne," Lonny said.

I laughed even though my hands shook. I called Dakota and put her back in my office. "The three of you stay here tonight like we agreed. Burk said he's never seen these intruders venture past the collections building. Whatever they're doing, it's a fast in and out. Lock the door behind me, keep the lights out, and try to get some rest."

George shook his head. "We're in the middle of a psychodrama, and she says get some rest. Good luck. I never signed up for Burk's bullshit."

"I hope that's all it is," I said. "Bullshit would be a big improvement."

CHAPTER 28

The office door clicked shut behind me. A nighthawk glided silently overhead in the midst of its evening hunt. Hank's windbreaker was hot, but I clenched my teeth to keep them from chattering. My legs felt stiff, like I'd exercised too hard. I inhaled deeply, holding my breath as long as I could, then letting it out slowly.

I crept down the ravine from the office and snuck part way up the opposite side toward the collections building. I tucked the edges of the windbreaker's hood behind my ears and listened. Something rustled in the sagebrush close by. I squatted, held as still as I could, and waited. An animal walked slowly toward me, picking through the foliage. With only moonlight for illumination, it was hard to make out details, but when it neared, I saw the spots on its back—a young fawn, spindly legged, probably on its way to the spring-fed watering hole to the west of the collections building. The breeze shifted. The fawn scented me and bounded off.

I moved up-slope, and hid behind a thick clump of sagebrush where I could see the back entrance. A breeze stirred the vegetation. Shadows moved in slow undulation. The back door to the collections building wasn't visible in the dark until the moon rose higher. An owl hooted behind me, followed by the soft flutter of its wings. I clutched the windbreaker to me, both for warmth and to keep the fabric from snapping like a sail in the desert breeze. The temperature had dropped a good twenty degrees from the heat of the day, and the absence of sunlight made the night seem even colder. I watched and waited and blinked back sleep, keeping well-hidden.

#

I awoke with a start, curled on the ground when the first traces of dawn broke into the ravine. No intruders had shown up before I drifted off. I wondered if Burk had seen anyone.

I pressed the button on the side of my watch. The watch's dial luminesced green, and the time read 5:17. I looked around and then stood and stretched out the stiffness from sleeping on the ground. I'd awakened to a quiet, empty morning. I yawned. I felt embarrassed I hadn't been able to stay awake all night, but grateful I hadn't had any trouble with night predators, animal or human. Maybe Burk had seen something. I hiked uphill to the office to check on Lonny, Hank, and George. Lonny unlocked the door for me. Dakota had been let into the main room, and she greeted me with exuberance, ears perked, tail wagging. I gave her a hug and let her outside. Hank, Lonny, and George lay awake in their sleeping bags.

"Anything happen last night?" I asked.

"Nothing," George said, sitting up. "I told you this was bullshit."

"It's only bullshit for one more night, George. Then the security team will be here, and you can go back to your tent. Anyone seen Burk?"

"Right here," Burk said behind me. "Saw you walking back to the office. See anyone last night?"

"No, but I fell asleep. Guess I'm lucky no one showed. What about you?"

"For once my insomnia was a good thing. Kept me awake

all night, but I didn't see anybody, either."

"You should go get some rest, Burk," I said. We have one more night like this ahead of us, and we both need to be sharp."

Burk yawned and took off for his tent. I told the other three I'd see them again at nine that night. I whistled for Dakota, and we walked back toward my trailer where I could have a private phone conversation with Henderson.

I wondered if the former site director ever regretted leaving his position at Moenkopi Ridge. Burk said he'd undergone surgery for melanoma. Skin cancer would be enough reason for most people to bag an outdoor job, but projects like Moenkopi Ridge could go on for years. Positions like a directorship came with the kind of job security enjoyed by only a handful of archaeologists—the ones that published—and Lyle had published plenty. He'd become the expert in a new technology for dating ancient ceramics, been at the top of his field—and likely at the top of his pay scale.

The trailer was cool and quiet when Dakota and I returned. I sat in the living room and called Lyle's cell.

"Have you had a chance to tell Gerry about the bone theft yet?" he asked.

"Yes, I met with him yesterday."

"How did he take it?" Lyle asked.

"Not well."

"Removing artifacts with a backhoe makes me cringe," Lyle said.

"Will you be back at the dig today, Lyle?" I asked, ignoring his comment.

"No, since the bone hash was stolen, I'll wait until Monday. Gerry and I talked earlier about using my new method to date ceramics from the kiva site. Now that you've made him aware of the theft, I'll ask him when he wants me to move forward."

I'd been excited about the idea of working with Lyle. Learning from a research method's inventor was a rare opportunity. Not something I'd be part of if I wasn't going to be running the dig much longer, and I didn't feel like talking to Lyle about my soon-to-end status with Rodgers & Associates.

"Okay, let me know when to expect you."

"Aideen..." There was a long pause. "I heard you were fired. Gerry called and told me. I suppose I shouldn't be telling you this, but I was impressed with your presentation at SCF. Maybe I can help."

I remembered the way he'd looked me over when I arrived at SCF. Was he coming onto me? Or was my suspecting him of that completely out-of-line?

I covered the receiver and took a deep breath.

"What could you do, exactly? Gerry acted like his mind was set."

"Yes, he can be that way. But we became friends during the years I worked for him. Maybe I can come up with an idea that will get him to reconsider."

I sat up straighter on the edge of the couch "You must know I'd really like to keep this job. What do you think I should do?"

"Sunday's your day off, right? Why don't you come down to my gallery in Sedona and we'll talk? I'll do what I can to help you come up with a new approach in your dealings with Gerry. Then you can ask him for another meeting. Besides, I'd enjoy showing you around my new gallery."

"I have work here at the dig I need to finish tomorrow and Sunday. Could I meet with you early Sunday and be back by noon?"

"Sure. Let's make it 8:30. That way I can get in a round of golf after our meeting before it's too hot."

#

"You planning another night of heroics?" George asked

when Dakota and I returned to the office that night.

"I'm standing watch again, if that's what you mean."

"Maybe another night falling asleep on the ground is what it'll take for you to dismiss Burk's ramblings."

"Could be, George."

George smirked and turned away. I'd had more than my fill of his disrespectful comments, but now didn't feel like the right time to challenge him.

Lonny and Hank arrived together and dumped their gear in the front room.

"Security team still set for arriving tomorrow?" Hank asked.

"Still on. How'd it go today at the kiva site?"

"We screened down to a section of the original floor, probably close to the fire pit." Hank nodded to George and said, "Janet may bring over a section of wood we extracted for you to look at. Could help with the dating."

"Will do," George said. Abruptly he stood, unlocked the front door, and slowly pulled it open. Sand swirled inside, peppering the bedrolls.

"What are you doing, George?" I asked.

"I'm going out to help Burk."

"Burk doesn't want any help," I said. "Now that it's dark, you need to stay inside."

"I'll ask him myself," George said. "I've had enough of this charade."

I shook my head. "This is not what we agreed to. The plan was to keep staff out of sight. If strangers show up, you could end up alerting them. Or risk endangering yourself."

"I'm done holing up here. This was a dumb idea."

George left without switching on his flashlight and headed in the direction Burk had stationed himself the previous night. Lonny shook his head and locked the door behind George, then he looked for him out the window.

"Do you see him?" I asked.

"Too dark," Lonny said.

I called Dakota into my office. "I'm going out again tonight to watch the back entrance."

Hank shrugged and Lonny unlocked the door for me. "Be careful," he said. "You could end up tangling with George." Hank laughed.

Rather than risk falling asleep again, I'd drunk enough coffee to keep a donkey awake, and now I regretted it. Every noise, even those common to the nighttime desert, made me jumpy—the rustling of sagebrush, pebbles dislodged by my boots, small animals scurrying away from my footsteps. I made my way back to the hiding place that had given me a good view of the collections building. The still-full moon rose and illuminated the back entrance. I sighed and hunkered down, wondering again if I'd made the right decision going along with Burk. So far, all I'd learned was how to get by on little to no sleep.

An hour passed, then another. When the moon was high, a light breeze brought the scent of something out of place: cigarette smoke. Neither Burk nor George was a smoker. I crouched low and stared into the darkness, searching for the telltale red circle, but all I saw were swaying shadows in the ghostly light of the still-bright moon.

The wind picked up, bringing another waft of smoke and something else: voices. Two masked figures ran around the corner of the building. I sucked air and flattened myself behind a bush.

Fire raged across my midsection. My mind yelled "scorpion!" and I screamed before I could stifle it.

"Did you hear that?" a man's voice said. "Somebody's out here!"

A beam of light swept the slope where I lay motionless. I clenched my teeth to keep from making another sound. My chest felt like I'd been stung by a swarm of wasps. I rolled to my side and ran my hand down the front of Hank's windbreaker. Dozens of spines protruded. I'd landed on a barrel cactus.

"Probably another damn deer," the same voice said.

"Deer don't scream."

"Who's out there?" The first voice again. "Stand up or I'll shoot."

I barely breathed.

"Here, take this flashlight," the first said.

The light moved to the side. A shot blasted into the underbrush a dozen feet from me.

"I said stand up," he said.

What were the chances he would hit me if I remained hidden? He couldn't know my exact location. But what if he got lucky?

The next shot barely missed. I tucked into a fetal position.

"Stand up or I'll blast the whole fucking hillside!"

If I stood, he'd likely shoot me anyway. I held my breath and dared a look between the branches of the sagebrush I was using for cover. Two men stood in the moonlight in front of the rear entrance, the taller one aiming his weapon into the hillside. He flicked a lit cigarette into the underbrush. The shorter one panned the hillside with a flashlight.

"Quit shooting!" the shorter guy said. "You'll attract someone. Let's get in and get out. Fast."

I prayed those shots *had* attracted someone. Burk should be close enough to hear gunshots unless he'd moved his hiding location farther away from the collections building.

The shorter man pulled something from his jacket pocket and poked it into the lock. Seconds later he had the door open. They entered cautiously, then the door closed silently behind them. Burk was right. It looked like one of them had a key.

Another shot disturbed the desert stillness, sounding

like it had come from up the trail. I scurried up the opposite side of the ravine to return to the office and call for help. The shoelace on my boot caught on a bush, tumbling me into the thicket. I banged my knee on a rock, sat, and grabbed it with both hands, my midsection still on fire. When I could breathe normally, I carefully unzipped the windbreaker, pulling out most of the cactus spines.

Someone grabbed me roughly around the waist from behind. A hard, calloused hand clamped over my nose and mouth, cutting off air. Pulse pounded in my ears. I grew faint. A voice inches from my ear commanded, "Don't scream!" He turned my head around to face him.

Burk. When he saw I recognized him, he eased up.

"You scared the hell out of me!" I rasped.

"What are you doing out here?"

"Watching the back entrance like I said I would. Two guys showed up and went inside. Did you try to shoot at them?"

"No. Didn't even see them. That last shot came from George. Caught him lurking around the front of the collections building and asked him what he was doing. He went for my gun. It went off in the struggle."

"You still have it?" I asked.

"No. George got it. Crazy son-of-a-bitch has a screw loose."

"Where is he?"

"No clue," Burk said.

"The men who went inside were armed like you said."

"Were they shooting at you?"

"Yeah, trying to drive me out of hiding."

"How did they know you were out here?"

"I screamed. Did you hear me?"

"No, too far away. You need to beat it, Aideen. I'm going in after them."

"Don't be stupid. You can't go in unarmed."

"Who said I'm unarmed? George only got one gun. I had another one stuck in my pack."

I grinned, despite my throbbing knee and burning midriff. "You should wait for law enforcement. I'm on my way to the office to call the sheriff's office."

"What makes you think anyone'll show up? I'm done waiting on them."

Burk scrambled down the gully. I watched him unlock the back door and sneak inside. Then I scrambled uphill to the office.

A dark shape shifted its weight high in a treetop near the office door. I looked up and met the eyes of a great horned owl. I knocked softly, but no one answered, so I tried the knob and found it unlocked. The white solar shades had been pulled down inside, and all the lights were out. I froze and listened. And waited. Dakota scratched and barked from inside my office. I locked the front door behind me and hurried to my office in back. Dakota bounded out when I opened the door. Hank and Lonny were gone.

I ran to the landline on my desk and dialed.

"9-1-1—what's your emergency?"

I told them who I was and said, "Two strangers shot at me and broke into the building where we store artifacts. One of our archaeologists went in after them."

"Are you safe where you are?"

"Hard to say. I'm more than half a mile from where the shooting occurred."

"Stay put. Help is on the way."

I called Frank as soon as I hung up.

"Where were you? I've been calling."

"I left my cell in the office so it wouldn't give me away. Two armed trespassers breached the collections building, and Burk went in after them. I just got off with 9-1-1."

"What's your location? Are you safe?"

"In my office. I don't know where the intruders are at

this point."

"What was Burk doing, acting on his own?"

"He has a bad attitude about the sheriff's office."

I told Frank about Burk's tangle with George.

"Where's George now? And the others?"

"Unknown."

"Okay, stay on the phone. I'll use my landline to see what else I can find out."

I heard Frank repeat what I'd told him. He finished and came back to his cell. "Okay, I've checked in with the county sheriff's office. The sheriff and two of his deputies are en route, and they know where you are. I also called an Arizona-based BLM agent for his help. Stay put while I see what else I can stir up." He disconnected.

Dakota sat panting beside me. I thought I heard voices and peeked out a window. No one.

A branch snapped.

The claw of my imagination raked across my back and brought up goose flesh. I crawled under my desk and crouched beside Dakota. When the phone rang, I banged my head on the underside of the desk trying to reach it and answered to a dial tone.

My muscles begged for a stretch. The knee I'd fallen on throbbed. A tree branch scratched against the window like ghostly fingers trying to get in. I slid out from under the desk and tripped over a metal trash can.

Someone pounded on the front door.

CHAPTER 29

DAKOTA BARKED NON-STOP. I felt around on the desktop for anything I could use as a weapon but came up empty-handed.

"Aideen are you in there?" someone called.

I opened my door into the main office. Dakota raced ahead of me.

"Who's there?" I yelled over her snarls.

"Hank. Let me in!"

Dakota would not let up. Sweat salted my upper lip.

"What's going on? Is Lonny with you?"

"No," Hank said, his voice tight. "Come on, Aideen. Let me in."

"Where's Lonny?"

"I don't know. We heard shots. Lonny and I ran out, but we didn't stay together."

I crept to the window closest to the door and looked past the edge of the shade. Hank was not alone. George Hargood crouched behind him with a gun rammed in Hank's back, and there was still no sign of law enforcement.

I crept away from the window. "Hank, I've barricaded myself in," I called. "I have to move some things."

I had no idea what I was going to do, but it no longer made sense to do it in the dark. I flipped on the lights and let Dakota bark all she wanted. I searched around for something heavy and spotted the perfect weapon: Jill's snow globe. The extra-large paperweight enclosed a scene of cherubic angels hovering around a manger. A red plastic banner announced "Peace on Earth" across the bottom.

"Aideen?" Hank called.

"I'm clearing a path. Hang on."

The phone rang again. Ignoring it, I gripped the snow globe by its hollow plastic pedestal, stood to the side where I wouldn't be seen, and reached over to unlock the door.

Hank stumbled inside, George behind, prodding him with the gun. Dakota snarled at George, and I slammed the snow globe down hard on his gun hand. He dropped the gun, and Hank dove after it.

Dakota advanced with her jaws agape and sank her teeth into George's butt. George bellowed. Hank twisted to aim the gun at George from his position on the floor. Dakota shook her head from side-to-side, a big wad of ass between her fangs. George yelled, "Get that fucking dog off of me!"

"Hands up, George," Hank yelled.

"Call off the dog!" George screamed.

A deep growl, like a heavy metal CD gone bad rumbled from Dakota's throat. George tried to shove the dog away, but she kept a firm grip on the butt wad in her mouth.

"I suppose I could call her off if you'd settle down," I said to George.

"Goddammit, do it now!" he yelled.

I motioned to Dakota to come sit beside me. She let go of George's bum and came over with her eyes glued on his face and her ears flattened against her head.

Hank ordered George to sit in Jill's chair. George winced when he sat down.

"Any rope in this office?" Hank asked.

My eyes stayed on George. "None I know of."

Hank stood, keeping several feet between himself and George. "How about duct tape?"

"Maybe. You sure you have him covered?"

Hank assumed a wider stance. "Yeah. I got this."

I scrounged around in the supply closet and found a roll of duct tape.

"Tape his arms to the arm rests on the chair," Hank said.

George's biceps bulged from weightlifting. I wasn't about to get close to him.

"Push that chair away from the desk, George," I said.

"That kid's not gonna shoot me," George growled.

"You could be right," I said. "Trade you," I said to Hank. I kept my eyes on George and handed Hank the duct tape.

"Aideen. I've got this," Hank said.

"Now would be a good time to hand me that gun," I said, holding out my hand.

Hank hesitated. I stared at him, my hand extended. Hank gave me the gun, and I pointed it at George.

"Hank might not shoot you, but I won't hesitate," I said, moving the safety back and forth a few times. "Push that chair away from the desk like I said. Do it!"

"You're such a bitch," George said.

"Thanks. I feel the same way about you, George."

Hank taped George's arms to the chair from behind, then walked around in front of him to start taping his legs.

"Watch out he doesn't kick you," I warned, only for George to slam a vicious kick into Hank's knee no sooner than the words left my mouth. Hank fell back on his butt, legs sprawled. His arms still taped to the chair, George leaned over, struggling to stand. I stuck the gun in the back of his neck and held it there until Hank stood up. He pushed George back down, then he moved behind him to secure his legs.

"Too bad," Hank said. "Not enough to cover his mouth."

Dakota stood within lunging distance. I reached down and untied the dusty bandanna from around her neck with my free hand and gave it to Hank.

Hank yanked the dog hair–coated cloth solidly between George's lips, grinning all the time while he grunted in disgust.

"That oughta hold him," he said.

Hank sat on Nova's desk. I swiveled her chair around and sat in it.

"Why did you and Lonny leave the office?" I asked.

"We split when we heard the shots. This site is so big, we figured we could hide somewhere less obvious. I came back later thinking maybe the office was safer after all. George must have seen me sneaking back."

"Why'd he come after you?"

"Said he needed a place to hide."

I looked at George. He grumbled something through the bandanna, so I yanked it down. "What was that, George?"

"You don't know what you've gotten yourself into, do you?" George said.

"What do you mean?" I asked.

George sneered and looked away. I wondered what he wasn't divulging.

To Hank, I said, "Law enforcement should be here by now. I'm calling for an update. Don't go anywhere."

Hank nodded. Dakota followed me into my office.

"Anything new?" I asked Frank.

"The sheriff and two deputies arrived on-site and are headed for the collections building. My friend, David Archer with the BLM is on his way. Did you get a call back from dispatch?"

"I don't know. A call came in, but I didn't get to it in time."

"I'll call them back," Frank said. He disconnected. I waited, and Frank called a few minutes later.

"Okay, here's the latest. Deputies know where you are, and they've entered the collections building."

"Did they see Burk?"

"Yeah, someone knocked him out."

I frowned. "How is he?"

"Starting to come around. Said he saw a perp breach the artifacts room and he went in after him, but a second guy jumped him from behind. Both perps got away. Possibly still on site."

I sat behind my desk and blew out a breath. "What's the plan now?"

"Find the perps. All-clear the site. The sheriff and his deputies are searching. They'll want to speak with you after the site is secured."

"Would you tell them George is here? He pulled a gun on us, but we have him immobilized."

"Why the hell did George pull a gun on you?"

"No idea. But something he said made me think he knows something. Maybe the cops can get it out of him."

"How'd you stop him?"

"With a snow globe."

Frank laughed. "A snow globe?"

"Yep, only heavy thing I could find."

"You sure you and Hank are all right?" Frank asked.

"Yes, we're going to the collections building as soon as I hang up. We'll leave George here for law enforcement."

"Bad idea, Aideen. You need to stay put until the site is cleared."

"How long is that likely to take?"

"Can't say. Doesn't matter."

"We need to find Lonny. Nobody knows where he is."

"True, and the sheriff's department is on it. You need to sit tight and think of your own safety for once," Frank said. "Let the cops find Lonny."

"Okay. I'll give it an hour."

"You need to give it as long as it takes. Until the site is cleared, the cops could mistake you for one of the perps. Worse, the intruders could find you, and you already know they're armed."

Across the ravine, lights came on inside the collections building. I told Hank we had to sit tight and wait until we got the all-clear to leave the office. I carried George's gun into the bathroom, intent on pulling out the last of the cactus spines. Dakota followed me, and I heard her lie down in front of the door after I closed it.

\#

Frank called much later to say a deputy found Lonny but no luck with the intruders. Two deputies would head to the office after the site was cleared. Hank and I should remain there with George until they arrived.

"Okay. Is Lonny all right?" I asked.

"Shook up but okay," Frank said. "He was hiding under a tarp beside one of your trenches at the kiva site."

\#

"We're supposed to remain here until the deputies show up," I said to Hank.

"I want out," Hank said. "We've waited for hours with all the lights on. If those thugs are still at the dig, it's plenty obvious that we're here. I'd feel safer taking my chances and high tailing it to the collections building where the cops are hanging out."

Despite what Frank had told me, my intuition told me Hank was right. We'd been in the office for hours, the lights broadcasting our presence the whole time. It was obvious, given all the little incidents lately, that someone meant to do me harm. If the deputies hadn't found the intruders yet, they could be anywhere. The dig was huge, dark, and our location was lit up like a Christmas tree.

I took a flashlight from my desk and handed it to Hank. We opened the office door cautiously and looked outside, waiting for our eyes to adjust.

"You can't just leave me here tied up like this," George muttered. "Cut this tape off me."

I turned and said, "Not on your life, George. We can't trust you after what you pulled. The deputies know you're here. They'll be here soon to cut you loose."

"I had to protect myself," he said.

"Protect yourself from what, George? Hank and me?"

"From the guys breaking in. C'mon, Aideen. I've seen them too. Cut me loose."

"What do you mean, you've seen them too?" Skeptical, I regarded him. "Why didn't you speak up in staff meeting?"

"Because Burk was there. I don't trust him."

"I don't trust *you*," I said.

He blew out a sharp breath. "You know I've done good work here."

"True," I said, "and yet, you just threatened Hank and me with a gun."

"At least give me some water. It's hot in here."

I nodded to Hank, and he went to the bathroom and returned with a paper cup of water. Hank held it for him, and George drank it down. I wondered if leaving George in the office was the right move, but freeing him after what he'd done seemed way too risky. George was strong, and I knew he could probably get his gun away from me if he decided to.

"We'll have to sort this out later, George."

I picked up my tote and turned off my phone. Then Hank, Dakota, and I ventured outside with George's unfamiliar gun heavy in my hand.

CHAPTER 30

NAVIGATING IN THE DARK proved treacherous on the steep, uneven trail. Every few steps, loose rocks threatened to send us sprawling. Hank doused the flashlight—no point announcing our whereabouts if any human predators were still at the dig. Dakota stayed close, her hackles up in the moonlight. The absence of animal activity added to the eerie silence. When we reached the bottom of the ravine, we stopped to listen. An owl hooted as a cloud moved across the moon. We waited until the cloud passed, counting on the moonlight to keep us on the trail.

When we finally made it down and then up the ravine, the front door to the collections building was locked.

"It's Aideen and Hank," I called, pounding on the door. Deputy Marston came to the door and unlocked it.

"What are you doing with a gun?" he asked.

"Returning it to its owner," I said, indicating Burk who stood behind him.

"Hand it over. Shots were fired," Marston said. "We'll need to check it before it's returned."

I handed the gun to the deputy.

"How did you end up with it?" Burk asked.

"Come in and sit down where we can talk," Marston said, waving us into the front room.

Although none of us were comfortable after a long night

and an equally long drive on Marston's part, we all found a place to sit among the scattered folding chairs. Hank and I told Burk and Marston the details of our tangles with George and that we'd left him taped to the chair.

"Someone needs to go to the office soon to cut George loose," I said. "I didn't feel right leaving him like that, but given how he'd pulled a gun on us, we didn't believe we had much of a choice."

"Sheriff Blackstone and another deputy are on their way there now," Marston said. "I may have more questions for you later, Aideen, but right now I'd like to finish up questioning Lonny Nampayu. He was pretty shook up when we found him."

"Lonny's okay?" I asked.

Marston nodded and headed down the hall to the lab.

I asked Burk how he felt.

"Head hurts where that bastard hit me, but I think I'm okay."

I studied his face. Pain showed around his eyes, but he seemed alert, and his speech sounded clear.

"George told me he's seen the intruders coming here late at night like you have. Has he said anything about that to you?"

"First I've heard of it."

"Have you ever seen George prowling around on one of your late-night jaunts?"

"Maybe once or twice."

"How come you never said anything?"

"You know George. Not exactly Mr. Social," Burk pointed out. "He could have been heading for the shower for all I knew."

"True. Have you spoken with Lonny?"

"Yeah, he's all right. Thing I'm worried about now is damage to the artifacts. Come take a look in the artifacts room."

I left Dakota with Hank and followed Burk to the artifacts room, wincing when I saw the sizable lump on the back of Burk's head. With all the bravado about his war experience, I couldn't help wondering why he'd insisted on going inside alone after the intruders.

A man in tactical attire with his upper body stretched across a deep shelf poked around on the wall with a pocketknife. He worked precariously close to an ancient ceramic cooking pot. The nine-hundred-year-old vessel had a rounded bottom designed to fit snugly in a cooking fire, and it jiggled whenever the man moved. A dozen or so artifacts lay in disarray on the floor.

"Who moved the pottery?" I asked. "It's not safe on the floor like that."

The man backed out and stood. He was a good six feet, dark haired, and surprisingly clean for someone who'd been wallowing around on a dusty shelf. "Who are you?" he asked.

"This is Aideen Connor," Burk said. "The project director."

"Special Agent David Archer, BLM," he said, extending his hand. "Frank Nakai from the New Mexico BLM office called me and asked for my help. Most of those pots were like that when we came in. Appears they were moved off that shelf I was just on."

I shook Archer's hand and then turned to Burk. "Did you move them?"

"No. The crooks must've moved them."

"We need to pack them up for transport right away," I said.

"Can't they be moved to a safe room on-site?" Archer asked.

"No, this is our only secure room. At least, it *was*. These artifacts should go to our controlled warehouse in Phoenix."

Archer took a step back. "Burk said he suspects drug activity here. Until we know what we're dealing with, moving anything is going to require my supervision."

"Then how about you approve moving them now?" I said. "We can't risk damage."

Archer frowned and didn't attempt to disguise the irritation in his voice. "How long will it take?"

"Several hours and a trained team to do it right." I looked at Burk. "You should go ice that lump and sit this one out. Did you see anyone when you went in earlier?"

He smirked. "Yeah, I saw the one that didn't hit me. He was wearing dark clothes with a black balaclava. Could have been just about anyone of average height and build."

"You sure you're okay, Burk?"

"'Yeah, but I'm definitely ready to bag it."

"Okay, I'll make sure one of us checks in on you every hour or so," I said. "Don't get cranky when we wake you up."

"Like I've told you, half the time I can't sleep anyway." He headed across the hall to the lab on his way out.

"Any news on finding the guys who broke in?" I asked the agent.

"No. The sheriff paused the search until the sun's up. They think they saw fresh tire tracks on the west side. They'll take a closer look when it's light. Do archaeologists typically use solvents in their work?"

"No. Why?"

"This room smells strongly of chemicals. Especially near that lower shelf."

I looked to where he pointed—the same spot where I'd noticed a chemical odor when I'd checked the artifacts room earlier with Nova.

"I smelled it, too, but it's not coming from anything we've used."

I moved the rest of the artifacts off the shelves and set them carefully on the floor. Archer then removed the shelves and pried off the supporting brackets with a crowbar. With shelves and framework gone, horizontal and vertical cuts in the drywall became visible. A loose section of drywall was exposed where Archer had been probing.

"What do you know about these cuts?" he asked.

"First time I've seen them."

Archer bent down and pried out the section of drywall with his pocketknife. By making the cuts close to the bottom of the brackets, but not directly underneath, anyone who knew the setup could move a few pots off the shelf and pry out the drywall section.

I looked over Archer's shoulder at the now visible cavity. Stacks upon stacks of bags containing dirty white powder crowded the space between the two-by-fours behind the wall board. A few of the bags showed rips and chew marks.

"Do you think those chewed bags are the reason for the chemical smell?" I asked.

Archer turned toward me. "Not something I should discuss with a civilian." He leaned the loose piece of drywall against the cavity, hiding its contents.

"I'm going to allow you to pack up those pots while I wait for my team. You need to get everything out of here as quickly as you can. Move the pottery across the hall to the lab first. You can pack it for transport from there. This room is now off-limits to all employees."

Archer pulled his phone from a holder on his belt and motioned me out of the room. I wondered what Rodgers would say when he got the call telling him a drug stash had been discovered at the dig.

#

Archer called for a forensics team within minutes of uncovering the drugs. While he waited for his techs to arrive, I said I'd like to speak with him about other suspicious activity at the dig. He locked the artifacts room with the key he'd taken from Burk and asked for mine. I reached into my pocket for the key attached to my clasp knife. "Here," I said, pulling the key off the ring and handing it to him. I tucked the knife back into my pocket.

We walked across the hall to the lab and sat down in a couple of straight-back wooden chairs. I described finding the slashed sheep under my trailer, and later, the picture of my late husband in its decayed blood.

"Do you have any idea if someone here at the dig would do that?" he asked.

I'd been asking myself that question. Who at the dig might want me out? Clearly George was no fan, but would he pull something that disgusting and elaborate just to intimidate me? And now he had what he wanted—Henderson was back at the dig. Since Rodgers fired me, maybe he had plans to bring Henderson back full time as director. Burk struck me as capable of pulling off an act like the sheep killing, but what was his motive? He'd been helpful since I'd taken over as director. Archer was looking at me, expecting an answer.

"I've thought about it, David, but I keep coming up short."

"Anything else before my team gets here?"

I told Archer about Alonzo's attack in Taos and the bloody *paho* staged in my car. Archer asked for more details and what a *paho* was, and I told him.

"This site is remote, David. Most people don't even know there's a dig here. Meanwhile, Alonzo—the guy who chased me at the pueblo—is wanted for murdering his wife. My hunch is that these events, including the murder are all connected."

When it came to hunches, I trusted my instincts. Sometimes artifacts discovered in the same strata didn't make sense, like parrot feathers unearthed at prehistoric Arizona sites. The high desert was hardly a natural environment for tropical birds. But when archaeologists confirmed trade routes between ancient Arizona settlements and prehistoric Mexican cultures, parrot feathers could be explained as a by-product of trade."

"Nakai already told me most of this. He said he was with you when you found this *paho*."

"So, you think there could be a connection to the drugs you just discovered?"

"It merits investigating," Archer said. "I'll want to interview you later. Be sure you stick around."

#

I called Janet and asked her to come in to help pack up artifacts. Janet, Lonny, Hank, and I spent the next several hours hard at work. We carefully crated up everything, locked those crates inside two company vans, and set the car alarms. Shortly before sunrise, Lonny and Hank retreated to their tents, and Janet drove back to her friend's place in Winslow. Lonny and Hank would drive the loaded vans to our warehouse in Phoenix after they rested a few hours and Archer gave clearance.

#

Exiting the collections building with Dakota, a huge orange sun rose from the east, and I took a few moments to enjoy the colors warming the mesa. Sunrise evoked the first feeling of peace I could remember in more than a week, and I feared it was likely to be short-lived. I was grateful no one had been seriously hurt at the dig, but the strange altercation with George had unnerved me. Why would someone as well-trained and smart as George risk his career pulling a gun on a co-worker? I'd discussed these concerns with Archer, and he'd assured me the sheriff and a deputy would attend to George and question him for answers that explained his behavior. After what I'd learned from Lucy, I couldn't help but to wonder if George was using drugs again.

The dog and I walked around to the front of the collections building to pick up the trail to the office and check on George. A man wearing a badge identifying him as the sheriff was inside talking rapidly on his phone when I opened the office door. An unfamiliar deputy blocked my view. When she moved aside, I was startled to see George. He still sat where Hank and I had left him, but his face was bloody and swollen—someone had beaten him senseless.

CHAPTER 31

The deputy ushered me out of the office doorway and down the metal steps. I sat on the ground and drew Dakota close to me, struggling to catch my breath.

"Deputy Dickens," she said. "Who are you?"

"Aideen Connor, the site director," I mumbled.

"What are you doing here?" she demanded.

"Trying not to pass out."

Dickens squatted beside me. "You're really pale. Put your head between your knees and breathe slowly."

I did as she said and counted silently. When I felt a little better, I stretched my legs out in front of me, and Dakota put her head in my lap with a sigh.

Dickens tucked a wisp of blonde hair behind her ear and said, "The BLM agent, David Archer, told us you and another employee were the ones who taped him up like that. You also the one who knocked him out?"

"No. George was alert and yelling at us when we left him. He must have known the person who beat him up, but it wasn't me and it wasn't Hank." I put my knees up and rested my head on them. "Please, I need some water."

Dickens gave me a penetrating look and said, "You thinking of running off?"

I looked up at her. "Do I really look like I'm ready to run somewhere?"

She gave me a sidelong glance and then went inside the office, quickly returning with a paper cup filled with water. I sipped it slowly.

Dickens squatted in front of me. "Why don't you tell me what happened?"

"George showed up here last night with a gun rammed in Hank's back."

"Who's Hank?" Dickens asked.

"Hank Benton. Field archaeologist," I said, and continued on. "I'd told Hank and Lonny Nampayu—another employee—to stay in the office last night, but when they heard gun shots, they ran off."

Dickens nodded slowly. "Maybe you should start at the beginning."

I told Dickens about Burk's claims, the shortage of motel rooms in town and the rest of the story. When I got to the part about George forcing his way inside with a gun, and that Hank and I were able to get it away from him, she interrupted.

"Only trouble with that," Dickens said, "is the person you're accusing is in no condition to rebut it. We've called to have him airlifted out of here. Where's that gun now?"

"I took it with me when we went to the collections building to give it back to the owner, Burk Trenton. Deputy Marston took it."

"How do you know it's Burk's gun?" she asked.

That brought me up short. "I guess I don't," I admitted slowly. "It's what he told me."

"Where's this Hank now?" she asked.

"Left him at his tent so he could get some rest. We were up most of the night and just spent several hours packing up artifacts to take to Phoenix."

My burner phone buzzed in my pocket. Frank.

"Let me answer it," I said to Dickens. "It's the BLM agent who knows me and knows what's going on here."

"Fine. Let me talk to him," Dickens said.

I handed her the phone, and she walked far enough away that I couldn't hear.

Several minutes later, she returned and handed me the phone. "He made an accurate description of you and also of your dog. He wants to talk with you."

"I've been calling your office all night," Frank said. "That deputy told me about George. You okay? I did some quick talking to convince her you're who you say you are, and promised I'd vouch for you."

"I'm way out of my element with all this, Frank," I said. "George looks awful. I feel somewhat responsible because Hank and I left him here, but what else could we do? He threatened us at gunpoint. And we both felt very unsafe staying there."

"I understand, but I wish you hadn't left him."

"What else could we have done?"

"Waited for the cops to handle it."

"Frank, George was badly beaten *after* we left. I'm glad Hank and I got out of here. It could have happened to us, too, if we'd stayed."

"Good point. You could be right. Listen, Aideen, what's done is done. When I talked with Archer earlier, he told me about the drug stash."

"Yes, and I think George might know something about that. He told Hank and me he's seen intruders here at night, like Burk has. Maybe he recognized them. Why else would someone beat him like that?" I paused, catching the low rumble of road noise on the line. "Where are you? Sounds like you're driving."

"Two hours out of Winslow. I've been reassigned to run BLM's drug investigation at your dig with Archer. I told that deputy to let you return to your trailer, that I'd take responsibility. I think she's good with that. Has the sheriff's department cleared that section of the dig site?"

"I don't know. Check with Archer. I'm scared, Frank. Last night was a nightmare from hell. I don't know what to make of George, and I'm really worried about Cha'tima and Chosovi."

"Why?"

"I think I know the identity of one of the intruders. I'll tell you more when you get here. Given all that's happened, I'm afraid the Honovis could be in danger. I want you to go up to Walpi with me to warn them."

"The sheriff's department will want you to stick around."

"You're a federal officer. Can't you help me with that? There's no food in my trailer. I've got to go into Winslow for supplies. Do whatever it takes to get me clearance, please. Then meet me in Winslow at the Two Horse Café as soon as you can get there."

"Okay. Put that deputy back on."

I handed Dickens the phone and waited while she talked with Frank.

"Seems you have some friends in high places," she said when she returned the phone.

Relieved, I thanked her and headed back to my trailer with Dakota before she could change her mind.

CHAPTER 32

DAKOTA AND I JOGGED back to my trailer where I showered and removed the last of the cactus spines. Dakota curled up, comfortable in the air-conditioning, and I was glad she seemed content to stay in the trailer. On my way to the rental car I ran into Burk. He'd ditched most of his black night watch garb and sported a faintly dusty, day-old look.

"Okay if I join you?" he asked, as I powered up the Jeep.

"Sure. Hop in if you're looking for breakfast."

Burk stretched out on the passenger's side and pulled the bill of his ball cap down over his eyes. I thought he was sleeping until a few miles down the road he said, "Did you call Rodgers yet?"

Deep in thought about all that had transpired the night before at the dig, I jumped at the sound of his voice. "No, Archer called him. I need food and caffeine before I can deal with Rodgers. I've never had a boss go so thoroughly sour on me."

A BLM vehicle raced past, spewing gravel and dust. I raised the windows and asked Burk if he'd look in the glove box for a cheap pair of sunglasses I had bought in Santa Fe. He found them and handed them to me, then he reclined his seat as far back as it would go, leaving me alone with my thoughts.

\#

Burk and I took a booth in the back of the Two Horse Café. The waitress who'd served Jill, Rodgers, and me yesterday morning wandered over in a retro-style yellow uniform with her hair in a long ponytail. Her look reminded me of the lead in a high school production of *Grease*.

"You two been up all night?" she asked.

I covered a yawn. "Yep."

"You work at night?"

"Not usually," Burk said.

I took the menu she offered, and she handed one to Burk.

"How about two mugs of coffee for starters?" I said.

When she left, Burk leaned forward. "I heard about George. Do you think he'll make it?"

I propped my elbow on the table and put my head in my hand. "I don't know, Burk. They air-lifted him to a hospital in Phoenix. Before someone beat him black and blue, he held Hank and me at gunpoint. Kind of hard to get that out of my mind."

"Who do you think got to him?"

"The only thing I can figure is the intruders found him and decided he was a threat. Maybe he knew who they were. He acted like he knew something when Hank and I were talking to him, but he was cagey. Something had him plenty worried to have pulled what he did, but you know all too well how dramatic he can be."

Burk nodded. "Yeah, that would be George. Mr. Dramatic. What're you going to do if Rodgers won't re-up on your contract?"

"He already said I was done in two weeks. Haven't had time to think much past that."

The waitress returned with coffee, took our orders and left. The bell on the door jangled, and Gerry Rodgers walked in. I let out a long sigh and said, "Speak of the devil."

Burk chuckled.

Rodgers located us in the back of the café and strode toward us. Burk scooted over to make room for him, and Rodgers slid into the booth beside Burk. "I heard," he said, looking at me. "A Fed named Archer called me before I left for Phoenix. Why didn't I hear about this mess from you?"

"We've been up all night dealing with it," I said. "I planned to call you after I had coffee and breakfast."

"Unbelievable about George," Rodgers said, and shook his head. "Heard he held you and Hank at gunpoint. That's a first."

"Glad to hear it," I said. "I sure wouldn't wish something like that on another dig director."

"Does this drug stash Archer found have something to do with what you wanted to tell me yesterday?" Rodgers asked.

"No, the drugs weren't discovered until late last night. I wanted your approval to hire a security company. Burk told me he's seen armed intruders going into the collections building at night, and I was worried about everyone's safety. After you left, I went ahead and hired a detail. I figured once you got the full picture, you'd be okay with it."

I looked at the boot-shaped salt and pepper shakers on the table, wishing they'd start a slow, disembodied dance while I waited for his response. "It's been a hellish night. I know you didn't approve it, but I hope you'll still allow me the rest of my probationary period to finish up. At least I'll have some closure."

Rodgers's shoulders slumped. He hadn't shaved, and I noticed the puffiness under his eyes. Neither fit with his usual buttoned-down mien. "You can have the rest of your probation time, Aideen. "I guess I've been too hard on you. Fiona let on she's divorcing me, and that's made me a bit off. And I'm sorry about the hellish night."

Burk cleared his throat. The waitress brought Rodgers a mug of coffee. He took a long swig. I watched him from across the booth and waited until he set the cup down and his shoulders relaxed a little.

"Gerry, given all that's happened, I'd like your written approval for hiring that security company."

He looked up. "For how long?"

"Maybe a few weeks. I'll ask the sheriff's department for their recommendation."

"Okay," he said. "Should be cheaper than a lawsuit."

#

There'd been a steady stream of customers since Rodgers arrived. The next time the bell on the door jingled, Frank Nakai strolled in. He glanced around and spotted me. I watched him approach without getting up. He looked the way he had the last time he'd driven all night—a little mussed up but alert, a slow, easy smile spreading across his face when he saw me. He walked to our booth and stood beside me until I scooted over.

"Who's this?" Rodgers asked.

"Special Agent Frank Nakai, this is my boss, Dr. Gerry Rodgers."

The two men shook hands, and Frank introduced himself to Burk.

"Are you working with Archer?" Rodgers asked.

Frank nodded. "The two of us will be running the drug investigation."

"Please keep me posted," Rogers said, handing Frank his card. He motioned to the waitress and ordered another coffee for the road. "I'll pick up the tab on the way out," he said.

No one talked until Rodgers left.

Burk looked at Frank, then at me. "I can drive your rental back, Aideen, if you want to ride with Frank."

"Thanks, Burk." I handed him the keys. As soon as he headed for the van, I said to Frank, "I'd like to leave for Walpi as soon as possible."

"What do you expect to find?" Frank asked.

"I've had an uneasy feeling about Cha'tima and Chosovi ever since I learned Tiponi was their granddaughter. Alonzo came after me when he thought I had Tiponi's photo. There's something about that photo that has nothing to do with sentimentality. And I know the Honovis have the photo—I saw it there on my last visit."

Frank said, "You think Alonzo has something to do with the drugs Archer found?"

With a nod, I said, "I think he was one of the prowlers last night. One of the two I saw was tall like Alonzo, and I think I recognized his voice. Something really has me puzzled, though. Remember when Alonzo showed up at my place and he acted surprised when I accused him of killing Tiponi? He acted like he didn't know she was dead. If he didn't kill her, who did?"

CHAPTER 33

THE HOPI MESAS ARE way off the main highway, but the remote location and the mounting heat did little to deter the tourists queuing up for a guided tour of Walpi. Across from the tourist office, pieces of yellow police tape still fluttered in front of Tiponi's home.

"We're here to visit the Honovis," I said to the woman at the ticket desk. "Please send someone to tell them Aideen Connor and her friend, Frank Nakai, are here." I handed her our cards, and we sat down.

The ticket seller made a call, but twenty minutes later we were still waiting. I asked her what could be keeping the messenger. The woman frowned and glanced at the clock above the door.

"You're right. Serena should have been here by now."

As if on cue, a young woman pushed her way inside with red-stained hands leaving a smear on the door. The ticket seller stood. "Serena?"

"Chosovi and Cha'tima didn't answer, and there was blood on their door! Look at my hands!"

Frank snapped open his badge wallet. "I'm a federal officer. Take us there now."

The ticket seller put her arm around Serena for a moment. Then she went to the door and flipped the hanging sign on the door from "open" to "closed."

"Tours are over for today," she told the remaining tourists outside. "We'll make good on your tickets tomorrow."

The few stragglers still in line headed for the parking lot, but had the grace not to grumble at her urgency.

"Are you going to be all right?" the ticket seller asked Serena.

The girl nodded, but her face showed pale beneath her dark hair.

"Go wait for me at home."

"She's your daughter?" Frank asked.

"Yes. You're not Hopi, are you?"

"No, Navajo."

"What's your name?"

"Nakai. Frank Nakai. Yours?"

"Lorraine Humetewa. My husband and Cha'tima are good friends." She was tall for a Hopi woman, and the long black shirt and skinny jeans she wore made her seem more so.

I introduced myself and asked, "Are you related to an Officer Humetewa?"

She nodded. "My husband's brother."

We ran across the land bridge and up the narrow stone-paved street into Walpi to Chosovi's home on the second level. A drying red-brown smudge coated the doorknob.

"Is there a Hopi officer on-site?" Frank asked.

"No, this is a ceremonial village." Lorraine said. "They don't stay here."

Frank went to the front window and tried to see in, but the white curtains were tightly drawn. "Is there another entrance?"

"No," I said. "There're only two rooms, and their home was built against a common wall in the back."

Frank took a bandanna from his pocket and tried to turn the blood-stained knob, but the door was locked. "I think I should break in."

Lorraine stepped out of his way. "Do it."

Frank kicked the door hard near the knob. It held. He backed up and kicked again. The jamb splintered with a loud crack, and the door creaked in. A trail of drying blood drops led from the entrance to the upturned green table. Katsinam lay scattered on the floor, some of them in pieces. The air carried the pungent odors of herbs and sweat and blood. I grabbed hold of Frank's arm, and he motioned me behind him.

Someone moaned. Through the door to their back room I saw Cha'tima sprawled on a rug at the foot of the double bed. Lorraine and I started to enter, but Frank held out his arm to stop us.

"Walk around the blood on the floor and avoid stepping on anything that could be evidence. Try not to touch anything," he warned. "Let me go first."

Frank squatted next to Cha'tima and checked his pulse then stood and said, "I'm calling an ambulance." He went into the front room and stood near the window for cell reception.

Lorraine and I walked gingerly through the front room and into the windowless bedroom. The right side of Cha'tima's head showed a large knot, and his thick hair around the swelling was matted and bloody. I sat on the floor beside him and held his hand. Lorraine went into the front room and returned with a pitcher of water and a clean dish towel. She dampened the towel, knelt beside Cha'tima, and gently bathed his face. His eyelids fluttered. He took a deep breath and slowly looked around the room.

"Chosovi?"

"She's not here, Cha'tima," Lorraine said gently.

Cha'tima turned toward her, and she took his other hand.

Frank returned and squatted close to the older man.

Cha'tima stared at Frank as if he knew him.

"Where's Chosovi?" Cha'tima croaked.

"We don't know where she is, elder." Frank said.

Lorraine went to open the curtains in the front room.

"He hit me," Cha'tima mumbled.

"Who?" Frank asked.

"Ray. He wanted her picture."

"Did you give it to him?" Frank asked.

"Yes. Didn't want him to hurt Chosovi… don't remember after that."

Frank turned to Lorraine and said, "Getting an ambulance up here is too precarious. I told the EMTs to meet us on the road to Tuba City. Aideen and I will drive him out to the highway."

Lorraine stood, picked up the pitcher and cloth, and set them on the wooden nightstand. "I'll go tell the neighboring families what we're doing."

"Try not to disturb anything else in the house," Frank said. Then he took off in a run.

I scooted closer to Cha'tima. He grabbed my arm with surprising strength. "Find Chosovi. I think Ray took her."

#

Frank was back some ten minutes later. "I left the van running. Let's get him out to it."

Cha'tima studied Frank's face, then he turned to look at me. He grimaced when he moved his head, then he closed his eyes.

Lorraine came through the front door and said she'd spoken to the neighbors on both sides.

Frank said, "I need a description of Chosovi."

"I have a picture of her," Lorraine said. "I'll bring it to the van.

"Frank, Cha'tima thinks Alonzo took Chosovi," I said.

"When we get on the road, I'll call her in as a missing person and possible kidnapping victim."

#

Two neighbor men recruited by Lorraine appeared with a long wooden board. They wrapped Cha'tima's rug around him, and Frank used it to gently pull Cha'tima onto the board. The neighbors helped Frank carry him to the BLM van. Lorraine met us with Chosovi's picture.

The three men lifted Cha'tima onto the floor of the van, and I sat down beside him. Twenty minutes down the highway, the ambulance from Tuba City approached from the opposite direction, red and blue lights spinning. Frank flashed his lights, and we stopped long enough for the EMTs to transfer Cha'tima into the ambulance. I climbed into the van's passenger's seat, and Frank and I followed behind the ambulance.

Frank reached across the console between us and took my hand. "That hunch of yours might have saved his life."

All I could do was shake my head and stare out the window. I held Frank's hand until we pulled into the hospital parking lot, silently praying the blood on the door of their home in Walpi was not Chosovi's.

CHAPTER 34

FRANK AND I WAITED at the hospital until Cha'tima's condition stabilized and his family was notified. Frank left his card at the nurses' station, and we asked Lorraine to keep us posted on Cha'tima's progress. Lorraine promised to sit with Cha'tima until his family arrived.

On the drive back, Frank told me he and Archer would be staying at the dig and had permission from Rodgers & Associates to bunk in one of the employee tents while they conducted their investigation.

"Burrows and I had a talk before I left, and he promised not to take me off this case again until BLM's part of it is concluded."

"That's a relief. And that reminds me, what was it you said to Dickens that got her to ease up? Something about knowing people in high places?"

"I told Dickens you were expected in Senator Benally's office in DC next week. To make a presentation on strategies to protect ancient sites on BLM-managed land."

"Senator *Lydia* Benally? Of New Mexico?" I echoed, tempted to pinch myself. "I admire her environmental work. How'd you come up with that idea?"

"Sometimes I get lucky."

"But what if Dickens calls the senator's office?"

"Don't worry about it. I already called her."

"You called Benally's office? Who'd you talk with?"

Frank reached over and squeezed my hand. "Relax, Aideen. Senator Benally's my mother. Why do you think I grew up in DC?"

\#

Frank dropped me off at my trailer and said he'd pick me up in a few hours to go to Winslow for dinner. I was out walking Dakota when my cell buzzed.

"Are you available to meet with Juanita Joshwecoma?" Nova asked. "She's here waiting for you."

I blew out a long breath. "It's not the best time, Nova. Ask her to schedule a meeting with me for early next week."

"I did. She's been here a while, and she's determined to speak with you."

"Did you ask her what it's about?"

"She'll only tell you."

I sighed audibly. "Okay. Tell her I'll be there in a few minutes."

\#

Juanita sat in the office waiting area, her face pale, her arms wrapped tightly in front of her, looking unlike the self-assured woman I'd come to know. She followed me into my office and sat down in the chair in front of my desk. I closed the door behind her, my feeling of annoyance vanishing in the face of her obvious distress.

"What is it, Juanita? You look like you've seen a ghost."

"Maybe I have. I heard those bones have not been recovered yet," she said.

"Where are you getting your information?"

"That's not important."

"Well, it's important to me. I'm in serious hot water over those stolen bones, and my boss thinks I'm leaking information."

"I can't tell you my source. I can tell you those bones

have to be reburied. You've got to find them and bring them back."

"This is far from our first uncovering of human remains, Juanita," I reminded her. "What makes these particular bones so important to you?"

"I found out those bones were stained red, right?"

"Yes, you're obviously well informed. Coated with red ochre, a natural substance." I folded my hands on top of my desk, took a calming breath, and looked directly at Juanita. "I understand you're concerned about the theft just like I am, but is that the pressing reason why you wanted to speak with me?"

She studied the back wall of my small office, and I thought she might be curious about why I kept a stocked gun cabinet.

"Why do you have that picture of Chaco Canyon on your wall? I've always hated looking at it," she said.

My back stiffened. *Why the sudden change of subject?* A photo hung behind my desk of an aerial view of Pueblo Bonito, a ruin in Chaco Canyon. I'd long admired the prehistoric architecture and the ancient settlement's unusual *D* shape.

"It's a famous archaeological site, as you know," I said. "I like the aerial view."

"Do you know what happened there?"

"In terms of…? A multitude of archaeologists have studied that canyon for years, and they're still sorting out all the things they believe happened there."

"There's a story in my family about that canyon that's been passed down from generation to generation. I've never told it to an outsider."

"And your family's legend has something to do with the bones stolen from this site?" I asked.

"Yes. We believe the reason those bones were stained red was because of something that started long ago. At

Chaco." She frowned at the photo, then back at me. "You're so much younger than that other director. It's taken me a while to trust you."

I waited. Either she'd decide to trust me enough to tell me what was on her mind, or she wouldn't. She was quiet for a few moments, as if gathering her thoughts, then she locked eyes with me and began.

"My grandmother told me this story when she lived with us. As the oldest living woman in our family, she passed it on to me, the youngest daughter of her youngest daughter, and as she explained, it would be my duty to tell it to the youngest daughter of my youngest daughter. I was maybe eleven at the time, and I thought she was a crazy old woman, but I remember quite well what she had to say."

I nodded and waited for her to continue.

"Our story began in the time of the migrations some nine hundred years ago. People from the south were showing up in our villages in small bands. Many of the great Mexican cities had already collapsed, and widespread civil unrest had become the norm. People knew of our settlements from the traders who made regular trips north. They were leaving their home cities in ancient Mexico in search of a safer place to live in the north.

"The people who migrated here were more advanced in farming and pottery-making than we were, and they offered to teach us if we would allow them to stay. Ultimately, many were accepted into our villages and assimilated.

"But there were others from the southern priest and warrior clans who came north and settled in Chaco Canyon. They quickly took control of Chaco's outlying settlements and ruled by inducing a state of constant fear. The warriors controlled the populace by conducting regular patrols in the villages—like they had on the causeways of Teotihuacán. The ultimate penalty for disobeying the priests at Chaco was human sacrifice—carried out by those same priests."

"So, your family claims that human sacrifice like that practiced in prehistoric Mexico also took place in Chaco?" I asked.

"Yes. And that wasn't all. Sometimes the victims' bodies were cannibalized."

I took a deep breath. Her story was consistent with current research by a number of archaeologists who'd studied the so-called Chaco phenomenon. "Juanita, your story parallels current research, but what does it have to do with the human remains stolen from Moenkopi Ridge?"

"My family believes a handful of those migrant priests settled near our mesas. My family and others from our old village knew that sometimes they sacrificed people *here* also—until my ancestors banded together with others in our village and drove them out. There's a reason Moenkopi Ridge was abandoned long ago. People living here many generations back believed the spirits of the sacrificed were not at rest. Before they moved on, the courageous ones exhumed the bones of the victims, performed rituals, and applied the red earth. Then they reburied the bones. The red earth warned others against future disturbance. Some in my family believe the ancients put a curse on anyone who touched those bones.

"You have to understand—they performed these rites at what they believed to be great risk to their own welfare. Those bones were never meant to be disturbed. You must make sure they're returned and reburied."

"Juanita, I'd like nothing better, but that may not be within my control."

Juanita sat erect and gave me a cool look.

"It's my personal duty to see that those remains are reburied, Aideen. I will do whatever it takes to make that happen. You have to recover them if you plan to continue working near our mesas. Without our support it will become difficult for you to continue your research here."

She had a point. It was unlikely local descendants would drive us out, but they could garner enough support to make further excavations by Rodgers & Associates difficult. Gerry Rodgers was especially sensitive to local opinion, and the last thing he wanted was for his company to be portrayed as anti-Native American. That wouldn't sit well with the multiple government contracts he was pursuing. And it certainly didn't bode well for recovering my status with the company, either. Juanita had already threatened a lawsuit, and it seemed to me Rodgers had decided to make me the scapegoat.

All that aside, I would like nothing more than to have the chance to help recover the bone hash. It had vanished on my watch, and despite the fact I didn't believe it to be my fault, I agreed with Juanita that the bones should be recovered out of respect for the descendants.

"At the moment, all I can promise is that I intend to do whatever I can to recover those remains and see to it that they are respectfully reburied according to your traditions," I said.

#

I walked back to my trailer wondering if there were other misfortunes Juanita had in mind for me. I knew she'd already had her discussion with Rodgers. At least he'd referred her back to me. He'd also fired me, which seemed misfortune enough, but I hadn't divulged that to Juanita.

I went inside my trailer to escape the heat and check on Dakota. She was acting like she was fully recovered from her entrapment in the crawl space. I kicked a book I'd left on the floor—a tome about guilt and forgiveness I hadn't been able to finish—and plopped down on the couch. Dakota rose to greet me, then curled up nearby on the floor.

The odds now looked to be a hundred percent I'd be leaving Moenkopi Ridge in less than two weeks, and I'd started to realize it wasn't only the job I was losing. The stark beauty of the high desert had gotten under my skin. Putting my life back together after Clay's death had been a primary motive for taking a position in a place as remote as Moenkopi Ridge. Diving headlong into my career had proven surprisingly satisfying. Before all the threats and problems started at the dig, I'd finally begun to heal.

Now my professional life lay in shambles, and although I suspected Alonzo was behind the threats against me, I hadn't figured out how the pressure he was putting on me was related to the murder up at Hano or the newly discovered drug ring. I believed it was all connected, although one thing made no sense: If Ray Alonzo was the murderer, why had he risked going back to Walpi when there was a warrant out for his arrest?

Yawning, I realized I couldn't remember my last full night's sleep. I sank into the couch, put my feet up, and closed my eyes. For a few moments, all I wanted was to listen to Dakota's even breaths, the soft ticks of the battery-run clock over the kitchen sink that had escaped the shotgun blast, the drone of a distant plane. Cleaning up any remaining debris in my kitchen would have to wait.

#

Slanted light filters through the leafy canopy and tells me it's afternoon. We stand on the storm-drenched trail at Dead Widow's Pass, Clay some forty feet up the trail ahead of me. He turns.

"Don't turn! Don't look at me!" I beg, but my voice sounds only inside my own mind, and the deadly sequence begins—the ear-shattering rumble—like a runaway train—portends the lethal downhill surge. Trees topple between us. Clay's wild gaze meets my startled eyes, just as it has every other time I've had the nightmare. He looks at me with incredible longing—a look long burned into my memory. But this time, the dream is different. This time, Clay says something in the heartbeat before the mudslide strikes him.

My heart pounded with such force I sat bolt upright, fully awake and striving to remember what Clay said. The generator kicked in with a loud thud. I jumped. The stress of the past week had taken a toll greater than I'd wanted to admit to myself. Even so, I wasn't leaving Moenkopi Ridge without a fight. Believing my reputation had been unfairly marred, I was determined to find out why I'd been set up and how the thefts of human remains were tied to the death of a young Hopi woman.

CHAPTER 35

AN HOUR LATER, I stood looking out the front window, ready to go to dinner, when Frank drove up. "It's been a long day," he said. "Glad I'm finally off-duty. You have anything to drink before we head into town?"

"How about some cold white wine—if I can find two intact glasses?"

He smiled. "Glad you didn't blow up your refrigerator when you fired off that shot when Alonzo showed up."

I took a chilled bottle of white from the fridge and handed it to him then went in search of glasses. All I found were a couple of dusty jam jars. I rinsed them out and handed them to Frank.

"Are you going to clean up the rest of this mess in case your boss shows up?"

I handed Frank the corkscrew. "I'm in so much trouble already, what's a china cabinet?"

Instead of opening the wine, he set the bottle and the corkscrew on the counter. "I'm worried about you, Aideen."

"Why?"

Frank rested his hands on my shoulders. "You're asking me why after all the break-ins you've had? Your living space is a mess, and it isn't secure." My back tensed. Not only was my trailer not secure, someone had gotten inside my trailer more than once and almost succeeded in killing my dog.

I stared into Frank's eyes, then looked away. Perhaps sensing my true emotions, he held onto me and drew me closer. I was aware of the strength and warmth in his hands, the scent of his hair that reminded me of desert sage, his confidence.

I enjoyed Frank's company—more than I cared to admit. But I would be leaving soon and probably wouldn't be seeing him much longer. I thought of the times Clay used to hold me when I was tense, like Frank held me now, giving me the time I needed to collect myself. Abruptly, I pulled away.

#

The only eatery still open in Winslow was the Cowgirl Bar and Grill—famous for well-used brown leather saddles mounted on posts in front of an antique wooden bar. Patrons sat astride the saddles—as long as they could hold their liquor. Usually, the kitsch of the Cowgirl put me in a playful mood. I'd yelled "Giddy up" when I blasted through the swinging bar doors more than once. But my earlier exchange with Frank had dampened my mood, and the hurt, confused look on his face only made it worse.

We followed the waitress to a booth. She handed us menus, and I noticed she was the same woman who'd served Burk and me breakfast at the Two Horse Café.

"What are you doing here?" I asked. "I thought you worked at the Two Horse."

"Yes, I do, but they don't serve dinner. So… I work here, too."

After she left, I reached across the booth and took Frank's hands in mine.

"I appreciate everything you've done for me," I said. "I hope you know that."

"Sounds like you're saying goodbye," he said. "Maybe you should wait on that."

"Why?"

"You still have another whole week here."

"Two." I held up two fingers and laughed.

"So have dinner with me again tomorrow night," he said. "You're kitchen's in no shape for cooking."

I smiled in spite of the little voice in the back of my head warning me not to accept.

"It's only dinner," he said. "I'll pick you up the same time tomorrow."

CHAPTER 36

A LOT OF PEOPLE expect the desert to be quiet in the early morning, but sunrise brings a symphony of bird calls and the scurrying of small animals beneath the gray-green branches of sagebrush. As dawn took the sky from a dark, star-filled canopy to purple, then bright coral, a lone eagle entered my field of vision and began its morning circle overhead.

Two of the three company vans in the lot were packed with the artifacts we'd removed from the collections building. Lonny and Hank had slept most of the day after the night's events and were in no shape to drive yesterday. They would take the artifacts to the company's secure warehouse in Phoenix later today. I'd already alerted Lucy to expect delivery that afternoon.

I'd given the keys to the two vans to Lonny for safekeeping and left a note on Nova's desk saying I'd taken the third van to run an errand and would be back around lunchtime. I unlocked the side door of the empty van for Dakota, climbed in and put my phone and my clasp knife in the middle console. I fired up the engine, and we headed for Winslow.

After a breakfast stop at the Two Horse Café, Dakota needed a walk. The band on my watch had torn almost all the way through so I took it off and slipped it into the front pocket of my cargos and stashed my phone in a side pocket. "A new watch is another expense I don't need right now," I said to her. She perked her ears and cocked her head to the side as if she understood every word, and I was finally able to laugh about possibly joining the ranks of the unemployed. Half an hour later we returned to the van and took the road to Sedona, arriving on the outskirts in ninety minutes.

Surrounded by its iconic red cliffs, driving down Main Street was like being dropped on a Western movie set. It was easy to understand why Lyle had come to appreciate living and working in such a colorful locale. Boot shops sat sandwiched between specialty stores selling a hundred different kinds of hot sauce. Stylish cafés with brightly colored umbrella tables stood ready for the noon rush. A life-sized bronze horse reared riderless in front of a prominent art gallery.

The Desert Rose, Lyle's gallery, was at the far end of Main Street on a large corner lot with private parking in back. I parked, slipped my clasp knife into my other side pocket out of habit and led Dakota from the van. We walked a few blocks, then returned to the parking lot. I tied her to a tree in a cool, shady spot on the edge of the lot and set out a bowl of water for her. When she cocked her head and looked at me, I held up my index finger in front of her alert eyes and told her to stay.

Lyle's gallery took up most of a city block. A large Navajo sandpainting dominated the lit storefront window that also showcased spectacular Navajo rugs on wooden display horses. Black velvet jewelry boards loaded with silver jewelry lay on the sand-covered floor.

I pushed the buzzer to the right of the door and waited. A male voice answered "Yes?" over the intercom.

"Lyle? It's Aideen."

"Hi, Aideen. I'll buzz you in."

Overhead lights jerked on as soon as I stepped inside. Lyle walked toward me, looking like a well-dressed cattle baron in his fancy cowboy shirt with mother-of-pearl studs, brown jeans and a leather belt sporting a buckle the size of Oklahoma. His polished look made me feel a bit underdressed in my black cargo pants and teal colored T-shirt.

"Welcome to the Desert Rose," he said. He reached for my hand and looked into my eyes and smiled. Somewhat taken aback, I pulled away and turned to take in the surroundings.

"Your gallery's beautiful," I said. "When did it open?"

"A little over four months ago. I finally have the displays the way I want them—just in time for peak tourist season."

The expansive showroom had an open floor plan with multiple free-standing glass and wooden display cases, each enclosing a different art form—Ancestral Pueblo pottery, Navajo weavings, ancient weapons from the early Basketmaker Period, traditional and contemporary Native American jewelry.

"Thank you for inviting me," I said. "Your inventory is impressive."

Lyle smiled and asked me to follow him. His cowboy boots gave him an extra two inches, making him slightly taller than I was in my hikers. His boots clunked on the bare wooden floor as he led me along a hallway to the rear of the building. There was an elegance about the man that went well with the studied layout of his gallery.

Halfway to the end of the hall, he turned right and motioned me into an office marked Private. "Have a seat," he said, gesturing toward a round conference table in the middle of the room. I sank into a red upholstered chair that reminded me of the furnishings at the Southwestern Cultures Foundation.

Lyle settled into his chair. "I'm so glad this worked out," he said. "Did you tell Gerry you were coming for a visit?"

"No. I didn't tell anyone. Thought I'd see what you suggested first. I'm still trying to make sense of Gerry's reaction regarding the bone hash. It's true the bones were stolen on my watch, but I feel he's being unfair blaming it all on me. I'd asked him to approve hiring a security team, but he didn't act on it until after those bones were stolen."

"Did you point that out to him?"

"Yes, but he was in no mood to listen. Then drugs were found hidden in the collections building after our meeting, as if the bone theft wasn't enough. Talk about a perfect storm! I get it Gerry has an overload of things to handle right now."

"You're right about that! I don't want to speak out of turn, but his actions toward you do seem harsh, especially in view of the rest of the chaos at that dig. Was it during that meeting with him that he fired you?"

"Yes, right before he stormed out, he told me not to expect continued employment when my probation ended. Apparently, someone on the NAAC is threatening to sue the company if the bones aren't recovered soon. I'm sure it was Juanita Joshwecoma."

"Could be. Sometimes she can be a little testy. And there's another threat for Gerry to handle. Anything else?"

"No, he left right after that. I didn't get a chance to tell him about the intruders Burk and I saw going into the collections building late at night. Of course, later we realized those intruders were part of the drug operations. I didn't know about the drug stash at the time Gerry and I met, but I did know about the intruders. That's why it still seemed necessary to me to hire security—for staff safety. But I never got to discuss that with him."

Lyle nodded. "Sounds like this situation started as a repeat of my last year at the dig. Burk told me a similar story about intruders. We called the sheriff's office, and a deputy came out, but they never found anything."

"Sometimes Burk does act a little strange, but this time his suspicions are vindicated—at least regarding intruders at the dig. Didn't Gerry tell you all this when he called you and said he'd fired me?"

"Actually, he did. That's why I called you offering my help. I'm going to grab a second cup of coffee. Would you like some?"

"Sure."

"How do you like it?"

"Cream and sugar."

He stood and excused himself and returned momentarily with two mugs.

"I put in a little sugar for you, but we seem to be out of cream." He handed me a mug.

"Thank you. No problem." I took a swig. The taste of burnt coffee beans overpowered the sugar, but I tried not to let on and downed half of it. Lyle sat down next to me and crossed his legs.

"So, what other reasons did Gerry give you for not re-upping on your contract?"

"May I be completely frank?" I asked.

"Yes, of course. I'll keep whatever you say in confidence."

"A few people at the dig have told me they believe Gerry and Jill Linden are having an affair. Then when I saw Gerry yesterday, he told me he and Fiona are divorcing. I think I caught him at a really bad time. I saw him in Winslow with Jill earlier the morning he fired me. That's on top of the NAAC threatening to sue and make things difficult for Rodgers & Associates. I think the theft of the bones just took him over the top—and that was *before* we'd discovered the drug stash."

"Yeah, Gerry told me he and Fiona are divorcing. I've been down that road myself. No question it can get ugly. Tell me something, Aideen. How would you characterize the quality of your work at the dig?"

I folded my hands in my lap underneath the table. "Honestly, I believe I've done a good job. I know better than to believe I could fill your shoes, but I've improved the process for keeping track of the artifacts in the short time I've been there, and I've implemented new procedures that have saved costs. For the most part, the other employees have been willing to follow my lead. There's no doubt in my mind I would continue to grow as director if given the chance."

"I see this job means a lot to you. You must know Gerry has a reasonable side. My suggestion—wait a few days to let him cool off and then give him a call. Set up a meeting at his office in Phoenix where he's more relaxed—then tell him what you just told me. Bring evidence of all the money you've saved the company. He's pragmatic—and he still has to answer to his board."

I raised the mug for another sip of coffee but thought better of it. I already had the beginnings of a sledgehammer of a headache, and although I didn't want to hurt Lyle's feelings, his coffee was god-awful.

"You still look a little leery," Lyle said. "Would it help if I put in a good word?"

I felt my shoulders ease a little. "That would be great. Everyone thinks so highly of you."

"Happy to do it," Lyle said.

A buzzer sounded in the front room, and he frowned. "I wonder who that is so early? Gallery hours are clearly posted." Lyle put his hands on the table and stood. "Let me see who it is. I'll be right back."

When he left the room, I stood up to stretch and leafed through a few magazines left in the center of the table—a brochure showing tours organized by the American Institute of Archaeology and a couple of magazines on coin collecting. I remembered Lyle was on his way to a coin show when I first met him and wondered if he was thinking of adding antique coins to his inventory.

The front door to the gallery slammed, followed by a stern rebuke to someone from Lyle.

"Put that out. There's no smoking in here."

A second male voice said something I couldn't understand.

"...later..." Lyle said. I sat down and rubbed my temples. The buzzer sounded again. Several minutes passed before Lyle returned to the conference room. He came through the doorway, shaking his head.

"Must be a new delivery man. Got his address wrong." Lyle stood by the table and added, "Aideen, I'm truly sympathetic to your situation. Gerry's a decent guy. If you remind him of your accomplishments at the dig, I believe he'll come around to a fair settlement. Just give him a few days to come to terms with what's going on. Gerry's been handling a lot at the dig as you know, and I'm sure he's stretched thin with a divorce on top of it."

Lyle headed for the door.

I stood and walked with him down the hall toward the showroom.

"Lyle, thanks for seeing me. May I use your restroom before I leave?"

"Of course. It's off the main gallery on the west side. Take your time. I'll wait for you up front."

My head throbbed. Cigarette smoke coming from the main gallery was faint but noticeable and made my headache worse.

I found the restroom and splashed cold water on my face. I didn't get headaches often, but when a migraine hit it could ruin the better part of a day. I blotted my face with a paper towel and tossed it in the waste receptacle—and missed. When I bent down to retrieve it, something behind the receptacle caught my eye—two elaborately beaded blue-and-white hair ties. I picked them up. One was still knotted. Caught in the knot were several long gray hairs. I thought back to whom I'd seen wearing hair ties like the ones in my hand: Chosovi.

My hands went cold. If these *were* Chosovi's hair ties, she must have been here. The ties hadn't been thrown in the trash can. They were hidden behind it. The can was full, nearly overflowing, and the restroom needed freshening—probably the reason the hair ties hadn't been discovered. Several vivid images from the last few days flashed through my mind. The red dot of a cigarette in the dark outside the collections building. The smell of smoke in the gallery. The muted voice of the delivery man who'd come to the wrong address this morning. His voice reminded me of someone.

I replaced the hair ties exactly as I'd found them, flushed the toilet, and pulled the cell from my pocket to call Frank. But my cell phone showed no bars. A cold chill engulfed me. I had to get out of there.

#

Lyle stood waiting for me near the front door. My head throbbed like evil little elves were standing behind my eyeballs pounding their way out. I exited through the front door Lyle held open and jogged around to the parking lot behind the gallery. I had to find a place where I had cell service fast and call Frank. I ran to the edge of the lot where I'd left Dakota, but her leash had been chewed in half, and she was gone! Panic over my missing dog and the acrid smell of cigarette smoke were the last things I remembered.

CHAPTER 37

I OPENED MY EYES in darkness so total that when I raised my hands in front of my face, I couldn't see them. I felt my own hot breath against my thumbs. My head felt ready to explode. My wrists were bound, palms together, my legs tied tightly at the ankles. I wanted to scream, but only a low moan came through the foul-smelling rag pulled tightly between my lips that tasted like motor oil. I jerked my head from side to side until I was dizzy. The gag didn't move.

Fear, like a venomous snake that knows it can move slowly, slithered the length of my spine and wrapped itself around my neck. It would be easy to choke, gagged as I was. If I wanted to live, I had to control my panic. I willed myself to breathe slowly, in and out, in and out, even breaths. I counted silently. One thousand and one. One thousand and two. When I'd counted to one thousand and fifty, I cleared my nose with a forceful exhalation.

I strained to sit up and promptly banged my head on a hard surface just above my head. Starbursts of pain exploded in front of me. Sitting completely upright was impossible. Panic seized me again. I slumped back onto the rough surface beneath me. My mind fought for control. My body shook. I groaned my despair.

Something groaned back.

I went absolutely still. I moaned again as loud as I could.

Something—someone—moaned in response. My mind spun in a dozen different directions. I squinted, hoping for a clue, but still saw nothing. I moaned again, but this time, I heard no answer.

Nightmarish memories took hold. Peru on the day Clay died. Had the end been like this for him? Unable to move. Struggling to breathe. But instead of this eerie stillness, Clay had seen and heard the swarms of black insects. Trees uprooting and tossed in the air like rag dolls. Clay knew the mind-numbing roar and the violence of the mudslide that killed him, not an all-encompassing darkness that made no sense. Clay's death had been loud and violent and quick. How long might it be before the thought of dying in this place might seem to me like a blessing?

Is it possible a person you loved can speak to you from beyond death? Not something we can know, but I believe Clay's spirit reached out to me from the boneyard of my own memory. His last act had been to shout something to me over the chaos. Lying bound and alone in the dark, I finally remembered what it was:

"Aideen, I love ..." And then he was gone.

The weeks we'd spent alone together that summer had built a new level of intimacy between us. Clay used everything he had to stay alive on that mountain. For both of us. Dozens of feet down the mountain, I saw his long arm push through the mud. But despite his strength of body and mind, Clay didn't make it.

Entombed in a space I could neither see nor comprehend, I finally accepted that there was nothing I could have done to save Clay. There was no shame in my surviving, even though Clay did not. Faced with the likelihood of my own death in a strange and unknowable prison a continent away, I felt the tight fist of guilt gripping my heart slowly open, and I forgave myself for being unable to save my husband's life. I knew if Clay were here, he'd do everything he could to save us both, no matter the odds. I had to do the same—and save myself.

With teeth gritted and stomach taut, I rolled onto my side and recognized the roughness against my face: solid rock. The red sandstone common to Sedona? Was I still there? My whole body tensed, and panic threatened to overtake me. I thought of Clay's resolve and knew allowing myself to panic would only increase my odds of dying here. I began the slow, mindful breathing exercises I'd learned to fight claustrophobia. Slow and even. Mindful. Peaceful.

I pieced together the last things I remembered after exiting Henderson's gallery. The cigarette smoke—first inside the gallery, then outside, right before I blacked out. I remembered how Alonzo acted surprised when he'd shown up at my trailer and I'd told him he was wanted for Tiponi's murder. He'd acted like he didn't know she was dead. But it was Alonzo who had gone to Walpi, attacked Cha'tima, and left him for dead. He'd gone there demanding Tiponi's photo, like he'd done when he showed up at my trailer. I wondered why he hadn't killed Chosovi. It must have been Alonzo who'd brought her to Henderson's gallery. Why?

I believed then that Alonzo was not the murderer of his ex-wife. He hadn't even known she was dead! Maybe he'd gone into hiding when he'd learned from me there was a warrant out for his arrest.

I squinted in the dark, reached my bound hands to my mouth, and tried to work my thumbs under the gag, but the cloth was too tightly wound around my head—so tight my jaw ached. The gag wouldn't budge.

Back on my side I rubbed the gag against the stone underneath me, breathing hard until the fumes trapped in the cloth forced me to stop. When my head cleared, I worked it again. Up and down, up and down, like a wind-up doll saying "yes."

I had to stop every few minutes. I'd had an asthma attack

when I painted our apartment in Philadelphia. Determined to make our living room a cheerful yellow respite from Philly's winter gray, I'd started painting on a sub-zero day without opening a window. No one would find me here, dizzy and disoriented, the way Clay had found me sprawled on paint-splattered newspapers in our living room. I slowed my pace. Every breath had to count. I fought to stay alert.

As I struggled to free myself, I wondered what would happen to my body if I died in this hellhole. Would an archaeologist in some distant century unearth my bones and speculate about the strange ritual that had taken place in this odd, confined space? I imagined how that scientist might assume my remains—bound and gagged as they were—to be a form of sacrifice, like the live burial of the Inca maiden, whose perfectly preserved remains I'd seen in an archaeological museum near Cuzco.

I willed these thoughts from my mind and gave my head an extra-hard thrust. The gag frayed apart. I spat out the remnants, took in a huge breath, and coughed. Clenching my jaw was the only thing that kept me from screaming. If my captors were nearby, alerting them to my gag-free state would not play in my favor. Remembering the moans, I spoke softly into the dark. "Is someone else here?"

Holding completely still, I heard another moan, so faint that I questioned if it was real. I called out again. Another muffled sound came in response—this time more distinct.

I jackknifed my body and stretched my bound hands toward my feet. My ankles were held together with something sticky; duct tape from the feel of it. My fingers had gone numb. I lay as I'd turned, worn out from all the effort and drifted off.

CHAPTER 38

I CAME TO IN the dark and was so disoriented I screamed until I was hoarse. Too late, I remembered the danger of being heard and fell silent. I heard another sound and held completely still to listen.

"Hello?" I called.

"Ummmmm."

It sounded as if the person moaning was as far away as another room. My voice hadn't sounded confined, either, the way it did in small spaces when I excavated. Like a blind worm, I inched my body toward the noise. I was unsure how long I'd been here. Without light, time moves in an unending circle, like a snake swallowing its tail. But there had to be clues.

I wasn't hungry. The last meal I'd had was breakfast at the Two Horse Café before driving to Sedona. And now, although I wanted to get to a bathroom soon, I wasn't desperate. That suggested I'd been tied up and unconscious for a matter of hours—not the days I'd feared when I first woke up. The realization gave me new energy.

I rolled onto my back and pulled my hands in opposite directions. They barely moved. Back on my side, I brought them to my mouth and nibbled at the binding on my wrists. It tasted like plastic-covered wire. Electrical wire? Rubbing that against the rock underneath me would never fray it apart like the gag. But somewhere around my bound wrists, the wire had to end—in a twist, perhaps, but there *would* be an end.

Bringing my wrists to my mouth, I bit at the plastic and explored the tight binding with my tongue. My hands throbbed. Something scratched my face. I traced the wire with my tongue and felt a sharp prick, tasting blood. I spat it out and then gripped the end of the wire with my teeth.

I tugged and pulled the end of the wire—around and around—spitting out blood and plastic. The length felt endless—until I freed my hands. The full flow of blood coursing back made my hands achy and warm. I flexed my fingers and twisted both wrists in a circle, lay back for a moment to stretch my arms, and took deep, life-giving breaths. I stretched until my arms regained full range of motion.

Encouraged by my success, I ran my hands down the front and sides of my cargo pants. My captors had taken my phone, but they'd missed the clasp knife I'd slipped into my side pocket. I tugged out the knife with a rush of excitement and laid it across my stomach. The pocket on the other side of my pants still held the digital watch I'd stuffed in there earlier. The watch's dial luminesced green. I felt around for the buttons on the side and engaged the one that lit the watch's face. The tiny light coming on in total darkness made me blink. The time read 4:17.

I pointed the light into the dark. By moving it around slowly, I was able to recognize the hard surface above me—the underside of a floor. I'd been left in a crawl space like the sheep killed under my trailer, the way Dakota had been left to die.

Dakota! What had happened to my dog? Softly, I said her name. At the sound of my voice, I heard another muffled response. Freeing my feet became an obsession. I pointed the watch toward my boots. The shadow of something small—two to three inches long—crept up the duct tape binding my ankles. The thing was so light I felt nothing even as it crept off the duct tape and onto my pants, but as it stepped closer into the dim watch light, I saw the raised stinger.

Tension ratcheted through my whole body. Slowly, tail in the air, the scorpion continued its path up my leg.

With the watch in my right hand pointed at the scorpion, I carefully reached with my left hand for the clasp knife resting on my stomach. Bark scorpions exhibit an unusual behavior: they hunt in packs. If there was one bark scorpion down here, odds were there were others, preying on roaches and other insects. And now, me.

The watch light suggested movement a little beyond my feet. A packmate? But my most immediate problem was the scorpion on my leg. It had crawled only inches south of my knee. Slowly, I raised the knife. I wondered how far I could flick it if I got the knife blade underneath it. But what if I missed? The knife was in my left hand, and I was right-handed.

I brought my hands together to switch the knife to my right hand, the watch to my left, moving ever so carefully. The scorpion stopped its slow march up my leg. I went rigid. It lowered the stinger in its tail. I held my breath.

Something crawled onto my neck from behind. I shrieked and swatted my neck convulsively and immediately felt a sharp stab worse than a dozen bee stings through the leg of my pants. I swiped with the knife blade. I had to get it off before it stung again! But a second sting stabbed my kneecap. I slashed across my knee with the knife... and cleaved the scorpion in two.

My leg hurt like hell and began to swell. I sat as upright as the coffin-like space allowed. Bark scorpion fatalities were rare in adults, but people allergic to bees were more likely to have a bad reaction. And I was allergic to bees.

Another moan sounded in the darkness.

My breathing grew labored. I struggled not to hyperventilate. I counted aloud slowly, concentrating on slowing my breathing and my racing heart. One thousand and one... One thousand and two. My swelling knee did nothing to ease my sense of urgency. Already, the fabric in my pants felt tight.

"I'm getting us out of here," I rasped. "Can you hear me?" I called, louder, and heard what could have been a faint response.

"I have a knife! I'm freeing my feet. Make a sound. Whenever you can."

This time, a sound came back louder, muffled, and forced. Carefully, I flipped to my side, fearing I could be risking another scorpion attack. Bending my knees, I pointed the watch's faint light at my bound ankles with my left hand and sawed through most of the duct tape with my right.

Footsteps sounded overhead! I held still and listened. The footsteps were loud, like cowboy boots on a wooden floor. The sound Lyle's boots had made crossing his gallery when I'd arrived. Was I under his showroom? In that moment the identity of the other person bound and hidden down here with me seemed clear: Chosovi.

She'd been missing when Frank and I found Cha'tima. Alonzo must have brought Chosovi to Sedona after he snuck out of Walpi with Tiponi's picture. But why? If she was down here in this crawl space, obviously he meant her harm like he did Cha'tima. So, had Alonzo been working for Henderson? It seemed an unlikely alliance. The educated former dig director hooking up with a doper with a record? Then I remembered *why* Alonzo had a record. He'd been arrested for cooking and selling meth. And drugs were just discovered at the dig—in a very well-hidden stash. Close to canyon country famous for harboring meth labs.

I thought back to the night I'd watched the rear entrance to the collections building and recognized Alonzo's voice. Alonzo had been the one shooting. And the other voice, the rational voice telling him to stop. Coming from an accomplice of average height and build. Henderson!

I remembered Henderson's bitter coffee and the way he'd watched me drink it, studying me oh so casually. The headache that started even before I left his galley. What a betrayal! I had trusted Henderson, looked up to him—and he and Alonzo had trussed me up like so much meat and stuffed me in this hole.

It took a lot of work to gag, tie up, and hide an unconscious person. Why hadn't he just killed me? I knew then Henderson had plans to dump my body elsewhere. And from the sound of the moaning, I wasn't going to be the only one dumped. I rubbed my hand on my leg where I'd taken the stings. The muscles around the welts had begun to cramp.

The fact I hadn't told anyone where I was going suddenly showed itself as the hubris it was. Why *hadn't* I told Frank what I was doing? In the honesty of the darkness, I realized I had strong feelings for Frank that I hadn't felt comfortable sharing with him. Frank was another reason that if there was even a small chance someone would open a door into this crawl space, I had to be ready. I blew out a breath, concentrated on ignoring my aching leg, and resumed my attack on the duct tape binding my ankles until I'd freed them.

The watch showed it was now after five. More footsteps. Softer this time, like a person wearing athletic shoes. Overhead someone spoke. "What're we gonna to do with that redheaded bitch?"

I flinched. *Alonzo's* voice.

"Take her to that remote cave in the Superstition Mountains like I told you," Henderson said. "And don't fuck this one up like you did with that archaeologist. He's still alive. You didn't hit him hard enough."

"He owed me big time for all his unpaid tweaks."

"Where did you get off selling meth to someone at the

dig? You are beyond stupid," Henderson scoffed. "And you shouldn't have brought that old woman here, either."

"Fuck you, Henderson. She cut me so bad I had to make her drive me here or I'd have bled to death. I'm tired of doing your dirty work. You owe me money."

"Shut up and get down in the hole, Alonzo. We have to get that old woman out before she dies down there. The Feds have cadaver dogs. We'll settle this later."

Wood creaked. I flattened and pushed the watch light button off' and shoved the remnants of duct tape cut from my ankles beneath me. Closing and palming the knife, I clasped my hands in front of me—like they were when they'd been bound—and I held my ankles together. The trapdoor creaked up.

CHAPTER 39

THE LIGHT FLOODING INTO the crawl space blinded me for a few moments, even with my eyes closed. I felt a sudden rush of air. The sounds of the trapdoor opening came from my left toward my feet. I barely breathed.

Through slit eyes I saw Alonzo slide into the hole, waving a flashlight. I forced myself to lie completely still and breathe slowly.

"The old woman still alive?" Henderson called down.

The beam from the flashlight moved further to my left. "She's still breathing but she's out. Looks like she pissed herself. Stinking bitch cut my arm. Want me to finish her?"

"No, I told you the Feds have cadaver dogs. You never should have brought her here."

"Like I told you, I needed her to drive me off that mesa after she cut me."

"Drag her to the opening. We'll roll her up in one of those old blankets and put her in my van."

I focused on my breathing—slow and even, slow and even. One gasp, one sound unlike someone unconscious, and my chance to escape would be gone. From the sound of the grunts and the expletives, removing a limp body took all of Alonzo's strength.

"Henderson! Come grab her and pull her up," Alonzo said. Henderson's footsteps moved closer to the opening. He grunted. Chosovi was silent. Alonzo moved up and out of the space.

The trapdoor slammed shut. Cowboy boots retreated. It took all I had not to scream. How long would I have before they came back for *me*? Ten minutes? Twenty? I flipped the clasp knife open in my right hand, raised the watch in my left and punched the watch light back on to get my bearings. The trapdoor had opened to my left. I shone the light overhead and crawled with my back as close to the underside of the floor as space allowed, looking for a cut in the pattern that would reveal the door's exact location. I saw something moving on the ground in front of me. I shone the tiny light down. Another scorpion crawled toward my knee—the knee that hadn't taken any stings.

"Not on your life, you nasty booger," I muttered, killing it with the clasp knife.

Footsteps overhead. They were already back! I hadn't had time to figure out exactly where the trapdoor would open. I crouched where I thought it would lift with the secured end in front of me, then switched off the watch light and tucked it in my pocket. With jaw clamped shut, I tightened my grip on the clasp knife. When their voices drew closer, the one word I recognized was "redhead."

I readied the knife. My heart pounded so hard, I feared it was audible.

The trapdoor creaked up. Light poured in from the gallery, throwing a man's shadow onto the crawl space floor.

"Okay, get down there and hand her up," Henderson said. "Fucking pain in the ass."

Alonzo landed in the crawl space in a low stoop with his backside toward me. I scooted toward him, feet first, and kicked him hard with everything I had. He sprawled face forward with a roar and banged his head on the rock floor. A dirty bandage encircled the upper part of his right arm.

"What the hell happened?" Henderson yelled down.

Before Alonzo could answer, I scrambled onto hands and knees and crawled forward as fast as I could toward the light. Alonzo moaned and rubbed his head. I made it to the opening. The trapdoor lay flat on the gallery floor above. Alonzo turned and saw me. He looked dazed, but he moved toward me. Before he could reach me, I stood up inside the hole. Henderson stood on top of the flattened trapdoor, but he was weaponless. I stabbed him in the thigh with my clasp knife. His hand shot to the wound, and he staggered backward. He jumped off the trapdoor and grasped the end of it in both hands, raised it up, and slammed it against me. I pushed back with all my strength. Henderson gained leverage on me, pushing down with a grunt of effort and forcing me into a squat inside the crawl space underneath the half-open trapdoor.

Alonzo grabbed me from behind. I pivoted and stabbed his bandaged arm. He screamed, lost his balance, and fell back holding his bleeding arm. Henderson had backed off the trapdoor, and I shoved it open in one clean push. It banged flat against the gallery floor. An ever-expanding red flower bloomed on the front of Henderson's pants where I'd stabbed him. He grabbed a large ceramic pot from a nearby display and smashed it on the floor. I palmed my knife and propped both hands on the floor behind me, then I boosted myself up and out of the crawl space.

Alonzo crawled back to the opening and stood up inside it. Standing above him, I took another swipe at him with the knife, but he jerked out of the way. I pivoted toward Henderson, who lunged at me with a jagged shard. Alonzo stood and pushed himself out of the crawl space.

I put a display case between myself and both men and backed against a wall. Alonzo pulled a knife from his pocket and switched it open. A rivulet of blood ran down his re-injured arm. Henderson advanced from the opposite side, feinting with the shard. I stood cornered between them.

"You've got the knife!" Henderson yelled. "Finish her!"

I braced myself, jaw clenched, pulse drumming in my ears. I knew in my fury I could take out one of them, but two—maybe not. I held my breath and braced for the attack, pivoting between Henderson and Alonzo.

"Did you know Henderson killed your ex-wife?" I shouted at Alonzo.

Alonzo jerked around to glare at Henderson.

"Don't listen to her bullshit," Henderson said. "I didn't kill Tiponi."

"He's lying. Help me stop him," I said. "He killed Tiponi because she knew about the drug ring you and Henderson were running. He stole your knife—the one with your prints all over it—and killed her the same night you came back to the motel room in Tuba."

"Shut up," Henderson said. He lunged toward me brandishing the shard. "Do it, Alonzo. Kill her!"

Hot outside air blasted across my face.

A snarling gray blur streaked across the gallery. Dakota.

She lunged at Henderson, knocked him down and stood with her forelegs on his chest. Henderson cursed and tried to push Dakota off. Dakota growled, her fangs inches from Henderson's face. An overhead track light glinted off Alonzo's raised knife. He looked back and forth between Henderson and me.

"Get the fucking dog off me!" Henderson yelled. He tried to scramble up. Dakota sank her teeth into his cheek, barely missing his eye. Henderson let out an agonized shriek and batted at Dakota with both hands. Dakota backed away from Henderson, letting him crawl away, bleeding profusely. Dakota stood her ground between the former dig director and me. When Henderson backed toward the gallery entrance, Dakota turned toward Alonzo and stalked him.

Alonzo waved the knife at the dog. "Call it off, bitch."

Before I could say a word, Dakota lunged for Alonzo's

throat. Alonzo brought his knife down hard before the dog was on him. With an awful sucking sound, the knife cut through flesh and cartilage.

Blood spurted everywhere. Dakota went down with a yelp but rose on shaky legs and lunged again. Before her legs gave out on her, she clamped her jaws on Alonzo's knife arm. He dropped the knife. It spun across the floor, a swirling silver circle drizzling blood. With a face full of pain, Alonzo pulled free from Dakota's weakening jaws and scrambled after the knife. Dakota sank to the floor, panting. My heart seized when Alonzo retrieved the knife and staggered toward my dog.

"No!" I screamed. Alonzo tried to push past me, but I hurled myself at him and stabbed him in the stomach.

He screamed and fell to the floor holding his gut.

I withdrew the bloody knife and ran to Dakota. I sliced off a strip of cloth from the bottom of my T-shirt and squatted beside her. She snapped at me from her cloud of pain. Her left ear had been slashed half off, dangling by precarious flesh and cartilage. I grasped her by the collar from behind her head to hold her down and put pressure on her wound, trying to stop the bleeding. Blood soaked the strip of cloth. I spoke softly until my dog whimpered and recognized me. My eyes darted between the dog and Alonzo.

Henderson pulled himself up and shuffled closer to the front door, his face swollen and bloody. Alonzo lay clutching his stomach and groaning. All my attention went to Dakota. She panted heavily. A string of drool puddled on the floor beneath her mouth. My eyes blurred.

I held Dakota down with my leg on her neck while I tore off more strips from my shirt and wrapped and tied them tightly around her head. I stroked her gently, told her I loved her and that she had to stay. It was the best I could do.

Henderson collapsed beside the front door. Alonzo had not moved and still lay holding his gut, blood seeping out between his fingers.

I left Dakota with a sob in my throat, praying Alonzo and Henderson were too wounded to hurt her anymore, and I ran to the phone in the gallery office to call for help.

As soon as the 9-1-1 operator had the location and details, I ran through the back door into the parking lot to look for Chosovi, my hands shaking, my heart filled with dread.

CHAPTER 40

An inert form wrapped in a dirty blanket lay on the floor behind the driver's seat inside the locked gallery van. Three police cars careened into the parking lot. An ambulance turned down the alley, killing its siren. Six cops rushed from their vehicles.

"Are you the one who called?"

"Yes. My friend's locked in the back of that van. Please hurry."

He looked through the window, then tried the door. "Stand back."

He pulled a nightstick from his duty belt, smashed the window on the driver's side then reached inside for the master lock and released it. Another cop opened the sliding door. Two medics entered the van and crouched beside Chosovi.

"Who's inside the building?" a cop asked.

"The two men who attacked me. Both in bad shape. One was beside the front door when I escaped."

"Is anyone inside armed?"

"One of them, Ray Alonzo, has a knife. He was lying on the floor when I left."

Four cops rushed through the back door of the gallery.

The policeman standing by eyed my tattered and bloody T-shirt. "You look like you could use some help yourself."

"I'm not injured, but I'm really thirsty," I said. "My dog was hurt helping me—it's her blood. I've got to get back inside and help her."

He went to his cruiser and came back with a bottle of water. I watched the EMTs cut away Chosovi's gag and remove the filthy blanket wrapped around her. They covered her nose and mouth with an oxygen mask connected to a tank carted from the ambulance.

Seeing Chosovi's wild, unbound hair, her stained dress, her shallow breathing, I thought how her family had done what they could to protect Tiponi, but they'd lost her anyway. I could only hope Chosovi would not be lost to them as well.

Another EMT rolled up a gurney, and two of them gently lifted Chosovi onto it. I reached for her hand, leaned close, and said her name. She opened her eyes and looked at me with a flicker of recognition.

"You family?" an EMT asked.

I shook my head.

"Sorry, we can't let you ride with her if you're not family."

He told me the name of the hospital where they were taking Chosovi and advised me to call later for a status update. They lifted her into the ambulance and sped from the parking lot, emergency lights flashing.

There was nothing more I could do for Chosovi. I squeezed my eyes shut for a moment and wondered in what condition I'd find my dog. I hurried to the back door to the gallery as more vehicles converged on the parking lot.

A Sedona police officer blocked me from entering.

"Please, I'm the one who called. I've got to get back inside to help my dog. She was hurt defending me."

"Sorry about your dog, but we can't allow you inside."

Exhausted and spent, my heart sank—until a voice behind me said, "This is a federal case, and I'm a federal officer. Let her in."

Frank flashed his badge, then he looked at me and said, "Aideen, it looks to me like the first thing we should do is get you to a hospital."

"No way, Frank. I wouldn't have made it without Dakota. It's *her* blood all over me. We have to save her."

We rushed inside together.

#

Dakota barely raised her head when we found her in the exact spot where I'd left her. We wrapped her in an old blanket left on the gallery floor that was probably meant for me.

Frank asked one of the cops on-site to help him gently carry the dog outside to his van while I made a beeline for the bathroom.

It was a shock seeing myself in the mirror. The skin on my face was rubbed raw from removing the gag. My eyes were bloodshot, my tattered clothes a mess of bloodstains and grime. The adrenaline rush from fighting off Alonzo and Henderson had begun to wear thin. My leg throbbed from the scorpion stings, but my breathing was even, and I knew from experience with bee stings that I hadn't had a serious allergic reaction. I used the restroom, splashed water on my face, and then ran as fast as I could to find Frank in the parking lot.

I remembered how Chosovi had looked at our last meeting in Walpi—her careful grooming, her shy and winsome smile, and her artful hand gestures. I vowed to hold that image of her in my mind like a prayer.

Frank sped down Main Street and pulled up in front of an emergency veterinary clinic. I jumped from the van, pressed the call button, and waited for the system to ring through. A sign in the window advertised 24-hour service, but the front lobby was dark. Two veterinary technicians responded minutes later and rushed through the door pushing a gurney. They wheeled Dakota into surgery while a third vet tech met us in the lobby.

After completing the clinic's forms, I sat with Frank in the waiting room, hoping for the best. Frank put his arm around me, ignoring the filth that clung to me. I'd rinsed off most of the dog's blood from my hands in the bathroom, but a dark red-brown line still showed under my nails. The sight of it brought tears to my eyes. I leaned into Frank's strength, and he just held me.

When I regained my composure, I asked, "How did you find me?"

"I went by your place early this morning and when you weren't there, I figured you'd gone for a run with Dakota. I went into town for breakfast, and when I walked into the Two Horse, that waitress who served us last night told me I'd missed you by several hours. Something felt off, so when I got back to the dig and you hadn't returned, I got a key to the office from Burk and found the note you'd left on Nova's desk. When you weren't back by three, I knew something had gone wrong."

"But how did you know where to find me in Sedona?"

"GPS. I called Nova at her apartment—Burk gave me her number. She came to the dig and figured out which van you'd taken and looked up the vehicle's ID. I called the GPS company and got them to locate the van. Why didn't you tell me you were coming here, Aideen? I would have come with you."

"Henderson said he'd help me strategize how to keep my job. I never expected to wind up in his crawl space."

"What a sicko," Frank said.

"Yeah. I knew something was off when I found Chosovi's hair ties hidden in the gallery bathroom. I tried to call you, but someone knocked me out in the parking lot before I had cell service."

"Alonzo may have been working for Henderson for some time," Frank said. "But that doesn't explain why Tiponi's photo was so important to him."

While we waited to hear about Dakota, I used Frank's cell to call the hospital where they'd taken Chosovi. Alonzo or Henderson had taken my phone when they placed me in the crawl space. Now who knew if I'd get it back. Chosovi was in intensive care, but the hospital refused to provide more details until her family was notified.

Exhausted and spent, I gave Frank his phone back and asked him if he would call Lorraine Humetewa. "Someone has to let Cha'tima know his wife has been found alive."

#

When the emergency vet came out several hours later, I was unable to read his face. My eyes filled before he spoke. I held my breath. He sat down beside us.

"I think we have your dog stabilized, Ms. Connor," he said smiling. "She's receiving fluids, and she'll have to remain in the clinic for a few days, but other than possibly losing that damaged ear, we think she'll fully recover."

I smiled and thanked him.

"Would you give us a phone number where we can reach you?" the vet asked.

I looked at Frank. "Would you give him your cell number?"

Frank kept one arm around me and reached with his other arm to give the vet his card.

CHAPTER 41

ON THE WAY OUT of the veterinary clinic, I finally told Frank about the scorpion stings. He shook his head and drove me to the same hospital where Chosovi was being treated.

The emergency room doc told us over twelve hundred species of scorpions live in Arizona, and only the bark scorpion is considered potentially life-threatening. Since I hadn't had an allergic reaction, I'd probably been bitten by one of the other eleven hundred and ninety-nine. Otherwise, I wouldn't have made it out of Henderson's crawl space.

The ER nurse cleaned and bandaged the stings. She cautioned that scorpion stings have a cumulative effect, each subsequent sting eliciting a worse reaction than the previous one, similar to bee stings. Her advice was that I should avoid them in the future.

Frank called David Archer and learned he'd driven up from the dig to the Desert Rose. He was on his way to the hospital to interview me.

I rolled my eyes. "Can't it wait? I have to get out of these filthy rags and soak off the last of that crawl space. The way I look is scaring people."

Frank laughed. "Yeah, I was worried that ER nurse would take one look at you and recommend the psych ward.

I asked David to wait till tomorrow, but he's hell-bent on interviewing you while the ordeal is fresh in your mind. Good thing this is a federal case, or the local cops would insist on speaking with you immediately as well."

"Nothing like punishment for being a victim."

Frank winced. We walked together to intensive care to check on Chosovi.

The charge nurse stared at me and asked, "Were you looking for the emergency room?"

Frank told her I'd been in an accident but was out of danger. We asked about Chosovi's status. Since we weren't relatives, the only information she could give us was that Mrs. Honovi's condition had improved. Frank left his card, said we were friends, and we would appreciate an update after her family arrived and gave consent.

Archer sat waiting for us in the main lobby and was visibly shocked when he saw me. He handed me the Penn Museum carry-all I used as a purse and said, "Found this outside in the parking lot. I thought bending the rules a little to bring it to you might help after all you've been through."

I peeked inside, relieved to see my ID, and thanked him.

"Sedona police found Henderson and Alonzo still in the gallery. Both were taken away in ambulances, Alonzo to emergency surgery," he said. "What motivated you to come down here to visit Henderson in the first place?"

"I was trying to save my job."

"Why would you think Henderson could help?"

"He's friends with my boss, and I looked up to him. He's both admired and respected in archaeology."

"Then why on earth would he start dealing drugs?"

"I've been told plenty of meth labs have been springing up out here in remote canyons. Henderson could have run into a lab in the back country when he worked at the dig. He saw an opportunity and figured out a way to exploit it. Could be how he funded that expensive inventory he has in his gallery."

"Frank said you claim Henderson murdered that woman in Hano," Archer said. "What made you come to that conclusion?"

"Henderson would have visited Walpi and Hano plenty of times as dig director. He probably met Alonzo in Hano when Alonzo and Tiponi were still married. I think he fed Alonzo's meth habit, partly as payment for cooking the drug and partly to control him. He figured Tiponi knew about their drug operation, and when she and Alonzo split up, he decided he needed to silence her.

"Henderson saw the perfect opportunity to pin her murder on Alonzo when he learned Alonzo was meeting Tiponi in Hano to pick up his belongings. That would place Alonzo at the crime scene like Henderson wanted.

"Alonzo had already left Hano long before Henderson arrived in Hano that night to murder Tiponi. Alonzo returned to the motel and found me in 'his' room. When he didn't get his photo back, he followed me to Taos a few days later, thinking I still had it. I believe Alonzo had no idea Tiponi was murdered that night," I added. "After Taos Tribal Police released him, he was able to get his truck off their land before a warrant went out for his arrest. After he confronted me in my trailer at the dig he must have gone into hiding. There are plenty of places on the Navajo Rez that most people don't know about—not even the Feds."

"Interesting theory, but at this point, Alonzo is still the primary suspect," Archer said.

"Tribal police found the murder weapon," Frank said. "Doesn't look good for Alonzo. His prints are all over it."

"Evidence exists that could prove Alonzo was not in Hano when Tiponi was murdered," I said.

"What kind of evidence?" Archer asked.

"Officer Humetewa lifted Alonzo's blood off the motel doorjamb in the room I had in Tuba City and took it to the

Arizona state lab. You could check the DNA for a match. If the medical examiner can pinpoint the time of Tiponi's death, Alonzo's DNA from the blood in my room could place him in Tuba City instead of Hano at the time of her death. Humetewa will have a record of the time he showed up to interview me after Alonzo escaped."

Archer considered that then said, "What about Tiponi's photo? Why do you think Alonzo came after you for that?"

"I have no idea," I said. "We have to find it."

"I think you've been involved enough at this point, Aideen," Frank said. "Why would you even care about that picture now that you're safe?"

"That picture is what got me into this mess in the first place. I want to know why."

"Frank and I'll look into it," Archer said. "You could probably use some rest at this point."

Frank and I stood to leave.

"Just one more question," Archer said. "What do you think the murder has to do with all the creepy activity around your trailer?"

"I don't think it was connected to the murder. Henderson wanted me gone so he could resume his drug operation. He knew I rarely left the dig. So, he decided to scare me off the job and discredit my reputation—maybe even get his old job back now that he's recovered from cancer."

"You believe Henderson carried out those threats?"

"Henderson and Alonzo. The timing was right for one of them to have been at the dig every time," I said. Henderson probably made the fake *paho* and stuck it in my trunk. He knew how they were made and how to construct it without the proper symbolism. And Alonzo must have killed that poor sheep under my trailer and put sheep's blood in the trunk of my car."

Frank stood and offered me his arm. "That's enough for now, David. I'll give you a call in the morning."

I stood, took Frank's arm, and laughed.

"What's so funny all of a sudden?" Frank said as we headed for the door.

"This has to be a first for you, offering your arm to a woman who looks like she escaped from a morgue."

"At least you escaped."

\#

Frank found us two rooms in an inn on Sedona's main drag.

"Do you have a change of clothes in that carrier Archer brought you?" he asked.

"No, and these rags I'm wearing deserve a bonfire."

"There are probably half a dozen tourist shops along the strip. I'll go buy you a couple of T-shirts and a pair of jeans. What's your size?"

I told him, and he said, "I'll get you settled in your room and be back in a few hours with clothes and dinner. Are you going to be all right by yourself?"

"As long as I know you're coming back."

\#

I answered Frank's knock a few hours later clutching the sheet I'd wrapped around myself sarong fashion.

"Nice outfit," he commented.

Frank strode across the room with an overflowing grocery bag full of deli treats, fruit, French bread, and bottles of wine. He set the bag on the table in the kitchenette. Then he handed me a second bag he'd tucked under his arm.

"I really like what you're wearing now, but if you want to go change, here's what I bought," he said. "Mind if I douse a few lights while you're getting dressed?"

I'd turned every light on even before it got dark.

"That's fine," I said. "The light helped while I was here alone."

I carried the bag into the bathroom. Inside were three

T-shirts, a pair of jeans, lingerie, and hiking socks. All fit perfectly, which delighted me and also embarrassed me a little. I chose the gold-colored T-shirt with a wine-colored graphic of Kokopelli on the front.

"Come drink to your resurrection," Frank said when I reappeared.

He'd found two wine glasses in the kitchenette and uncorked a bottle of red. I slipped into the small dining nook—even smaller than the one in my trailer—and Frank sat down opposite me and poured the wine.

"How're you feeling?" he asked.

"Relieved. Betrayed. Afraid in the dark. Have you heard anything about Alonzo's condition? Is he likely to make it?"

"He's still in surgery. Gut wounds are tough, but I heard there's a chance he'll pull through."

I looked down at my hands, one wrapped around the wine glass, the other on the tabletop. My nails were ragged, but they were clean. I'd finally soaked off all the blood and the crawl space grime. "I've never attacked anyone before."

Frank regarded me for a moment, reached for my hand, and said, "Not like you had much choice. How was it for you being alone here after I left?"

"I would have felt a lot safer if I'd had Dakota with me ..."

"Would you like me to stay here with you tonight, Aideen? The room has a rollout. I can give you some privacy but be close by."

"Yes, I would really like that, Frank. I'm not quite myself yet."

He smiled. "Happy to oblige. You'll be glad to know that while you were soaking, I wrangled an update on Chosovi."

"How'd you do that?"

"I had to use my BLM creds to get someone at the hospital to talk to me. She's improved with the intake of fluids. The ICU nurse said they're hopeful she'll regain consciousness soon."

"That's good news. Anything about Cha'tima?"

"Called Lorraine. Her brother-in-law is on his way here with Cha'tima. The medicine man was released from the hospital late yesterday, and he's doing pretty well."

"The Humetewas really came through for us."

"I'll drink to that," Frank said. We clinked glasses. Frank saw my hand shaking and asked if I was all right.

"I guess it's starting to sink in how tonight might have ended. I could still be down in that hole or dead by now if Henderson hadn't planned on dumping Chosovi and me elsewhere."

As the wine worked its magic and I began to relax, I told Frank some of the insights I'd had while bound up in the dark. The unshakeable guilt I'd finally been able to release because I couldn't save Clay. The hope I'd had for putting my life back together in a place so wild and different from the one I'd left behind.

Frank held my hand while I talked, and I realized his ability to listen was something I truly valued in him.

I looked into his eyes for a long moment and knew Frank was another reason I regretted that I'd be leaving soon. I was just beginning to get to know him. I withdrew my hand and changed the subject. "You sure you're willing to stay with me tonight?" I asked jokingly. "I can't promise I won't have another nightmare!"

"I figured that might come with the territory," he said with a laugh. "Maybe we should leave a few of those lights on."

CHAPTER 42

IT WAS PAST NOON when I woke up in my Kokopelli T-shirt. I slipped on the new pair of jeans, stumbled past the folded-up rollout, and found Frank on his phone in the kitchenette.

He saw me and disconnected. "You look almost like yourself except for those scrapes on your face. Did you sleep well?"

"I did. Thanks for staying with me. I doubt I would have slept at all if I'd been alone last night."

He smiled. "Not such a bad assignment, pinch-hitting for Dakota."

I rolled my eyes. "It meant more than that and you know it, Frank."

Frank laughed, and when he looked at me, he was smiling. "I made some coffee," he said. "Why don't you come sit down and have some and I'll tell you what I've learned."

I filled a cup from a carafe by the sink and sat opposite Frank in the small booth in the kitchenette.

"I just got off the phone with Archer. Our team found Alonzo's pickup ditched a few blocks from the Desert Rose. Archer asked me to meet him by the truck in about an hour to do a cursory search of the vehicle. Right now he's tied up with the Sedona police."

"Frank, you've got to take me with you to look at

Alonzo's truck. They haven't found Tipono's photo in the Desert Rose, have they?"

"Not so far," he said slowly. "Why are you so obsessed with that photo?"

"I need closure, Frank. The events tied to that photo have cost me my job—could have cost me my life. I want to know why Alonzo was so determined to get it back."

"You can ride with me, but you'll have to stay in my van if Archer's around."

"Then why don't we leave now while we have some time before he gets there? Just give me a minute to brush my teeth."

"Might as well brush that wild mane of yours while you're at it," Frank said. "You look like a redheaded lioness."

I gave him an amused look and headed for the bathroom.

#

The black truck had been parked in a little-used alley a short distance from the Desert Rose. Frank checked the VIN number against the information Archer emailed, confirming it was Alonzo's truck.

"He must have dropped off Chosovi then moved his truck to hide it from Henderson," I said.

"Next thing I know you'll be applying for my job." Frank said.

He pulled a fresh pair of latex gloves from the glove box in the van.

"Don't get your hopes up too much, Aideen. If Archer gets here early, remember to beat it back to the van, and be sure not to touch anything. If you see something interesting, let me handle it. Don't even brush up against the vehicle."

We circled the dusty black pickup and looked through the windows. A picture of the Virgin Mary dangled from the rearview mirror. A plastic Jesus rode on the dashboard, his arms stretched upward as if reaching for the Madonna. The truck had a super cab with four doors—two normal-sized doors in the front of the cab, two smaller ones behind. Frank tried the door on the driver's side.

"That's odd. He left it unlocked."

"Maybe he was high," I said.

The floorboard on the passenger's side was littered with empty cigarette packs spotted with blood, and there was blood on the seat. "Alonzo said he'd made Chosovi come here because she cut him. She must have been the driver."

Frank nodded and motioned me to stay behind him, and I followed him around.

He opened the passenger door and checked the glove box. There were receipts from maintenance, but nothing out-of-the-ordinary.

Frank returned all the papers and reached around from the front to unlock the small door behind the passenger's side. A sunscreen lay folded on the back seat. He felt around under it in the spaces between the seat cushions, pulled out a pocketknife and a handful of spare change, all of which he returned.

We walked back around to the driver's side of the truck. A dozen or so dog-eared girlie magazines littered the floor behind the driver's seat. Frank flipped through the pages of the one on top.

"Having fun?" I asked.

"Not yet," he said with a smirk.

He looked through a few more magazines, found nothing of interest, and then put them all back. The cab appeared clean.

"What about the carpet?" I asked.

Frank used his pocketknife to work the carpet out from under the seat track, grasped it in both gloved hands and yanked. A framed photo lay face down underneath the carpet. Frank turned it over, and the black-and-white image of Tiponi stared back.

"That's it," I said. "Never thought I'd be glad to see it again."

Frank turned the frame over and looked on the back, held it up, and inspected the edges.

"Whatever its secret, it's not on the outside or the frame," I said. "I looked it over when I first saw it in the motel room. You've got to take it apart."

"I can't do that, Aideen. This is evidence. This truck will be impounded, and the techs'll go over anything and everything inside it with every gadget they have in their high-tech arsenal. We need to leave it for them. If there's something important inside, they'll find it."

"What can it hurt, Frank? You're wearing gloves. We aren't going to remove anything. This is my one chance to know why Alonzo tried to kill me for that damn photo."

"The techs will let me know."

I looked into Frank's eyes. "There's no guarantee of that. Frank, and you know it. I've been through hell because of that photo, and I want to know why."

Frank set the photo down on the back seat, looked at his watch, and turned toward me. His face was so close I could smell his aftershave. Then he closed the small gap between us and kissed me. I surprised myself and kissed him back, no holds barred.

"I thought you were worried about time," I said, pulling away.

"Hell yes, I'm worried about time. I'm only doing this for you."

"I know. How much time you think we have before Archer gets here?"

"Not much."

"Let's take it to your van and use your pocketknife."

We made a dash for the van and piled into the front seat. Frank worked each of the four prongs up on the back side of the picture frame and removed the cardboard backing. Inside another piece of white cardboard protected the back of the photo. A thin plastic container about two inches square was taped to the white cardboard. Frank carefully lifted the small container off the cardboard and held it up.

"What is it?" I asked.

"Looks like a coin holder," Frank said. "This type allows you to see the coin on all sides, even the edge. They're used to protect valuable coins."

Frank looked at his watch. "We're out of time, Aideen. Stay here. I need to put this back."

"Wait a minute. Let me hold it up at eye level so you can get a photo with your phone."

Frank grabbed his cell from a holder on his belt. "Hurry," he said. Hold it still."

The silver coin was larger than a quarter and showed a majestic-looking woman seated behind a shield that read "Liberty." She held a pennant on a staff in her left hand. The date "1870" stood out in large numerals at the bottom of the coin.

A BLM van turned down the alley. Frank handed me his phone and gathered the cardboard pieces from the picture frame and reassembled the photo as we'd found it. I pocketed his phone and jumped out of the van.

"Where are you going?" Frank asked.

"Go put the photo back and ditch those gloves," I said. "I'll take care of Archer."

Archer didn't bother to hide his surprise when he rolled to a stop. He parked his van on the opposite side of the street and jumped down. "What are you doing here?" he asked.

"Hi, David. I asked Frank to bring me along. I guess I'm still feeling a little shaky after that ordeal. I'm also wondering about the van I drove down. Frank said the BLM techs would probably search it?"

"I'll have to get back to you on that. It was still in the

gallery parking lot when I left. Where is Frank?"

"Waiting on you," Frank said, sauntering up. "Let's take a look at the vehicle."

CHAPTER 43

IF ARCHER SUSPECTED ANYTHING, he didn't let on. He checked the truck's VIN against the email from his office and confirmed the numbers matched, then he handed Frank a pair of latex gloves and slipped on a pair himself.

"Let's do a quick search before the techs arrive," he said. "I've already called for the tow truck to pick it up and take it to impound. Aideen, you should wait in Frank's van."

"Couldn't I just look over your shoulders?" I asked.

Archer looked at Frank. "I don't think we should allow it. You know how up-tight Burrows gets about this stuff."

"Aideen, you really should wait in my van," Frank said.

#

Frank went through the motions with Archer and asked him to hand-deliver the photo to the forensics team to make sure it arrived intact. Archer agreed.

While Frank and Archer were inspecting Alonzo's pickup, I was busy on Frank's phone searching the internet for a picture of the coin we'd found hidden inside Tiponi's photo. I learned it was an 1870 Liberty Seated Dollar, one of the most highly valued coins minted in the United States. Coins certified in mint condition were rare, but if the coin we'd found was certified, it could be worth as much as two million dollars. The coin still had high value even in less than mint condition, starting at close to $200,000. I remembered Henderson mentioning his coin collection and saying he was going to a coin show in Salt Lake when I'd first met him. Alonzo had probably stolen the coin from Henderson. No wonder he wanted Tiponi's photo back.

"All good?" I asked Frank when he returned to the van.

"Yeah, we're good," he said. "Archer agreed to wait for the tow truck."

I asked Frank to see about getting the photo out of evidence at some point, knowing the Honovis would want it back. He said that it was possible once the case had been wrapped up.

"Where to?" he asked.

"I'd like to visit Dakota."

"How did I know you were going to ask that?"

Frank headed for the veterinary hospital, and I reached across the console for his hand. "What are your plans now?" he asked.

"Return to the dig when I get my ride back and finish out my week."

"You called your boss yet? You should let him know you'll be delayed getting back."

"I'll call him after we check on my dog."

#

Dakota was doing as well as expected, but she was still too weak to move around much. The vet tech let me go back to where they were keeping her and pet her for a few minutes while Frank waited for me in the lobby. Dakota started thumping her tail the minute she saw me, and she managed to sit up. I threw my arms around her, gave her a huge hug, and thanked her for helping save my life. She gave my cheek a lick, as if to thank me for saving her life as well. The bandage on her head brought a tear to my eye, but Dakota licked it away.

#

I called Rodgers from a quiet spot in the veterinary lobby and filled him in on what had happened.

"Christ, what an ordeal," he said. "Did you go to the hospital to make sure you're all right?"

"Yes, they checked me out thoroughly enough. I'll feel a lot safer when my dog's back with me, though."

"I guess it's a good thing you didn't get rid of her," he said.

"If I had, I wouldn't be here. She goes where I go."

"This explains some things about Henderson that have been nagging at me," Rodgers said. "Lyle did excellent work, but there were some odd things about him."

"Like what?"

"Sometimes he'd just disappear. When I'd ask him to explain, he'd tell me he had to get away to de-stress and was going out to hike the backcountry. I'd have fired him if he hadn't been doing such a good job."

"Speaking of doing a good job, I'll be back at the dig to finish out as soon as BLM clears the company van," I said. "It could take them a few days, and I wanted you to know why I've been delayed."

"Take your time, Aideen. Why don't we consider this time as part of your vacation?"

"Vacation? What vacation? You fired me."

"Actually, that's on hold for now. I told the board about my plan to let you go, and they asked me to reconsider. I'm not promising anything, but I'll re-evaluate your performance when you get back. The accountant on the board was impressed with the amount of money you've saved the company in the short time you've been with us."

"What about the NAAC? They still planning to sue us?"

"I promised Juanita I'd do what I could to get the bones back. I'm hoping she'll ease off when she learns about Henderson."

At that moment, something clicked. Juanita had probably gotten her information about the bone hash theft from Henderson! People on the NAAC were very loyal to Henderson and respected him. I thought how ironic it was that his advice had been spot-on for me as well—stress the money I'd saved the company. I thanked Rodgers for the extra time and disconnected.

"Looks like good news," Frank said.

"Maybe. I might be able to keep my job, but it's not certain."

We climbed into his van and headed for Main Street. Frank parked in front of the inn and walked me to my room. I motioned him inside and closed the door behind him.

"Not sure this is a good idea, Aideen. Do you know how hard it was for me to leave you alone last night?"

"Why did you?" I asked.

Frank looked surprised. "You'd been through so much... I didn't trust myself to let it end with a hug..."

"I *was* pretty tired."

"How do you feel now?"

"Like I slept fourteen hours."

I looked up into Frank's dark eyes, and for the first time, I allowed myself to get lost there for a few moments. I took in the strong set of his jaw, the warmth in the way he was looking at me. He was so damned handsome, I shivered.

"What?" he said.

"I wish you'd stop talking and kiss me again."

Frank laughed. He swooped me up in his arms, and I wrapped my arms around his neck and pressed my face against his. He smelled delicious.

"No problem," he said. "Where would you like me to start?"

EPILOGUE

One Month Later

THE MUSTANG HUMMED ALONG. Dakota sat in the back seat flashing a big doggie grin as we drove east to visit Frank in Santa Fe. The insurance company had come through for me and authorized repairs rather than declaring the car "totaled." I'd argued with the adjuster that the 1967 Mustang was an American classic, not just any antique car, after he'd seen its state in the impound lot. The Mustang was my one last tie to Clay, and although I'd begun to move on, I wasn't ready to part with it.

Frank came out to greet us when I pulled in front of his house. He reached through the open back window to pet Dakota as soon as we stopped. "Looks like she's healing nicely."

"Her injured ear is a little shorter than her other one, but I'll take that over a one-eared dog," I said, exiting the car.

Frank walked around and gave me a big hug. We stood smiling at each other in a loose embrace until I said, "Showing off in front of your neighbors?" Frank laughed, then he pulled my roll-on out of the Mustang's trunk and the three of us headed inside.

Rodgers had asked me to stay on while he ran a national search for an interim dig director. He'd convinced Juanita

Joshwecoma to go along with his plan to keep me on in a reduced role, and he'd gotten her to promise not to sue Rodgers & Associates.

He'd been surprisingly sympathetic after hearing the details of my ordeal in Henderson's crawl space. We'd agreed that I'd work part of my time assisting BLM in their effort to recover the bone hash. If the whereabouts of the bones were discovered, he'd consider reinstating me as dig director. Frank convinced Burrows to put him in charge of BLM's search for the missing human artifacts. Occasionally, we would be working together.

Frank helped me set up my laptop on his dining room table and brought in his computer so we could compare notes. I was surprised when I opened Rodgers' email. He'd attached an article from an international archaeological journal that looked like it could pertain to the theft.

"Take a look at this article Rodgers just sent," I said.

Frank leaned over my shoulder to read it.

International News Journal
Ancient Bones Spawn Mystery over Origin

Lascaux, France. A noted antiquities dealer has turned over a unique collection of human remains to French authorities for identification. René Dernier, known for his independent work procuring artifacts for European museums, described the skeletal remains as those of a woman who died in her early twenties, two older males between forty-five and fifty, and a male child of about five years. Other remains in the collection have not been analyzed for gender or age.

In an interview with INJ, Dernier said he suspected the bones had been stolen and brought to France illegally when the broker who sold them to him was unable to produce an ATA Carnet that would have allowed public display of the bones for up to a year without going through customs.

Dernier became interested in the human remains when he learned the bones were stained with red ochre. The red coating originally led Dernier to believe the remains were from a Paleolithic European site, like the "Red Woman" discovered in a cave in Northern Spain, but DNA testing on the skeletons proved a genetic link to Native American tribes living in the American Southwest. Further tests established the age of the bones at closer to 1,000 years, not from the era of the Red Woman dating to Paleolithic times in Europe some 19,000 years ago.

Dernier reported to INJ that the bones bore unusual markings that a French forensics anthropologist claimed were cuts inflicted shortly after death. The Hopi and Tewa tribes in the state of Arizona in the United States have since laid claim to the remains and are demanding their return.

"Do you think Rodgers believes these bones they found in France are part of the bone hash stolen from your dig? Is that even plausible?"

"It's certainly possible given the estimated ages of the people when they died, the DNA link to Southwest tribes, and the red stain on the bones. Looks to me like I could be going to France."

Acknowledgements

Thank you to these exceptional writing teachers Mark Spencer, author, MFA program instructor and Associate Vice Chancellor at the University of Arkansas. Steven James, prolific best-selling author and creator of the Novel Writing Intensive Workshop. Sarah Elizabeth Schantz, thoughtful instructor at Lighthouse Writers in Denver. Best-selling author, Pam Houston for her excellent writing workshops. Thank you to the Taxi Writers Critique Group: Paul Esposito, Nancy Kern, Sarah Lindauer, Bill McBean, Jim McMaster, Karyn Sader, Adam Scanlon, Linnea Tanner and Sarah Zook. Thanks to Joan Jacobson and Grace Budrys for early beta reads. A big thank you to Artemesia Publishing and their great supportive staff. Thank you to my friends Annie Zook and Alexandra Ross for their on-going encouragement. And most of all, thank you to my husband, Gary for his love and support, and especially for all the wild back country adventures.

About the Author

Award-winning event producer and passionate explorer, Skye Griffith debuts her talent for storytelling with *Bone Hash*, a gripping mystery inspired by her explorations of archaeological sites and rugged backcountry across the American Southwest. Before turning to fiction, Skye orchestrated large-scale events—including Denver's first world championship, the Stanley Cup celebration. Her articles have appeared in the National Endowment for the Arts newsletter, I. E., the international events magazine and other industry publications. She lives in Denver with her husband and their 115 lb. Malamute and can be reached via her website, www.skyegriffith.com.